Notorious

Also by Kiki Swinson

Playing Dirty
Wifey
I'm Still Wifey
Life After Wifey
Sleeping with the Enemy (with Wahida Clark)

Published by Kensington Publishing Corporation

Notorious

KIKI SWINSON

KENSINGTON PUBLISHING CORP.

www.kensingtonbooks.com

DAFINA BOOKS are published by

Kensington Publishing Corp.
119 West 40th Street
New York, NY 10018

All Kensington titles, imprints, and distributed lines are available at special quantity discounts for bulk purchases for sales promotion, premiums, fund-raising, educational, or institutional use.

Special book excerpts or customized printings can also be created to fit specific needs. For details, write or phone the office of the Kensington Special Sales Manager: Kensington Publishing Corp., 119 West 40th Street, New York, NY 10018. Attn. Special Sales Department. Phone: 1-800-221-2647.

Dafina and the Dafina logo Reg. U.S. Pat. & TM Off.

ISBN-13: 978-0-7582-2837-6
ISBN-10: 0-7582-2837-6

First Printing: September 2009
10 9 8 7 6 5 4 3 2 1

Printed in the United States of America

Lil Jay and Kamryn, y'all almost ran me crazy while I was trying to write this book. Next time I'm gonna have to get me a nanny to keep y'all occupied, or get me a new husband. Something has to give. . . . LOL! Don't worry, though, because Mommy still loves you.

To my editor, Selena James. I took your advice and ran with it. Thanks for your undying patience. And to my agent, Crystal L. Winslow, I'm taking you to Hollywood with me. As business savvy as you are, I've got to keep you by the hip. That's a must.

Life in VA

I can't believe that just a week ago I was living in my man Lance's beach house in Barbados. I had plenty of money to burn on whatever I wanted—jewelry, clothes, anything. That may sound like the good life, but it wasn't. I was hiding out in Barbados, on the run from the Feds, the Miami-Dade police, and my client, Haitian mob boss Sheldon Chisholm. The Feds and police were trying to pin a whole bunch of shit on me, including the murder of my best friend, Maria, who was a DEA agent, and the murder of my housekeeper. And Sheldon wanted my head for promising him an acquittal and dropping the ball on his case. I'd been my firm's most successful attorney, and I'd had dozens of police, court clerks, ADAs, judges, you name 'em, on my payroll, but someone got to them all, and my career took a serious hit.

When Lance got murdered outside a night club last week, I knew I couldn't stay at his house in Barbados. I didn't think his murder was random; I knew that whoever killed Maria and my housekeeper and got to the people on my payroll also killed Lance. That meant someone was on my trail.

Since the court had confiscated my passport, I used an illegal one to re-enter the US. My plan was to head to Virginia, where I had family, and lay low until I put together a plan to prove my innocence and get my old life back.

I'd crossed a lot of state lines to get to my father's hometown in Virginia. During my travels, I picked up a newspaper in Texas that had my picture plastered across the cover. At that moment, my world stopped and I thought back on my life. Just a few months ago, I'd been a successful attorney in Miami with millionaire clients and an expensive appetite for the lavish lifestyle. I was at the top of the food chain. I was an unstoppable force with judges and DAs on my payroll. But then that all went up in smoke when I allowed greed and a cocaine addiction to take control of my life. Damn! I wished I could turn back the clock. But since I knew that was unrealistic, I folded the newspaper in half, stuffed it underneath my arm, and got the hell out of there really quick.

Instead of hopping on another flight, I rented a Toyota Highlander from Enterprise, stuffed all my things into the back of it, and drove the rest of the way to Virginia. It took me approximately twenty-two hours to get to my destination. Along the way, I prayed that my father's people hadn't heard about my brush with the law and the reward that they were offering. It had been a long time since we had been together, so I was like a stranger to them, which I'm sure would have made it easy for any one of them to turn me in. I knew what I had to do, and that was to keep my eyes and ears open. And the first time I sensed that something wasn't right, I was going to haul ass without even looking back.

I was tired as hell when I finally arrived in Norfolk, so I stopped at the Marriott hotel downtown near Waterside Drive to get me some rest. It was around three in the afternoon, so I was able to wear my sunshades in front of the hotel clerk without looking suspicious. After I paid the man with cash, I headed up to my fifth floor room to unwind. I started to call my cousin Carmen right after I unpacked, but then I decided to wait until I got me a nap. So that's what I did. But my rest didn't last long. I got a call from the front desk asking me if I wanted concierge services, and after I told the woman on the other end that I wasn't interested, I immediately hung up the phone. But for the life of me I could not go back to sleep. I looked at my watch and realized that it was a little after seven, so I got up from the bed and decided to make the call to my father's family. The only number I had was the number to my father's mother's house. My grandmother has had that number for as long as I could remember, and it has never been disconnected. So, I figured that when I called her, I could get Carmen's number and we could hook up.

The phone rang about four times before someone picked up. I hadn't been in contact with my relatives in ages, so I didn't know what anyone's voice sounded like. I said hello and asked to speak with Mrs. Hattie.

"Can I ask who's calling?" the woman asked.

"This is her granddaughter, Yoshi," I replied.

"Wait a minute now. I know this ain't my cousin Yoshi from New York."

"Yes, I am the one," I said, grinning.

"Oh, my God. I can't believe it's you."

"Is this Carmen?"

"You damn right it's Carmen. Who else would it be?"

I smiled. I'd almost forgotten how Carmen could be. "How have you been?"

"I've been doing okay. What about yourself?"

I couldn't tell her the truth—that I was on the run. So I said, "Nothing has changed. I'm still a lawyer, winning case after case, trying to make a name for myself."

"Wow! I remember when we were kids and we used to talk about how when we grew up we were going to be lawyers. But you were the only one who stuck with it. You must be living the life."

"Trust me, Carmen, life as an attorney isn't a bowl of fucking cherries. Girl, it's a constant grind, doing a lot of research, staying on top of your paralegals to make sure they are doing their work, and then on top of that, you've got to make sure you keep away from psycho-ass clients. They will try to kill you." I couldn't help thinking back on the shit I went through in Miami with Haitian mob boss Sheldon Chisholm.

"Ahh, it couldn't be that bad. Shit, I would love to have your life any day."

"You can't be doing *that* bad."

"Yoshi, I am thirty plus, working as a fucking waitress at the IHOP on Twenty-first Street. I live with Grandma and I don't have a car. Now tell me I am not in a fucked-up situation?"

Before I responded to her question, I thought about it and the answer was clear. She *was* in a fucked-up situation. Not as fucked-up as mine, but she was right behind me. I never would have pictured Carmen's life to be like this. Before my father died, he and I used to visit his people during the summer. Back then, everyone thought Carmen was the smarter one. She was prettier, too. All the boys wanted her to be their girlfriend, and they never considered looking at me. I was an attractive little girl growing up, but the boys couldn't get over the fact that my eyes were really chinky and I was bony as hell. Those little neighborhood bastards chose Carmen over me every single time because she had all the right curves and a really big butt. I wondered where those boys were now. Probably strung out on drugs, in jail on drug charges, or deployed over in Iraq, fighting a fucking war that Bush started. Whatever their status was right now, it sure wasn't helping Carmen out, because the way she just laid out everything, shit was really messed up for her. I just hoped she didn't try to come at me with her hands out because I was strapped. I only had enough money to last me until I could make my next power move.

Now don't get me wrong. I'd help her as much as I could, but I would not purchase her a car, and I would not put her up in her own apartment, so she'd better not ask.

So instead of making any comments about her situation, I said, "You're going to be all right."

"Easy for you to say. You're the big-time lawyer, living the life of a celebrity, and probably got a man with a lot of money, too."

"No, I don't. In my profession, you can't keep a relationship because men are always intimidated by success. So for the most part I've been single."

"So, what's going on? Last time I heard, you'd gotten hired on to some big-time law firm, making seven figures a year."

"Yes, that's true. But I think I've gotten kind of burnt out with all the mind-numbing cases. It's really hard trying to compete with other attorneys, especially when you're trying to make partner in your firm. People don't play fair. So anyway, I decided to get out of there for a while and take some time off."

"So, what are you going to do?"

"I wanted to come and see you guys."

"Come on and see us, because we ain't going nowhere."

"Well, give me thirty minutes and I'll be there."

"What do you mean, you'll be here in thirty minutes? Where are you?" Carmen got excited.

"I'm in Norfolk at the Marriott hotel downtown."

"Oh, my God! Are you serious?"

"Yes, I'm serious. So let's get together so we can continue to catch up. I would love to see how everybody else is doing."

"Are you driving?"

"Yes, I have a rental."

"Okay. Well, you can come by the house and pick me up. That way you can see Grandma and the rest of the family."

"Does Grandma still live in the same house from when we were kids?"

"Yep, she sure does. The house is blue now, but other than that, ain't nothing changed but our ages."

The thought of my grandmother still living in that old house made me cringe. I honestly couldn't imagine anyone living there for as long as she had. I remembered back when I used to visit her how the floor would squeak because the hardwood flooring was old and had never been maintained. I also remembered her having wood paneling on her walls, space heaters in every room of the house during the winter months, and one big air conditioner in the living room during the summer months. Everybody used to pile up in that small-ass living room when it was hot. I just hoped conditions at that house had gotten at least a little bit better. Because if it had gotten any worse, then the house sure needed to be condemned.

"Okay," I said. "I'll be there in thirty."

"Okay," Carmen said; then we hung up.

It only took me about thirty-five minutes to hop in the shower and get dressed. I could not let on that I was a fugitive, so I slid on a pair of dark blue Chip & Pepper jeans, a black wool Max Mara turtleneck, and a pair of black Fendi riding boots. It was kind of nippy outside, so I also threw on a wool blazer with patches on the elbows. After making sure my weave looked straight, I headed out.

A Reunion I
Will Never Forget

The distance from the hotel to my grandmother's house was a total of seven miles. From the looks of it, a lot of things had indeed changed since I last visited. I saw that several new high-rise developments had gone up, while a lot of the low-income housing projects had been torn down. I figured that was a good thing. But then while I was driving down Church Street toward Huntersville, where my family grew up, I noticed that some of the houses seemed to be condemned. I wasn't really liking this setup at all because the farther I drove into the neighborhood, the more ravaged it became. To make matters worse, there were at least five bums or drug addicts on every corner. The neighborhood's small-time drug pushers weren't too far away from them, so there was no question that there were hand to hand deals in the works. I wanted so badly to turn around and go back the way I came, but I figured that being among my people would probably be the only way I could stay clear of the police. No one around here looked like they'd watched the news in a very long time, so I was sure they wouldn't recognize me.

Continuing my journey to my grandmother's house, I drove one more block and made a right turn on Washington Avenue. When I finally pulled up in front of the house, I looked up and realized that it was exactly how I remembered it, except the vinyl siding was blue instead of white, and the front porch was packed with living room furniture instead of your normal outdoor furniture. I was sure that old cloth fabric sofa and love seat were filled with mold and mildew from the rain and outside moisture. I knew for sure that I wouldn't be sitting on that godforsaken looking thing. After surveying the front of the house, I realized I was going to keep my visit here short and carry my ass back to my hotel. So much for hiding out in the hood.

As soon as I got out of the truck and closed the door behind me, the front door to the house opened and Carmen ran onto the porch. "Oh, my God! I can't believe it's you." She smiled and raced toward me.

We embraced each other and then I pulled back so I could get a good look at her. Sorry to say, I wasn't too impressed with how Carmen was looking. She wasn't pretty like she used to be. She used to have beautiful skin and long, healthy-looking hair. Now, her skin looked stressed, she had bags under her eyes, and she looked like she needed Botox. Her figure was the same, although she had put on a few pounds, but somehow or other she looked like she was at least ten years older than me. And her taste in clothing was at least five years behind the times. She wore this old, red, hideous Enyce velour sweat suit with lint balls covering the entire jacket. The Reebok sneakers she had on looked a little better than the sweat suit, but not by much. Her hair was combed back into a ponytail, but the edges near her scalp sent a clear message that she needed a relaxer ASAP. I wanted to be the one to tell her, but it was too early in the game for me to be giving her advice without her taking it personal. I did not want us to fall out over my critique of her appearance within the first five minutes of us reuniting. So, I smiled and said, "I can't believe it's you either. You definitely look the same, just with a little bit of weight on."

"That's all the good cooking. Grandma be putting it down in the kitchen with all the fried chicken, meat loaves, collard greens, and macaroni and cheese. I can't ever get enough."

"I can tell."

"You look good, too," she said as she circled around me to check me out.

I smiled. "Thanks," I said, then I threw my Prada handbag over my shoulder as if to say, "Let's proceed into the house, please."

Apparently she got the hint, because not even a second later she grabbed onto my arm and said, "Come on in the house."

We treaded over the porch's weak wooden planks and then went inside. Carmen walked ahead of me and led me straight to the back room, which was where everyone hung out. It was like the meeting room for the family. Along the way, I looked at the pictures that hung on the walls. I saw a few photos of my father from when he was younger and a couple of photos of myself. My God, things had definitely changed. I looked like an innocent little girl then, with my two long pigtails. But look at me now. Who would have ever thought that I would have turned out the way I am today?

My grandmother was sitting in a recliner facing the television when I walked into the room. I would bet every dime I had stashed away that she was seventy-two years old, but she looked like she was every bit of fifty-five to sixty. She had not aged one bit. She kind of reminded me of Martin Lawrence's Big Momma character from the movie *Big Momma's House*. When she saw me, she smiled and said, "I see you're not a little girl anymore. Come on over and give me a hug."

I leaned over and hugged her. "How have you been?" I asked after I stood back up.

"I've been doing fine. Now, take a seat," she instructed me, and pointed to the sofa next to her.

I sat on the sofa and crossed my legs while Carmen took a seat next to me. Both of these women seemed like they were very happy to see me. "I see you haven't changed a thing around here. This house looks just like it did back when I was a little girl," I commented, looking around the room. It wasn't a compliment.

"Honey, please. This house looks a mess now," she replied, and threw her hands up to wave me off. "Over the past eight or nine years, my family has put a hand or two into tearing this house down. I would have never thought my house would look like this one day. If your granddaddy was alive right now, there wouldn't be a soul living in here and this house would look like it did the day we bought it. But since I am here by myself to fight off all these demons everybody in here has, I've allowed them to come in here and tear down what your granddaddy built. I've been trying to keep all my kids from coming back in my home for years, but they don't listen. They all get out there in those streets and get on those drugs and forget all about they got bills. And when they get kicked out their houses, where do you think they come? Here. And their trifling tails don't ever offer me any money. And on top of that, they come up in here and steal me blind," she continued, with a disgusted look on her face.

"Wow! It sure sounds like you've got a lot on your plate." I couldn't believe it. She deserved better.

"Honey, let's just put it like this. Grandma Hattie got more drama than your mama," she said with a smile. Better her than me.

"So, who's staying here with you besides Carmen?"

"Carmen's mama, Sandra, and her little sister, Rachael."

"How long have they been living here?" I asked.

"For about six months now. But before they moved back in here, your uncle Reginald was sleeping on that sofa you're sitting on for three years. I just put his butt out a couple of weeks ago because he kept bringing those nasty drug addict women in here all times of the night so he can sleep with them."

"Oh, my God! That's awful."

"Child, you ain't seen nothing. Be around here longer than a week and you gon' see what Grandma Hattie be going through."

"You need to get out of here and go on a vacation."

"I sure do, but I can't go nowhere and leave my house."

"Why not?"

"Because I might not have a house when I come back. I would bet every penny I've got saved up in my pickle jar back there in my closet that if I left this house for more than two days, I'd probably come back and this place would be burned down to the ground. Or it would be empty from Sandra trying to sell everything out of here."

"Why would she do that?"

"To support her drug habit. What else?"

"Are you serious?"

"Grandma don't be doing no lying. That's one thing you're going to learn about her," Carmen blurted out.

"What is Sandra's drug of choice?"

"She's on that heroin stuff. And that mess got her looking really bad, too. You should see her; she does not look like the daughter I once had. She looks like a total stranger to me, especially since her face is all sunk in and she done lost all that weight."

"I am so sorry to hear that."

"Honey, all we can do is pray for her because she ain't gon' stop running them streets until something powerful stops her in her tracks."

I really didn't know what else to say about that situation with Carmen's mother. I mean, who was I to pass judgment?

I was a recovering cokehead myself. Thankfully, I had not gotten as bad as my Aunt Sandra, but the fact that I'd used drugs still lingered in my mind. So I decided to leave that subject alone.

Right before I was about to extend a dinner invitation to Carmen and Grandma Hattie, I heard what sounded like the front door to the house bursting wide open and the door-knob tearing a hole into the wall it smashed into. The shit scared the hell out of me, and the very first thought that popped into my head was that my time of freedom was up and in the next few seconds I was going to be handcuffed and hauled downtown to Norfolk city jail until an extradition order was processed for me to be sent back to Florida. As I sat there and waited for my fate, my mind was telling me to stand to my feet and jump through the window behind me, but my feet wouldn't move. I was completely numb. And the fact that my heart was about to leap through my chest made my situation feel even worse. I closed my eyes.

I heard my grandmother and Carmen jump to their feet. "What in the world . . . ?" my grandmother said, then her words faded out. Two seconds later, I heard loud thumping noises in the hallway, heading toward where we were sitting. There were at least two or three sets of running patterns going on at the same time. Then I heard a woman scream and a man's voice saying, "Bitch, you gon' die this time!"

I opened my eyes, and to my surprise, I witnessed my Aunt Sandra being tossed up against the wall near the entrance of the den area where we were, staring down the barrel of a .357 Magnum. Tears were pouring down her face while she pleaded for her life. I honestly couldn't believe my fucking eyes. This young-looking street thug, who looked like he wasn't more than twenty-one years old, seriously had some balls running up in here like this. I sat back in awe and watched the whole scene as it unfolded.

"What in the world is going on?" my grandmother cried out.

"This bitch gave me some fake money for my dope! And this is the second time she done did this shit, too!" he roared, still pointing the pistol at Sandra's temple.

Grandma Hattie snapped out, "How much does she owe you?" while she dug inside the secret compartment of her bra.

"Forty dollars," he said.

"Please don't kill her. I'll give you the money," she pleaded, and then pulled out several five-dollar and ten-dollar bills. After she counted it to make sure it was the correct amount, she handed it to the guy.

He took the money and counted it to make sure it was all there, then mashed Sandra in her face really hard, sending her straight to the floor. "Next time ain't nobody gon' be able to save you," he warned her, and then he exited the house.

I stood there in complete fear, not knowing what to say or what in the hell to do. I did know that this was too much fucking drama for me and that I needed to get out of there and go back to my hotel. I was starting to think that coming to Virginia was the wrong thing to do. I mean, I thought the niggas back in Miami were crazy. But now I saw these motherfuckers here weren't playing with a full deck. Here they had the balls to run up in your house with a gun in their hand and threaten to kill your loved one behind forty dollars. I didn't know what that guy was going through before Aunt Sandra tried to play him, but whatever it was, it was serious. In all my years, I had never seen anything like this—and I used to live in New York. Maybe since we were in a recession, people were becoming more and more hard up. I just hoped for Sandra's sake that she didn't try that shit again, because homeboy already told her that if she did, she was going to be a goner.

After what I had just experienced, I really wanted to get out of there. I jumped to my feet to leave, but I got side-tracked when Carmen's little sister, Rachael, walked in the house. As soon as she turned the corner and entered the den, she looked at me and smiled. She was unbelievably beautiful. She looked just like Raven-Symoné from the hit television show *That's So Raven*, but she was not as chunky. She looked like she was at least five foot eight, which meant she was one inch taller than I was. She wore her hair long, and from the two different textures, it didn't take me long to figure out that she wore extensions. Her attire was pretty much that of a young hip-hop video chick. It was evident that she was up on the latest fashion because she was sporting an entire ensemble by Ralph Lauren.

"What the hell just happened? And why is Mama lying on the floor looking stupid?" Rachael asked.

"Your mama tried to beat one of Maceo's boys for some drugs," Carmen explained.

Rachael looked back at her mother and said, "You ain't tired of getting beat up?"

Aunt Sandra didn't respond. She continued to lie there on the floor, acting as if she was in major pain.

"Leave her alone, Rachael, and come on over here and meet your long-lost cousin, Yoshi," Grandma Hattie said.

Rachael turned back in my direction and smiled. She took two steps toward me with her arms extended. We embraced one another.

"You are so pretty," I said.

"You are too," she replied.

"Thank you, sweetie!"

"You're welcome."

"Hey, listen, I would love to chat with you and Carmen, pick your brain about how life is treating you, but I'm gonna have to run."

"Okay, we can talk later."

"Sounds good," I told her, and then I turned toward Grandma Hattie. I kissed her on the cheek. "I am glad to see you, too," I told her, pulling back from her so I could leave.

She apologized to me at least ten times. "Grandma, you don't have to keep apologizing," I insisted. "What just happened was completely beyond your control. So stop beating yourself up behind it."

She hugged me. "I know this wasn't the best homecoming, but we are all glad to see you."

"The feeling is mutual," I said, and then I turned to leave.

Trying to Regroup

My grandmother walked Carmen and me to the front door, while Rachael followed behind. When we stepped out onto the porch, Grandma gave me another hug. I sensed that she didn't want me to leave, but there was no way in hell I was going to sit in there another minute. My nerves would not have allowed it, so I kissed her once again and slid her a couple hundred dollars after she mentioned she didn't have the money to get her front door fixed.

I didn't say a word to my Aunt Sandra. I was too disgusted with her ass to even part my lips to curse her out. With all that damn drama, she just caused some serious damage to my grandmother's home and damn near gave me a heart attack, so I looked the other way when I passed her. Carmen, on the other hand, looked at her and told her how stupid she looked lying on the floor. She even nudged her with her foot and told her to get her dope fiend ass off the floor. Aunt Sandra just yelled out and told Carmen to leave her alone.

When I reached inside my handbag to get out the keys to the truck, Carmen poured a little guilt trip on me about the fact that I was running off so fast. She suggested that we at least needed to hang out and get a bite to eat or something so we could catch up a bit.

"What about Grandma?" I asked. "Wouldn't she feel safer if someone was here with her until she got someone to come by and fix her front door?"

"Grandma is all right. This ain't the first time her front door got knocked off the hinges."

"You have got to be kidding me!" I commented, shocked by Carmen's words.

"Nah, cousin, I'm dead serious. The police bust it down about a couple of months ago looking for Rachael's boyfriend."

"That's a lie!" Rachael blurted out. "They were looking for Rodney's friend Calvin."

"Well, did they get him?"

"Nope," Carmen interjected. "And Grandma was pissed, too. But what was even worse was the city refused to pay for the damages. So she ended up getting Uncle Reginald to come around here to fix it himself, which he finally did. Come to think about it, he's probably on his way now."

"Think we should wait and see if he comes? I mean, we can't just leave her standing there with her front door dangling like that. What if somebody tries to go in there to rob her?"

Before Carmen got a chance to answer me, my grandmother walked to the edge of the front porch and smiled at us. "Why y'all standing there looking like y'all don't know what to do?" she asked.

"I'm just wondering if you're going to be all right with your door like that," I answered.

"Oh, honey, don't you worry about me. I'm gon' call my son Reginald to come on over to fix it. He's probably around the corner somewhere. It'll be fixed shortly."

"I told you she was fine," Carmen insisted. "Uncle Reginald is right around the corner at the bootlegger's house getting him a couple shots of whiskey. So, as soon as Grandma goes back in the house and picks up that phone to call him, he's going to be right here."

"Carmen's right," Rachael said.

"What are you going to do in the meantime?" I asked Grandma, ignoring what Carmen and Rachael had just said.

"I'm gonna run in the house and get my cordless phone and come back here on this porch."

"Grandma Hattie, don't you think it's too chilly out here for you to be waiting around for Uncle Reginald? Your best bet is to wait inside before you mess around and catch a cold."

"Sweetie, I'm gon' be fine. Now you go ahead and get out of here before it gets too late."

"I'm gonna hop in the truck with her and show her around town for about an hour," Carmen said as she circled to the front passenger side.

"Well, you girls go on and have fun."

"All right," Carmen replied, and climbed into the passenger seat. I, on the other hand, was still uneasy about leaving my grandmother under the circumstances. But what else could I do? She was adamant about me leaving, assuring me that she would be all right since my uncle would be pulling up at any moment.

When Carmen and I both closed the doors behind us, Rachael asked, "Can you drop me off at my best friend's house? It's not far," then hopped in the backseat. I turned the key in the ignition, said good-bye to Grandma, and sped off.

As we traveled down one of the many one-way streets in Huntersville, Carmen sat back in her seat and started pointing out all the drug dealers she knew. A few of them looked like pure shit. Low budget thugs wearing colorful embroidery with the name Coogi plastered all over their attire. The shit looked ridiculous to me, but Carmen thought they looked like big-time celebrities. "Yoshi, look over to your left. The guy with the black leather jacket and the black skully on his head. That's Hard Boy. Chicks be going crazy over that nigga."

"Why?" I asked with utter disgust.

"Because he drives a BMW and he's got plenty of money. Not only that, look at him. He's cute as hell and he's big as a motherfucker! Chicks from around here love cats who are big and tall. That shit is a turn-on."

I slowed down to get a better look at him. I tried desperately to see what it was she saw, but I couldn't. He was not my type, though he was kind of handsome. That was as far as I would take it.

Moving along, we passed by a few more clowns wearing the colorful Coogi label. I guessed that was the going trend for these young guys. And what was so funny to me was that they thought they were clean, parading around on the block twirling their dope for some cash. I laughed to myself because it felt like I was watching a circus.

During the drive, I had a chance to break the ice with Rachael. She was a very impressionable young lady, so I attempted to get inside her head before she got out of my truck. "How is school coming along?" I asked.

"It's okay. I'm in my last year and I can't wait until it's over."

"How does it feel to be a senior?"

"It feels good."

"So, what are your plans after graduation?"

"Well, I'm not sure," she said, and then she paused. "I mean, I might attend TCC and take a couple of general courses until I make my mind up. And then again, I may end up joining the military."

"That might be your best bet right now, since the economy is screwed up."

"I keep telling her the same thing," Carmen interjected.

"You better listen to your sister because she's telling you some good stuff. It's really hard out there and a lot of companies aren't hiring right now. So, you are definitely going to need to come up with a good plan, and do it now."

"I am," she replied nonchalantly.

"Your boyfriend's name is Rodney, huh?"

She smiled and said, "Yes."

"How long have you guys been together?"

"It'll be a year next month."

"How old is he?"

"Nineteen."

"Is he out of school?"

"Yep."

"So he graduated?"

"No, he got kicked out like a month after we started going out."

"What's he doing now?"

"Out here on these streets selling drugs," Carmen interjected.

"Carmen, you don't know what Rodney does. He just be out there hanging out with his friends."

"That's a lie, Rachael, and you know it."

"Don't listen to her. She doesn't know what she's talking about."

"Oh, I know what I'm talking about. And the police do too. That's why they always got him hemmed up against a building—so they can search him. They know he's out here making plucks. They ain't stupid!"

"Stop it, Carmen, and please mind your business. Yoshi was talking to me."

"Look, baby sis, I'm just telling you some good shit because I am tired of you wasting your time with him. He is a high school dropout. He is a drug dealer and he's disrespectful to you. You need to wake up and smell the coffee and realize that that boy ain't no good for you."

"Carmen, you know you ain't never heard Rodney disrespect me, so why you gon' say that?"

"Yes, I have."

"Now why you gon' tell that damn lie? You know you ain't never heard that boy say something slick out of his mouth to me."

"Cut it out, Rachael, because you know I did. Don't let me put you out on front street!"

I spoke up. "All right, ladies, there's no need for arguing."

"I'm not arguing with her. I'm just trying to open up her damn eyes so she won't end up like me."

"Oh, that'll never happen," Rachael replied sarcastically.

"Never say never," Carmen fired back.

"Yeah, whatever!" Rachael sighed, then took her focus off Carmen. "Can you drop me off at this next corner?"

I said, "Sure," and pulled over to the curb. We were at the corner of A Avenue and Church Street.

Rachael got out of the truck and closed the door. "Thank you for giving me a lift."

"No problem," I told her. "So, when am I going to see you again?" I asked her.

"Well, I'm not going to be at my best friend's house long. I just came over here to get a pair of shoes I lent her a few days ago and then I'm gonna go back to the house. So, I guess I'll see y'all when y'all come back."

"Okay, so we'll talk more then," I replied, then pulled off.

"You are wasting your time if you think she's going to listen to you. She doesn't take anyone's advice, especially when it comes to that boyfriend of hers. That guy has got her wrapped around his finger. He can do whatever is it he wants to do and she won't do anything about it."

"It's her life. All you can do is let her make her own mistakes so she can learn from them."

Carmen sighed. "I know."

When we exited the Huntersville neighborhood and made a left turn onto Church Street, Carmen suggested that we get a bite to eat at this local eatery called Kincaid's. She said a lot of guys hung out there. And even though I wasn't in the mood to catch the eyes of any of the cats in the area, I said okay.

After we pulled up to the front of the restaurant, which was located on the bottom floor of the MacArthur mall, we hopped out of the car for the valet service.

Carmen chuckled. "I like this shit here!" she commented.

"What are you talking about?" I asked, after the valet attendant handed me my ticket.

"I'm talking about this valet shit! I've never been with somebody and they let somebody else park their car. Everybody I hang out with drives up in the garage and parks their own shit, so they can save some money."

I raised my eyebrows and said, "You have got to be kidding."

"No, I'm not."

"Well, you need to change your circle of friends."

"Grandma Hattie tells me the same thing all the time," she replied as we entered the mall. She led the way and I followed as she made a left turn to enter the restaurant. The hostess greeted us at the entrance, then she led us to our table. While we were taking our seats, the hostess placed two menus in front of us and said, "Your waitress will be with you shortly." The moment she walked off, Carmen started blabbing out the mouth about how this place was the hot spot. I glanced at the menu and then I looked around the entire restaurant and wondered if she was making a joke. Don't get me wrong, the place was nice and cozy, but it wasn't a five-star like I was used to. But I figured I had to make the best of it.

Finally, our waitress joined us and took our order. Carmen ordered crab cakes and fried shrimp. I decided to try a bowl of she-crab soup along with a side order of fried shrimp. While we waited for our order, I got the waitress to bring us both a glass of sangria. Carmen gulped her glass down in three swallows. I looked at her ass like she was losing her damn mind. "Carmen, we're in a restaurant, and that is not a glass of fucking Kool-Aid. You're acting like a pure slush." I paused as Carmen let out a disgusting belch and gestured to our waitress to bring her another glass. "Carmen, did you hear me? We are in a restaurant, not a redneck sports bar."

"I know that," she interjected.

"I don't think you do, because women are not supposed to belch out loud like you just did. That type of behavior is repulsive, and whether you know it or not, you just embarrassed the hell out of me."

Looking dumbfounded as hell, Carmen apologized as her face turned red. "Oh, my God! I am so sorry. Please forgive me, Yoshi. I never want to embarrass you. Oh, my God! Was I that bad?"

I sat back in my chair. "Yes, you were. Please don't let that happen again."

"Oh, I won't. And like I said, I am sorry. I mean, me and my girlfriends do that all the time and no one ever said anything to us about it."

"Well, like I said before, you need to get yourself a new set of friends because those type people aren't going to get you anywhere."

"It's funny that you say that, because my girl Foxy is ghetto as all outdoors. She and I be fussing all the time about how trifling she is and about all the stupid-ass niggas she be fucking with. She got two kids by two different niggas and they be treating her like shit. They don't take care of her kids and then on top of that, she's fucking around with this cat named J.R., who just whipped her ass after she confronted him for giving her a damn STD. Now tell me that ain't some sick shit?"

"Is she still with him?"

"Yep."

"Well yes, that is some sick shit!"

Carmen burst into laughter, but I was serious as hell. She went on to say that she had more friends like Foxy, but I made it perfectly clear that I wasn't interested in hearing any more of that foolishness. We started talking about the family. Her mother, Sandra, was the main topic I wanted to jump on and I made it known.

"How long has your mother been on drugs?" I asked.

Carmen sighed heavily and said, "It's been so long, I done lost track of time. Let's just say I remember being in junior high and she came up to my school to have a conference with my principal and after the meeting, she asked the man if she could borrow five dollars. Girl, my mouth fell wide open. I was so fucking embarrassed."

"What did you do?"

"All I could do was hang my head down."

"Oh, my God! What did your principal say?"

"He looked at her like she was crazy and told her he couldn't do it. So, she sat there with this stupid-looking expression, until he told her she had to go because he had to meet with another parent."

"Wow! That's crazy! I know you wanted to just disappear into thin air, huh?"

"I sure did. I'm just glad he shut her ass down and sent her flying out of his office, because I was so angry with her. She never did that bullshit again." Carmen took a sip of the second glass of wine.

After she swallowed what beverage she had in her mouth, she cleared her throat. And turned her attention to the entrance of the restaurant. I turned around, too.

"It seems like every time I see that nigga he's got a new chick."

"Who is that?" I asked, looking directly at this six-foot-three Black guy who had to be knocking on the door of three hundred pounds. He put me in the mind of Suge Knight, but he was darker in complexion. He wore his hair in a perfectly cut ceasar with long sideburns and a goatee. He was somewhat handsome and I must admit that he dressed the part as well. Sporting a brown leather jacket, a black Burberry polo shirt, black denim jeans, and a pair of brown ACG boots, he took the lead and followed the hostess while his date followed him. She, on the other hand, was an average-looking chick. A little over five-foot-five, she had brown skin and a ton of blond and auburn deep waved hair extensions attached to her head. She wore a short black leather jacket and a black fitted sweater dress that came down two inches above her knees, but it clung to her body like it was spandex. She also wore black spandex leggings and topped the whole ensemble off with a pair of black thigh-high boots with a three-inch heel. If you'd asked me, I'd tell you that she was a hooker because that's how she carried herself.

While Carmen and I gawked at these two temporary lovebirds, Carmen ran down the history of this cat. She gave me an earful and she definitely had my undivided attention. "That's the infamous Sean Barnes. He's got everybody around the way calling him Maceo. He runs all the blocks in my neighborhood. Everybody you saw hustling out there on them corners works for him. And when I tell you that niggas don't fuck around with him or his money, believe me."

"How old is he?"

"About thirty-one or thirty-two."

"So you mean to tell me that a thirty-something-year-old man put the fear of God in those young guys like that?"

"Yep, he sure did. And not only that, somebody told me that he's got a couple of police from this city on his payroll, which is why he can't be touched."

"That ain't hard to do," I muttered underneath my breath.

"Whatcha say?"

"Let's just say I had a lot of people on my payroll. Everyone had a position to play and a purpose to serve. If they couldn't make me any guarantees, they weren't getting paid. It was just that simple," I explained, taking a sip of my wine.

Carmen kept going on and on about how powerful this guy was and that he had an older brother who wasn't as mean as he was. She even mapped out all the locations of his stash houses and drug spots. She emphasized that no one dared try to rob him because there would be heavy consequences due to the fact that he was a fucking mental case. I just sat and listened to the nonsense. I was not at all impressed by that wannabe. I was not fazed by his three-hundred-dollar leather jacket and the many women he'd been seen with or the fact that he had a couple of local cops on his payroll. He was a peon in my eyes; he had absolutely no clue what real money and power was, like I did. All the men I'd ever dealt with were millionaires and they knew how to carry themselves. He had a lot to learn.

"Girl, look at him. Ain't he fine?" she continued, lust pouring from her eyes.

"He's okay," I replied nonchalantly.

"Come on now, Yoshi. Look at him. That nigga is fine!"

"I just looked at him," I assured her, turning my attention back to her. "And to me he looks *okay*."

"Well, I think he's sexy and fly as hell!"

"Well, if you think he's all that, then why don't you try and slide him your number?"

"Been there, done that already."

I burst into laughter. "You mean to tell me you've already been out with that guy?"

Carmen smiled. "Yes, I have. And I had the pleasure of fucking him, too."

"How long ago was this?"

"About a year ago."

"Well, damn! That was a quick courtship!"

"Girl, please! What courtship? That nigga took me out to dinner one night and then we ended up at the fucking Extended Stay out Virginia Beach off Independence Boulevard and that was the end of it."

"So you're saying it was basically a one-night stand?"

"Exactly! The motherfucker played me!"

"Well, if you feel like that, then why are you praising his ass like he's God or something? You should be throwing dots at his ass right now."

Carmen smiled. "I should, shouldn't I?"

"Yeah, you should."

Carmen continued to smile and gave every excuse in the world why that Maceo character was still cool with her. I listened to her until I couldn't bear the conversation anymore and then I got up from the table. I told her I was going to the ladies room to tinkle, but truth be told, I had to get the hell away from her ass. She was wracking my brains with that bullshit. I hated hearing women make excuses for men. That shit drove me crazy! And sooner than later, I'd have to let it be known.

When I returned to our table, our food was there, so I dug into it immediately. Carmen sunk her teeth into her entrée as well. We both devoured our food in record-breaking time. Afterward, I paid our tab and tipped our waitress and then we headed for the door. On our way out, Carmen broke her neck to speak to homeboy. I was so upset with her for doing that. But what made me even madder was that he refused to speak back. Instead, he looked at her ass like she was crazy. I started to say something to him, but I held my tongue and snatched her by her left arm and told her to bring her ass on. "It was going to kill you not to speak to him, huh?"

"I just wanted him to see me," she answered.

"But for what? He's a loser. Can't you see that?"

"He may be a loser to you because you're so used to dating those rich guys from Miami, but Maceo and his brother are like the cream of the crop around here. And every chick around here would die to be in his company."

I sighed in disgust. "I am truly sorry to hear that," I replied, then walked out of the restaurant and headed straight to the valet service area. I figured it was pointless to continue talking to Carmen about that fake-ass baller back in the restaurant. It was clear that she wasn't used to anything better, so why pound it in her head that she could do better? Bearing the thought that I had some silly-ass relatives began to bring on a headache, so I knew it was time to head back to my hotel room and retire for the night.

As soon as we got into the truck, Carmen asked, "Why are you so hard on men?"

"I'm not hard. I just don't like the ones who got a lot of shit with them."

"But you don't know Maceo, so how can you say he's full of shit?"

"Wait a minute, are you sticking up for that loser back there?"

"No. All I am saying is that you don't know him to be saying that. He is really a cool person once you get to know him."

"Look, Carmen, I hate to be the one to rain down on your parade, but I don't have to know that guy back there to say he's a loser. Remember, you are the one who told me that he played you into having a one-night stand with him. And then on top of that, he just saw you in public and didn't even acknowledge you. Now you want to tell me that he's a cool person. Are you that in denial about who this guy really is?"

"No, I'm just saying that right before we had sex, he was really nice to me. He took me out to eat and we laughed the whole entire night."

"Yeah, you just didn't know he was setting you up the whole time."

"That may be true. But I did have a nice time with him. So, I wished things could've been a little different."

"But they were't. So snap out of it. There are more men out there who will appreciate and treat you right. Now get off that low self-esteem trip and get with it."

Carmen smiled. "How come you don't have a man?"

"Because they are draining."

"Draining how?"

"It's kind of complicated. But I will say that relationships take a lot of hard work and sometimes the person you are with doesn't want to work as hard as you to keep it alive. So, I'd just rather be by myself. That way I can eliminate all the drama."

"Have you ever been married?"

"No."

"What's the longest you've been in a relationship?"

"Umm, I think it was two years."

"Why did y'all break up?"

"Because he was an alcoholic and he cheated on me twice."

"Were y'all living together?"

"No."

"Did he ever try to get back with you?"

"Several times, but when he finally saw me out with another man, he knew that there was no coming back."

"How long ago was this?"

"About seven years ago."

"Have you been in a relationship since then?"

"Well, sort of. See, after my two-year relationship with Carlos, I laid low and did a few dates here and there, since I really didn't want a commitment with the long hours of being an attorney and all. But not too long ago I dated one of my old clients and I must admit that I fell in love. It didn't last long, though. But it was fun while it lasted."

"What, he cheated on you, too?"

"No, he got killed."

Carmen placed her hand over her mouth. "Oh, I am so sorry."

"No, it's okay. Lance was a good man. And he definitely knew how to treat me."

"Would you have married him?"

"I'm not sure. But I would have seriously considered it if he'd asked."

"Do you still think about him?"

"Of course I do. Every day."

"How long has it been since that happened?"

"It's been about a month now," I lied. I couldn't tell her that Lance was killed last week and that I was on the run.

Carmen looked at me really weird, as if a thought popped into her head. "Wait a minute . . . Is that the real reason why you came here? You wanted to get away to get over what happened to him?"

I hesitated for a second. What she had said made sense. I didn't want to let on why I was *really* there, so I latched on to what she said and ran with it. It definitely sounded better than the truth.

We talked the rest of the way back to her house. I was glad I got to spend time with Carmen, even though some of the things she said annoyed me. Before she got out of the truck, she leaned over and gave me a great big hug. "I love you, girl!" she said, smiling.

"I love you, too, Carmen," I replied. And after I told her that I loved her, I sat back and thought about it. Did I truly love her? Or was I saying it because she told me first? My heart was fighting with my emotions because of what I'd been through trying to love people. How could I love a cousin I hadn't seen in more than a dozen years? Was it because she always had my back when we were children? Or was it because that was just the right thing to do?

Damaged Goods

I sped off from Grandma Hattie's house because I was more than ready to get back to my hotel room. I was exhausted. But my plans went out the window when I heard a loud scream from behind me. I looked in the rearview mirror and saw Carmen running down the block behind my truck, flagging me down with wild arm motions. I hit the brakes, put the truck in reverse, and backed up. When Carmen ran up to the passenger side window, I rolled it down and when I did so, I realized she was pretty upset.

"Yoshi, I need you," she said, out of breath.

My heart raced. "What's the matter?" I asked.

"Rachael is in the house beating the shit out of my mother and I need you to help me break them up," she panted.

I backed the truck all the way to the front of Grandma Hattie's house. I put the truck in park and hopped out. Carmen ran ahead of me, but before she went inside the house, I yelled, "Where is Grandma Hattie?"

"She locked herself in her room," she yelled back.

"Oh, my God! What the hell did Aunt Sandra do now to be getting her ass kicked again?" I questioned as I ran behind Carmen.

The moment I entered into the house, I heard a loud commotion upstairs. I assumed it was coming from Rachael's bedroom, so I ran upstairs and down the hall. The closer I got to all the chaos, the more troubled I felt.

"I am so sick of you! I wish you wasn't my fucking mother!" I heard Rachael scream. And right when I was about to step over the threshold into the bedroom, I witnessed her hammering down at her mother's face with her bare hands. She was straddling Aunt Sandra, sitting on her stomach and punching her in her face with all the force she could muster up. Aunt Sandra was trying to block every blow Rachael threw her way. Carmen was trying to pull Rachael off her mother, but she was having a hard time doing so. Carmen yelled for me to help her. I quickly snapped out of it and ran to her side to assist her.

"Get this crazy bitch off me!" Aunt Sandra screamed.

I scrambled to the floor and grabbed hold of Rachael's left arm while Carmen grabbed the right one. She and I both used every muscle we had to pull her off Aunt Sandra. Right after we pulled Rachael off Aunt Sandra, Rachael kicked her directly in her mouth while Aunt Sandra was trying to stand to her feet. It was unbelievable how the force from Rachael's boot knocked teeth out of her mother's mouth. It all happened so fast. Blood squirted everywhere. And when Aunt Sandra saw the blood pouring from her mouth like a faucet, she immediately covered her mouth with both of her hands. I heard her scream behind her muffled mouth.

"Oh, my God, Rachael! Why the fuck you do that?" Carmen yelled.

I stood there frozen because I didn't know what to say, much less what to do. But Carmen rushed toward Aunt Sandra. "Ma, run to the bathroom and get a towel," Carmen instructed. They both ran out of the room.

"That's what the fuck she gets. Don't help that fucking

crackhead because she's gonna stab you in your back next and then you're gonna go upside her fucking head, too!" Rachael clowned the situation.

I turned and looked at her because I was completely taken aback by this whole ordeal. I would not have ever believed that I would witness a daughter jump on on her mother and beat her like I just saw Rachael do. And to add fuel to the fire, she cursed her out while she was attacking her. So with all this in mind, I couldn't pass up the chance to ask her what prompted her to react the way she just had. Curiosity was killing me inside. "What is wrong with you?"

Rachael stood there in front of me. "Ain't nothing wrong with me. I'm fine."

"Well, why did you just go off on your mother like that?"

"Because the bitch is disrespectful," she replied, and then she started looking around her bedroom for something to get the blood off the hardwood floor.

"What did she do?"

"While I was downstairs getting my boyfriend, Rodney, a cup of Kool-Aid and a plate of food, he was up here chilling on my bed watching TV till I got back. So when I came upstairs with his drink and stuff in my hands, I found my mama's crackhead ass down on her knees begging him to give her ten dollars and she'd suck his dick."

In total disbelief, my mouth dropped wide open. "You saw her doing what?"

"I saw her on her damn knees begging her daughter's boyfriend to let her suck his dick for ten dollars. Now, how embarrassed do you think I was when I walked up on that bullshit?"

"I can't imagine," I commented.

"What did Rodney do?"

"I saw him push her back and tell her to go away with her silly ass! But she kept right on begging him until I scared the shit out of her and told her to get the fuck out my room."

"So how did you two start fighting?"

"Well, we started fussing first and since Rodney didn't want to hear it, he told me he was going outside to eat his food. I gave him his plate and he left. And right after that, shit just got out of hand."

"What do you mean?" I asked.

Rachael got down on the floor and started wiping up the blood with an old holey shirt. "Yoshi, my mama told me straight to my face that if Rodney wasn't in my bedroom, she could've gotten him to give her ten dollars to suck his dick because they've done it before in one of these abandoned buildings around here."

"She told you that?"

"Yeah, she told me that bullshit. That's why I went off and smacked the hell out of her."

"Oh, my God, Rachael! Do you think she was telling you the truth?" I wondered aloud.

"Hell, nah, I don't believe that shit! Rodney wouldn't dare do something like that, and especially with her."

"Well, why do you think she would say something like that? Those are some touchy accusations."

"She just wants some fucking attention and since nobody is giving her any, she's gonna try everything within her power to make herself be seen."

"Do you think you'll be able to forgive your mother for what she did tonight?"

"Probably not! I just want her to stay as far as possible away from me. She is like a thorn in my side. She ain't never been there for me or Carmen. All she wants to do is hang out in those streets and get high. I wish she would just disappear and never come back." Rachael got back on her feet with the bloody shirt in her hand.

She walked over to a small trash can that stood next to her nightstand and threw the shirt inside it. Then she reached for the handbag on her bed. "I got to go." She sighed.

"Where are you off to?"

"I'm going outside to see where Rodney is."

"You be careful then."

"I will," she assured me, then stepped into the hallway. She stood by the door and waited for me to follow her out so she could close it behind us. When I did so, she pulled the door shut and locked it. I stood in the hallway and watched her as she walked down the stairwell and headed outside. It was clear to me that she was one hurt individual. She hadn't just gone off the deep end on her mother because of what Sandra said to her boyfriend; she did it because of old hurt, unhealed wounds from her past. This left me to wonder if Carmen and I hadn't come when we did, would Rachael have done even more damage than she had? I shook my head in dismay because this family was in desperate need of some serious counseling.

After I watched Rachael leave the house, I started toward the bathroom to check on Carmen and Aunt Sandra, but at the last minute I decided to go check on Grandma Hattie first. Her bedroom was a couple feet from the hallway bathroom, so I moseyed right in that direction. I knocked on the door and announced who I was. Several seconds later, I heard her unlock the door to let me in. When the door opened, I saw her bedroom was dark except for the tiny light she had underneath her lampshade beaming from her nightstand. She looked like she was very weary. Her eyes were really puffy, so I grabbed her hand and said, "Are you okay?"

She sighed heavily and said, "Baby, I don't know how much longer I'm gon' be able to keep taking this mess around here."

I walked inside her bedroom and closed the door behind me. She shuffled back to her bed and took a seat on the edge of it and I took a seat next to her. "Do you want to get out of here for a while?" I asked her.

"No, baby. All I need is to spend some alone time with my God and I will be just fine."

"Are you sure?" I pressed the issue.

Grandma Hattie patted me on my thigh and nodded. So I put my arm around her shoulder and kissed her on the cheek. "You are so sweet!" she told me.

"No, Grandma. You are. I mean, you are one of the nicest women I have come in contact with for some time now. On top of that, you are a strong woman, so to sit right here next to you and see how upset you are really does something to me."

"Yoshi, I've tried so hard to deal with all the crap that goes on around here. But when I saw my granddaughter jump on her own mother and beat her down like a dog, that really took something out of me. My heart couldn't take it. I wanted God to take me away from here that very moment. That's why I ran in here and locked my door."

"I'm sorry you had to witness that, Grandma. But what's done is done. Rachael has gone outside and Carmen has Aunt Sandra in the bathroom trying to clean her up."

"I hope no one was hurt really bad."

"Rachael is fine. But she did knock out a couple of Aunt Sandra's front teeth."

Grandma Hattie placed her hands across her mouth. "Oh, my God! What in the world has gotten into that girl? Is she insane?"

"No, she's not insane. She's just hurt. And when people are hurt, they will do the unthinkable."

"I see right now I'm gon' have to pray harder for this family because everybody has allowed the devil to get in their heads."

"Well, pray for me while you're at it."

She and I talked for a few more minutes and then I made my exit. I kissed her once again on the cheek and told her I had to head back to my hotel. "Call me if you need anything," I told her.

"I will." She smiled and then I closed her bedroom door.

While I was heading toward the stairwell, I noticed the bathroom door was open but Carmen and Aunt Sandra were nowhere to be seen. I looked over at Carmen's bedroom door and it was closed, so I walked downstairs. When I reached the bottom, I called out Carmen's name, but she didn't answer, so I opened the front door to leave. And when I did, I realized she was standing outside on the front porch talking to her mother. I had every intention of giving them their space and walking right by them, but Carmen was not having it. She grabbed my arm and pulled me into their circle.

"Where you going?" she asked.

"I've got to get back to the hotel. I am so tired and I need a hot shower."

"Well, I ain't gonna hold you. I just wanted you to know how sorry I am that you had to get involved with all that drama. But you saw how crazy it was, so you knew I wouldn't have been able to break it up by myself."

"There's no need for any apologies. You guys are family. End of story," I replied, pulling away from Carmen's grip. Aunt Sandra had taken a seat on a chair. I guess she didn't want to be in the company of Carmen and me as we exchanged words. I did get a chance to look in her face before I stepped foot off the porch, but she couldn't look me straight in the eyes. It was apparent that she was embarrassed by what had just happened to her. And from the way I saw it, she should have been. I mean, how can you get up enough nerve to approach your daughter's man and ask him to give you ten dollars for a blow job? That is degrading and nasty! Not to mention you get busted and then you get your ass kicked. How fucked-up is that? I swear, there's a lot of shit out here they need to learn.

A New Day

When I woke up, I felt refreshed. All the drama I had en-
countered the previous night went right out the window.
But in the back of my mind, I knew I was about to embark
on yet another adventurous day. I showered, slipped on a
light blue and gray Puma sweat suit with a pair of Puma
sneakers to match, then combed my hair back to another
ponytail. The weather report indicated that it was fifty-
eight degrees outside, so I slid on a heavier jacket, grabbed
my handbag, and headed out the door.

I hadn't called Carmen or Grandma Hattie to let them
know that I was coming over. I felt the urge to sneak up and
surprise them. Surprisingly enough, Grandma Hattie was
outside on her front porch when I pulled up. She smiled at
me the moment she laid eyes on me. I smiled right back at
her, noticing that she was not wearing a coat. She stood at the
edge of the porch with her hands pushed down inside the
front pockets of her robe.

"Where is your coat, Grandma?" I asked the moment I
hopped out of the truck.

"Honey, Grandma don't need no coat. I'm used to this
crazy weather," she told me.

I walked up the steps to greet her, leaned over and kissed

her. "It sure is crazy," I agreed right after I pulled back from her. "So, what are you doing outside?"

"Waiting on the mailman. Around here you got to get your mail straight from the mailman's hand to yours, if you're waiting on some important stuff like a check or something. 'Cause folks out here in this neighborhood would walk up to your mailbox and take your mail clean away from you without even blinking an eye. I know because I done had it done to me."

"Are you serious?"

"Yes, ma'am. I am. Not too long ago, my SSI check walked right out of my mailbox, and I never found out who stole it from me either."

"Did you report it to the Social Security office?"

"Yeah, I did. But those folks down there didn't do anything about it."

"Wow! That's sad."

"It sure is. But let me tell you something, sweetheart. My God loves me! And he has always taken care of me, too. So, all the mess those people took me through down there at the Social Security office and all the chaos my children and grandchildren take me through on a daily basis—I try to deal with it as best as I can because I know the Lord ain't gonna put on me more than I can bear."

I shook my head in disbelief because I couldn't fathom putting up with the shit she put up with every day. I'd always known her to be a strong woman, but I never imagined she had to be this strong. I patted her on her shoulder and said, "All I can say is, may God continue to bless and watch over you because I wouldn't be able to walk in your shoes."

"He will, sweetie! He will," she assured me.

Now while she and I continued to chat, the mailman finally walked up and handed her the mail she had waited so patiently for. She smiled at him, bid him farewell, and told him to be careful as he continued his route. He assured her that he would.

"Come on, let's get inside before you freeze your butt off," she said, and turned around to enter the house.

"Good idea," I replied, following her.

The house was so quiet you could hear a pin drop. I assumed that whoever was there had to be asleep. I followed my grandmother and ended up in the kitchen.

"Hungry?" she asked.

"Sure. What did you have in mind?"

"When was the last time you had some good ol' corned beef hash with two eggs cooked over easy and a bowl of hot grits?"

"Probably the last time I visited you."

"Well then, it's time to get you back into the groove of things," she said. She grabbed a can of corned beef hash and a box of grits from the pantry. Then she reached inside her refrigerator and retrieved a carton of eggs.

"Want a glass of apple juice or a cup of coffee?" she asked.

"Coffee is fine," I told her. "So, where is everybody?" I continued, as I watched her take a mug from a cabinet to prepare me a cup of coffee.

"Carmen is upstairs, asleep. And my Rachael just left to go to Thomas Market up on the next block. I think she said she was going down there to get her a box of cereal and some milk. She's one of them youngsters who likes to eat that Fruity Pebbles mess instead of a healthy breakfast."

"Where is Aunt Sandra?"

She sat the cup of coffee on the table directly in front of me. "Honey," she began, "I haven't seen her since the fight last night. But I'm sure she's all right, though, because no one has come and knocked on my door to tell me they found her body laid out in one of these back alleys. All I can do is pray that she wakes up and decides she wants to get her life together."

I shook my head before I took a sip of my coffee. From the looks of things, all three of her children, including my father, had done absolutely nothing with their life. And what made matters even worse was that her grandchildren had followed down their parents' same path. I mean, look at Carmen. She looked like she'd been through the rough. She had drug use written all over her face when I first saw her yesterday. She may not have used them in a while, but there was a lot of evidence in her whole appearance that lead me to believe that she was a heavy user. So, she definitely followed her mother's footsteps. Now, I can't say for sure who Carmen was before I resurfaced, but people have always said that an apple doesn't fall too far from the tree. Shit, look at my life and compare it to my late father's. He was a drug user and a fucking alcoholic. So, there you go. Now, my uncle Reginald's only son, I'm not sure about. But from what I heard about my uncle's alcohol addiction, it wouldn't surprise me if his son had one as well.

"When was the last time you seen Uncle Reginald's son, Alonzo?" I asked, changing the subject.

"Oh, my God! It's been about five years now. But your uncle Reginald said the military got him stationed out there in Iraq."

"Oh, so he's in the military?"

"Yes, honey, he sure is. And I heard he's doing good, too. He sent us some pictures not too long ago of his wife and three kids."

Shocked, I said, "Oh really."

"Yep, he sure did. And his children are so beautiful. He done went out there and married a Spanish woman."

"How old is he now?"

"I reckon he's about thirty-eight or thirty-nine because he was running around here at least four or five years before you and Carmen came into this world."

"So, where are his wife and kids? Because I know they aren't in Iraq with him."

"Oh, no. They live in California."

"Oh, okay. Sounds good," I commented, then I took a sip of my coffee. And as I was about to make more inquiries about my father, I heard the front door open.

"There's Rachael right there," my grandmother announced as she continued preparing the hot pot of grits and the frying pan filled with corned beef hash.

When Rachael walked into the kitchen, her face lit up. I smiled at her and said, "Good morning."

"Good morning to you, too," she replied, then took a seat at the table.

"How are you feeling this morning?"

"I'm kind of sore. But I'm cool."

"She knows she better not try that stunt again because God don't like ugly. I don't care how your parents treat you, you are supposed to always respect them and your days will be longer," Grandma Hattie said.

"Don't tell her nothing, Grandma, because Mama is gonna show her something the next time she puts her hands on her," Carmen interjected as she walked into the kitchen to join us. She wore a pair of old shorts and a Mickey Mouse T-shirt and a pair of old socks. She waved at me and headed straight to the refrigerator and grabbed the bottle of apple juice.

"She ain't gonna do a thing to me," Rachael snapped.

"You think you're so bad, but walk up on the right one and they're gonna knock you out!" Carmen told her. Then she stood behind Grandma, waiting for her to hand her a glass from the cabinet.

"Why don't you be the first?" Rachael roared.

I took another sip of my coffee and before I could utter a word to defuse the argument that was about to come on, Grandma Hattie spoke up first. "Now, y'all stop that mess. I ain't trying to hear it this morning. I want peace and quiet. You both understand?"

"Yes, ma'am," Carmen replied. But Rachael remained quiet and rolled her eyes as if she was truly disgusted. Grandma didn't press the issue. She just wanted everyone to get along.

"You hungry?" she asked Carmen as she handed her a glass.

"Yeah. Whatcha cooking?"

"Corned beef hash, eggs, and grits."

"Oh yeah, make a plate of that as quickly as possible," she said as she poured herself a glass of the apple juice. After she put the juice container back into the refrigerator, she took a seat at the table with me and Rachael. "What's on the agenda for you today?" she asked me.

"Well, I hadn't planned anything."

"How long do you plan on being in town?" Rachael asked.

"For a while," I said.

"What's 'a while'?" Carmen asked.

I took a deep breath and then sighed. "Well, I was going to surprise you guys, but since we're on the subject, I was going to find myself a place out here and settle down for a while. Who knows, I may make this my second home."

Shocked by my response, Grandma Hattie turned around from the stove and said, "Oh, my God! Are you serious?"

"Yes, ma'am," I replied.

"So, where would you like to live? Because we have a lot of nice places around here," Carmen said.

"They just built some new condos downtown near Waterside and I'm sure you'll like them," Rachael said.

"Oh yeah, those condos over there are pretty," Carmen added.

"By any chance would you know how much they are running?" I asked.

"Nope," Carmen replied. "But they shouldn't be that much since the economy is screwed up and ain't nobody buying anything."

"Would you mind running with me by there a little later, so I can check them out?"

"I sure can," she continued.

"I wanna go, too," Rachael said.

"Sure, sweetie. You can ride with us," I said.

"Oh, so you ain't trying to be up in Rodney's face today?" Carmen teased.

"Why are you always worrying about me and my man?" Rachael snapped.

"I'm not worried about you and Rodney!"

"All right girls, now I told y'all stop that mess!" Grandma interjected. "I'm not in the mood for it this morning."

"Tell her to stop worrying about my boyfriend and get her own."

"Carmen, please leave your sister alone," my grandmother pleaded as she placed a plate of food in front of me and one in front of Carmen. And then she handed us both a fork for our corned beef hash and eggs and a spoon for the bowl of grits.

"Grandma, this looks delicious," I complimented.

"Yeah, Grandma, you put your foot in this," Carmen said, and then she dug her fork deep into her plate.

Rachael got up from the table and grabbed herself a bowl and a spoon from the dish rack. Immediately after she sat back down, she filled her bowl up to the rim with cereal and milk. When Rachael mumbled a few things underneath her breath, Carmen didn't react. Instead, she ignored Rachael and continued her conversation with me. While we sat and ate, Grandma joined us. For the rest of the meal, everyone sat in harmony until Aunt Sandra arrived. She had some clown with her when she walked into the kitchen. Both looked like they were high as gas, and Grandma Hattie was not pleased at all.

"Sandra, what have I told you about bringing folks into my house?" my grandmother snapped.

"Stop tripping, Mama! You done let me bring Smoke up in here before," she replied as she marched to the stove with her right hand covering her mouth. I knew right off the bat that she didn't want anyone to see what her mouth looked like, so I turned my head. When she approached the pots on the stove, she removed the lids from them to look inside.

"Girl, if you don't get out of my pots.... You ain't washed your nasty hands."

"My hands are clean," Sandra protested as she leaned over the stove and into the open pans.

Disgusted by Sandra's lack of cooperation, Grandma Hattie abruptly got up from her chair and got Aunt Sandra away from the stove. "Move your butt out my way!" she said, and pushed her to the side.

I sat back and watched Sandra as she gave her mother the most vicious look she could muster up.

Carmen saw it, too. "Don't be looking at Grandma like you gon' do something to her," she blurted out.

Grandma Hattie kept her back turned to Sandra as she prepared Sandra's plate. But she did acknowledge what was going on. "I don't care how she looks at me, just as long as she doesn't try her luck," Grandma said.

With her arms folded as she leaned against the refrigerator door, Sandra said, "Y'all too paranoid around here for me!"

"You made us like that," Rachael joined in.

"You need to mind your business and stay out of grown folks' conversation," Sandra snapped.

"Mama, ain't nobody trying to hear that mess you talking," Rachael snapped back, waving her hand in the direction of her mother like she truly didn't matter to her.

With his two-week-old clothes, smelling like he needed to be sprayed down with a fire hose, Sandra's friend Smoke stood there like he wanted to jump to Sandra's defense, but he kept his mouth closed. I was surprised no one said anything about the odor the two brought in the house with them. Thank God they didn't stay long. As soon as Grandma Hattie handed Sandra that plate, Sandra raced out of the kitchen with her drug addict friend Smoke in tow.

I sat there in total disbelief as I watched how dysfunctional my father's side of the family was. Carmen and Rachael had absolutely no respect whatsoever for their mother. But how could they when Sandra had no respect for herself? What I did admire about Carmen and Rachael is that they had a lot of love and respect for Grandma Hattie.

After we all ate breakfast, Grandma started cleaning up the kitchen while Rachael made her way to the hallway bathroom and Carmen headed upstairs to shower and change into outdoor attire.

Once Grandmother and I were alone, I stood up from my chair and walked over to where she was standing. I slid my arm around her shoulder. "Grandma," I began, "I know you are a strong woman and you can handle your business. But I also know that there's got to be something I can do to lift some of this burden you got on your shoulders."

"I'm fine, darling. I am fine," she insisted.

"Grandma, I don't care what you say, but while I'm here, I am going to take care of you. That's the least I can do," I told her. Reaching down into my pocket, I grabbed the ten hundred-dollar bills I took from my hotel room safe and shoved them into her robe pocket.

She jumped back and reached into her pocket. Her eyes nearly popped out of her head when she looked at the money she had in her hand. "My God! How much is this?" she wondered aloud.

"One thousand dollars," I said.

"A thousand dollars! Oh no, I can't accept that," she replied, trying to hand the cash back to me. But I put up a huge resistance.

"I will not take that money back, Grandma. I want you to keep it and do something nice for yourself."

"Like what?"

"Why don't you let me take you to the mall so you can treat yourself to a nice dress. And who knows, maybe you could buy yourself a new pair of shoes to go with it."

"I don't know about that," she said hesitantly. "It's been a long time since I went to the mall and bought myself something. I probably wouldn't know which stores to go in."

"Don't worry about all of that. Just put the money away before anyone sees it. Go to your room and slip into something else so we can get out of here."

"Okay, but I ain't gonna spend all this money in one place because I gotta pay a few bills," she said, and stuffed the money back into her robe pocket.

I smiled. "Just take care of what's important and I'll handle the rest," I assured her as I watched her head out of the kitchen. She seemed excited about having a few bills in her pocket, and I was pleased to see her mood change.

My Ghetto Ass Family

I sat downstairs and waited for everyone to take care of their business so we could head out. After about fifteen minutes everyone was ready to go.

Grandma Hattie took the front seat, while Carmen and Rachael sat in the back. Carmen gave me instructions on how to get to Lynnhaven Mall in Virginia Beach. It took me only twenty minutes to get us there and when we arrived, I parked near the food court entrance.

"What store are we going in?" Rachael wanted to know.

"It doesn't matter to me," I said.

"It doesn't matter to me either," Grandma Hattie said.

"Let's go inside Macy's. They always have a sale," Carmen decided for us.

Grandma, Carmen, Rachael and I climbed out of the truck and made our way inside Macy's department store. Macy's was a little too small-scale for me, considering I normally shopped at high-end stores like Saks and Neiman Marcus, but I made do. I saw a few things I needed, like a new robe and bedroom slippers. I even picked up some cosmetics and a bottle of perfume called Unforgivable by Sean John. Grandma Hattie found a nice dress in the full-figure women's section. Rachael helped her pick out the dress and the accessories to go with it before we left the store. Carmen stood at a distance and complained the entire time about how long we took to pick up the items we purchased. Rachael shut her down with a few comments and told her to stop hating because she didn't have any money to spend. "Stop messing with broke-ass niggas and you'll have some money to come and shop with!" Rachael told her.

"Now, why you gotta front on me like you dating a baller? Rodney ain't nothing but a fucking block hustler! So don't get it twisted!"

"Call him what you like. But at least he gives me what I want."

"That little bit of shit he be throwing your way? You acting like he put your silly ass in a fucking 2009 Benz and got you living out here in one of these big-ass houses in Virginia Beach. Shit, you're far from status like that. So please get off your high horse and come back down to earth. Because you ain't all that."

"Bitch, you ain't all that!" Rachael roared.

Grandma Hattie was a couple of feet away from them, browsing through the glass display case at a set of pearl earrings with the necklace to match, but she swiftly rolled up on Rachael and Carmen and stood between them.

"What is the matter with y'all mouths? Every time I turn around, y'all are fighting like cats and dogs! Y'all need to stop that! It ain't right. Y'all are family. Family ain't supposed to treat each other like that. Straighten your acts up before I go upside both of y'all heads."

Rachael sucked her teeth while Carmen rolled her eyes. I stood behind all three of them and laughed so hard underneath my breath, I nearly choked myself.

"Instead of y'all standing there looking stupid, let's go before these people in here start talking about us really bad," my grandmother suggested, and walked out of Macy's and into the mall.

I followed behind Grandma Hattie, while Rachael and Carmen followed me. We went into a few more stores and then we stopped in the food court. I got in line at the sushi stand and Grandma Hattie and Carmen stood in the Chick-fil-A line, while Rachael got in line at McDonald's. I was the first one at the table. Grandma Hattie and Carmen sat down right after me. But Rachael was still in line waiting on her order.

"What's taking that girl so long?" Grandma Hattie asked. "By the time she get over here to this table and try to eat her food, we gon' be getting ready to leave," she continued, taking a sip of her beverage.

"It looks like she's waiting on her order," I spoke up.

"This ain't nothing new. She's always the last person to get her food because she wants her fries hot and fresh out of the grease," Carmen interjected.

"I'm like that, too," I began to say, but was cut off by a loud commotion. Carmen, Grandma Hattie and I looked in the direction of the commotion and saw Rachael facing off with two other young girls who had to be her age or maybe a year or two older. My heart dropped at the sight of the altercation that was about to take place. I immediately noticed how Rachael stood her ground, with her mouth going sixty miles per second. It was apparent that she was not about to back down from those two young girls, so Carmen and I hopped up from the table.

"Please go and get your sister before somebody gets hurt!" Grandma pleaded.

"We are, Grandma," Carmen replied. "Oh Lord! Rachael is about to go upside one of them chick's head," she continued, as she picked up speed.

"Who are they?" I asked, sounding out of breath as we raced to Rachael.

"Meka and Mee Mee. They're sisters who live out Tidewater Park, which is not too far from where we live. They are always fucking with Rachael because Mee Mee used to mess with Rachael's boyfriend, Rodney. And Rachael supposedly took Rodney from her."

I frowned with disgust. "Are you kidding me?"

"Nope," she replied.

"Come on now, Mee Mee. You know you don't want none of me because you know I would stomp your ass all around this damn floor," I heard Rachael say.

"Bitch, do it!" Mee Mee dared her.

"Yeah, bitch! Try it!" Meka chimed in as she moved closer to Rachael.

As we approached these two young girls, I got a better look at them. The two girls were identical twins. Both of them had caramel complexions and they were about five foot eight, so they were pretty tall. They were kind of attractive young women with their multicolored Mohawk spiked hair styles, but I could tell that they were hood chicks because of the way they were dressed and the way they were carrying on.

"All right, now there ain't gon' be no double banking 'round here," Carmen announced, making her presence known.

Both girls looked in our direction. "We ain't got to jump this bitch! Mee Mee can fuck her up by herself," Meka snapped.

"Break it up, ladies! Break it up!" yelled a White male security guard, approaching with another security officer in tow.

Luckily, I didn't have to say a word. But I grabbed Rachael

by the arm and pulled her in my direction before anyone could throw a blow. "Girl, come on, because it is truly not worth it," I whispered in her ear.

Thank God she didn't throw up any resistance. She willingly came with me and allowed me to escort her to our table, where Grandma Hattie had been waiting. When I looked back to check up on Carmen, she was in a heavy conversation with both of the security officers. I guess she was trying to plead Rachael's case about why she was about to go head to head with the ghetto twins. Speaking of which, when I looked to see where those two sisters were, they had disappeared.

Back at the table, Grandma Hattie had a few choice words for Rachael.

"What in the world is your problem today? You are always finding trouble. Why is it that you like to fight all the time?" she asked.

Rachael rolled her eyes and sucked her teeth. "Grandma, you know I don't be going around messing with people. They got to say something to me first before I go off on them," she explained.

"Well, who were the girls you were fussing with, and what were y'all about to fight about?"

"They're twins named Meka and Mee Mee from Tidewater Park. Mee Mee was messing with Rodney and then when they broke up, he got with me. She thinks that I was the reason they broke up. And every time she sees me, she wants to run her mouth and threaten me like she's going to beat me up or something."

"Well, are you sure you're not the reason why they broke up?"

"Yes, ma'am! When I met Rodney at the skating rink one night, he told me he had just broke up with his girlfriend like a couple of days ago. So, their breakup had nothing to do with me," Rachael replied defensively.

"Did you tell her that?"

"Yes, but she doesn't believe me. And every time I turn around she's always trying to get in my face with that dumb mess! I am tired of it."

"Well, it's evident that they don't really want to fight you," I interjected, "because if they did, they would've hit you a long time ago."

"Yoshi's right. Those girls don't want to fight. They just want to intimidate and scare you. That's all," Grandma Hattie said.

"Well, they should know by now that they can't do that," Rachael said.

"Believe me, they know it. That's why when they see you they try to be a little more aggressive. The next time you run into them, just go the other way because you're only making yourself look bad by standing there and arguing with them. Be the bigger person and tell them you ain't got time to be wasting on them," Grandma Hattie said.

Rachael burst into laughter. "Grandma, I can't tell them that. They will laugh in my face and call me a chump! And if other people are around, I'd really look like a clown saying something like that."

"So, whatcha want to do? Stand there, argue, and get into a fight, so you can end up getting arrested and going to jail? You don't want that, sweetie. Jail is not a good place to go. Ask your sister, Carmen. She'll tell you."

Hearing my grandmother say that Carmen spent time in jail kind of shocked me, in a sense. I mean, Carmen did look kind of worn down when I first saw her. You know, like she'd been through a lot in her life. So, I guess street life and the jail cell would go hand in hand. Allowing my curiosity to get the best of me, I unconsciously said, "Oh, my God, Carmen been to jail!"

Rachael turned around and looked at me. "Everybody in our family been to jail except for me and Grandma," she said nonchalantly.

"And so what?" Carmen blurted out the moment she arrived to the table. She sat a McDonald's bag down on the table. "Here's your food," she said to Rachael before taking a seat.

"So, what did the security guards say?" Grandma Hattie asked.

"They just wanted me to reassure them that I was going to keep Rachael with me so the other two girls wouldn't bother her. They want to try to avoid all altercations and the paperwork that goes along with it."

"What did they do about the other girls?" I asked.

"They said that they were going to escort them out of the mall since they were the ones who started the whole mess with Rachael."

"That's good," Grandma Hattie said.

"They ain't gon' do nothing but go back to Tidewater Park and tell everybody they chomped me down."

"Who cares what they say!" Carmen interjected. "Just as long as they don't put their hands on you."

"I second that motion," I commented.

We sat there at the table for about fifteen more minutes so Rachael could eat her food. I sat back and listened to the advice Carmen and Grandma Hattie gave Rachael about her ordeal. Some of it I agreed with, the other part of it, I thought was unrealistic. But once the family counseling session was over, we headed back to the parking lot so we could return to Norfolk.

I had to admit that it was one interesting day. The time I spent with my grandmother was wonderful. But those incidents with Rachael and Carmen fussing in Macy's and Rachael about to fight those young girls were a bit much. I was thinking I'd had enough of my two cousins, at least for a couple of days. I couldn't bear the thought of hanging out with those two at the same time anymore. It was too much for me to handle. Next time, they would have to be separated. No exceptions.

Shopping around Town

Yesterday was a pretty bizarre day. I had to endure a lot of bullshit I would not have otherwise dealt with if it wasn't my family. Thanks to them, though, I never got out to look for a place to live. I decided this morning that that mission would be accomplished today, so I called Carmen and asked her if she could escort me on this errand. She happily obliged, so I picked her up around noon and we headed out.

It was a chilly afternoon. The weatherman said it would be thirty-five degrees today and he had not lied. With the wind blowing like mad, it felt like twenty degrees. I prepared for the brisk weather before I left the hotel, throwing on a pair of leg warmers, D&G jeans and a wool turtleneck and a pair of D&G snow boots with fur lining. I topped it off with a cream-colored wool pea coat by Chanel.

Carmen was sweating the hell out of me when she first laid eyes on me. "Girl, you got to let me borrow some of your clothes," she said.

To which I replied, "I don't lend out my clothes. Never have and never will." And then I quickly changed the subject. "So, where are you taking me?" I asked while I was driving out of her neighborhood.

"I am going to show you where they just built some nice-ass condos down near Waterside. Now, I know they're expensive, but I also know you can afford it with all that money you make being a big-time lawyer."

"Yes, it has its perks." I said, knowing damn well my ass was on a fucking budget. Those million dollar checks I used to get were long gone. And being on the run didn't help my situation because I had to pay for the hotel and shell out money to continue riding in the damn rental truck. I wanted to spread my wings and live like I used to live, instead of watching every fucking penny I spent. This money had to last me until I could clear my name.

"So, what are you trying to do? Buy or rent?" Carmen asked.

"I only want to lease a place right now because I'm really not sure about how long I'm going to be in the area. More importantly, since the economy is so bad, I shouldn't jump on the first thing smoking. Never act like you're desperate around real estate agents because they feed off shit like that. So, I am going to be easy and lay back and see what's going on."

"How much are you willing to pay?"

"I'm not sure. I guess it all depends on the area and how the place looks."

"Okay. Well, I know this man who owns a couple of the duplexes out there where I stay—" Carmen began to.

"Oh no, honey. I hate to be the one to break the news to you, but I wouldn't ever move in your neighborhood."

Carmen burst into laughter. "I wasn't talking about you getting a spot out there where I live at, silly. What I was about to say was, the guy who owns a few of the spots out Huntersville told me he had a few in some other neighborhoods, too. So, make a right turn on the next block and I'll get his phone number off one of his FOR RENT signs he got posted up in front of his properties."

I made a right turn at the next block as Carmen had instructed.

"You see that FOR RENT sign to your left?"

"Yes."

"Okay, pull over right in front of it so I can write down the number," she said.

I pulled over to the side of the curb in front of an old, run-down ass apartment building while Carmen scribbled the number on the back of an old receipt she found inside her handbag. And while she was doing that, I looked at this two-story building with a fire escape on the side. From the looks of it, the building had four units and only two of them were occupied. The front doors of the two units that had tenants were filthy as hell. They looked like there was mud plastered all over them. The sight of it was disgusting.

What made matters even worse was when Carmen and I witnessed one of the front doors to a unit open up and a fairly decent-looking, light-skinned, full-figured women with short hair who looked like she was angry with the world came out holding an armful of clothing. She stepped to the edge of her porch and threw the clothing down on the ground. Moments later, a man who was about the same height as she was came behind her yelling to the top of his voice. It became very clear that those were his clothes she had thrown to the ground.

"Why the fuck you throwing my shit outside?" he roared, as he rushed by her to gather his things up.

"Because you are getting the fuck out!" she screamed. "I'm tired of your no good cheating ass!"

"This is my house, too. I'm not going anywhere," he protested.

While he was bent over picking up his clothes, homegirl snuck up behind him and attacked him. She threw punches at his head like a wild woman. And immediately after he felt the first blow, he dropped his clothes, covered his head with his arms, and ran for cover. "I hate your lying ass!" she screamed as she ran behind him.

Carmen and I looked at each other and shook our heads in disbelief. But I couldn't resist making a comment. "This is another reason why I wouldn't live out here," I said.

She laughed at me and said, "Let's go."

After what I had just witnessed, I was a little apprehensive about her making the call to this realty company, but I sat back and let her do her thing while I got us out of her neighborhood.

"Can I speak to Ed Williams?" I heard her say and then fall silent. "Can you tell me when he'll be available because I am looking to rent one of his properties," she continued, and then she pressed the speaker phone button so I could hear the entire conversation.

"What area?" I heard the woman asked.

"Anywhere but Huntersville," Carmen said.

"Okay . . ." the woman said, and then she paused for a second. "What kind of rental property are you looking for?"

"Tell her a condo," I whispered.

"Does he have any condos?" Carmen asked the woman.

"Yes, ma'am, he has a couple of condominiums in Virginia Beach and Chesapeake."

"What part of Virginia Beach?" Carmen asked.

"He has two condo units in Newpointe Condos, right off the Newtown Road area. And he also has several units in a development called Columbus Station, which is right off Virginia Beach Boulevard near the Towne Center and Columbus movie theater."

"Oh, you're talking about the Pembroke area of Virginia Beach Boulevard."

"Yes, that's exactly where I'm speaking of."

"How much are the condos renting for in Newpointe?"

"The upstairs unit is renting for nine hundred a month. And the downstairs unit is renting for eight-fifty."

"Can you tell me why one place is higher than the other?"

"The upstairs unit has a fireplace so you're actually paying for that amenity."

"Well, how much are the units in Columbus Station?"

"They all are going for twelve hundred."

"Ask her when can we see the unit in Newpointe," I whispered.

"Can I set up a time with you so I can check out the place in Newpointe?"

"You sure can, but which one are you referring to?"

"The one with the fireplace," I whispered to Carmen, who repeated what I'd said.

"You can see it today if you like. I can meet you there in about an hour, if that's okay with you."

"Yes, that's a good time." Carmen took down the address and thanked the woman.

"You are most certainly welcome! And so you know, my name is Cindy Radcliff," the woman said.

"And my name is Yoshi," Carmen said, then hung up.

I was driving around in circles waiting for Carmen to get off the phone and when she finally did, I went straight into question mode. "How far is Newpointe from here? Is it nice out there? And how is that neighborhood?"

"I haven't been out there in a while, but it was nice when my homegirl used to live out there."

"How long ago was that?"

"About three years ago."

"How far is it from where you live?"

"It's about a fifteen-minute drive if you take the highway. Now if you want to rent one of those new condos down near MacArthur mall, then you are going to definitely come out of your pocket with at least twenty-one hundred a month."

"I'm not trying to pay someone else's mortgage."

Carmen laughed. "I know that's right!" she commented.

"So, will this lady ask to run my credit?"

"Girl, please! That company is so bootlegged, it's ridiculous! All they gon' ask you is if you work. You say yeah. Then they gon' ask you where. Just tell her you're an attorney and you're here visiting your family, but you want to rent a place while you're here."

"I don't want to get into all of that with her. Where I am from and why I am here isn't any of her business. I just want to keep it simple and keep from telling her more than she needs to know."

"Well, shit, just tell her you own a business."

"Wouldn't I have to show her proof that I owned one?"

"Didn't I just tell you that company was bootlegged? All they care about is the money. They gon' make you fill out an application, but they don't do credit checks. All they need your information for is so they can file it in their records, just in case they get audited. That's all. There's nothing else to the process. I mean, do you know how many niggas who sell drugs get places from them? They don't give a damn about where you get your money from. All they care about is that you pay your rent on time."

"Sounds good to me," I said, wondering what kind of lie I was going to tell the rental agent. I thought about asking Carmen to get the place for me in her name, but I decided against it because I didn't want her asking me a whole bunch of fucking questions, getting suspicious.

To kill the length of time we had to wait to see the rental property, Carmen and I got a bite to eat from Ruby Tuesday on Newtown Road. I ordered the lump crabmeat sandwich with fries and a sweet ice tea. Carmen ordered the firecracker fried shrimp with a baked potato along with a glass of sweet ice tea.

Now that I had Carmen alone, it was killing me to know what she went to jail for. But before I eased that question out, I said, "If you could change anything about your life, what would it be?"

Carmen thought for a second, then said, "I would have finished school and went on to college."

"Is there anything else?"

"Well, if I would have finished school and went on to college, I wouldn't have gotten mixed up in the streets."

"What do you mean? I don't understand."

"Yoshi, I used to be in those streets hard. I dropped out of school and became a stripper at this club called Platinum. I was eighteen years old then. I worked there for about two years, and while I was there I started getting high, tricking, and doing private parties. The side money got good, so I left the club scene altogether. Now, why did I do that? From that moment, my life turned upside down. I turned to the streets and became a full-fledged prostitute. Niggas were disrespecting me and beating my ass and I even got raped."

Shocked by the thought of Carmen getting raped, I looked at her with as much sympathy as I could muster up. "Oh, my God, I know that must have been awful."

"Yes, it was a traumatic experience, but I've learned to deal with it."

"Where's the guy who raped you?"

"I couldn't tell you where that bastard is. That White man beat me so bad he knocked me out cold. He damn near killed me, if you want to know the truth."

"So the police didn't make any arrest?"

"I don't think the man was from this area because when I looked in the mug shot book, his picture wasn't there."

"What about DNA? Couldn't they use that?"

"No, they couldn't because I'd slept with three other men before I tricked with him."

"Oh, my God, Carmen, you mean to tell me you didn't use condoms?"

"I normally did, but that particular night I ran out."

I reached across the table and grabbed hold of Carmen's hand. "What did you learn from that experience?"

Carmen sighed and said, "I learned that I need to value my life. So after I got out of the hospital, I vowed never to return to the streets, and I didn't."

"I heard Grandmother say you went to jail. Is that true?"

"Yes, I did six months for grand larceny. At one point, I used to steal clothes and sell them on the street, but that all ended when I got busted."

"Girl, you were a tough cookie, huh?"

Carmen smiled. "I was just reckless with no sense of direction."

"Well, I'm glad you finally came to your senses because life is too short to be making foolish decisions."

"You ain't ever got to worry about that again. I have been clean from drugs for over six years now and I don't plan on ever going back to that lifestyle. It feels good to be able to walk around with your head held high and cats in the street aren't calling you a ho or a crackhead."

"I'm sure it does," I told her, and I meant every word of it. We chatted for a few more minutes and before we knew it, it was time for us to head on over to meet the agent.

From the restaurant, it took us only five minutes to get to our destination. And when we arrived, Cindy Radcliffe was standing outside the residence waiting patiently. She was a petite woman with the frame of a high school cheerleader. Her eyes were blue and her hair was styled in a bob cut with blond and copper brown highlights. She was very pretty and her attire was well put together.

After I parked the truck in the visitor's parking space, I pulled out my Gucci sun-shades and placed them over my eyes before Carmen and I got out and headed toward Cindy.

She smiled and greeted us with a warm hello. "Thanks for coming out. Hope you like the place because it is really nice, especially with the new amenities."

"What are amenities?" Carmen whispered to me.

"She's talking about new appliances," I whispered back.

Cindy pushed the key inside the front door and opened it up, with Carmen and I following. The living room area was right inside the front door, and the dining room area was only a few feet away from the living room, so the place wasn't as big as I had imagined. There was a skylight over the living room, plus there was a fireplace as Cindy had mentioned. But it wasn't top of the damn line. Next, we entered the kitchen. That too was small as hell, but I figured it would do. Thankfully, the master bedroom was really big and it had a vanity area with a walk-in closet, so I smiled when I saw that. There was also another bedroom. It was kind of small, but the way I looked at it, it could serve the purpose of either a guest room for Carmen, when she wanted to come by, or office space. Either way, it would come in handy.

Once the tour was over, Cindy escorted us back to the living room area. "What do you think?"

Carmen looked at me and said, "I think it's nice. But it's up to my cousin here."

Cindy took her attention off Carmen and looked at me. "So, what do you think? Is this someplace you would like to live?" she asked.

"It's a bit small from what I am used to. But I guess it will do," I replied hesitantly.

"Where do you live now?" Cindy asked.

"I'm currently at my grandmother's house," I lied.

"Where is that?" her questions grew.

"In Norfolk."

"So what do you do for a living?"

Hearing her go into question mode got me a little nervous, but I remained calm and answered her. "I'm in retirement right now."

She smiled. "Aren't you a bit young to be retired?"

"Trust me, I'm not as young as you think I am," I told her, and turned to walk away. I walked back into the kitchen area, hoping she would get off the fucking subject about what I did for a living. Shit, I couldn't tell her I was a fucking big-time attorney from Miami. I'm sure she watched the news, I didn't want to blow my cover.

"I like the fact that there's black appliances in the kitchen."

"I know. Isn't it pretty?" Cindy replied.

"Yes, it is," I said.

"So, what do I need to do to get the place?" I wondered aloud.

Cindy took a piece of paper out of her briefcase and handed it to me. "Take this application and fill it out," she said. "And when you're done with it, call me and I'll pick it back up along with a check for the deposit and first month's rent."

"How much is the deposit?" I asked.

"Same as the rent," Cindy replied.

"Would it be possible to get a six-month lease?"

"Sure, that'll be no problem."

"Could I pay for the entire six-month lease when I return the application to you?"

"Oh, most definitely," Cindy said with excitement.

"Okay. Well, that's what I want to do."

"That'll be no problem. We have a lot of new applicants who prefer to do it that way," Cindy added.

"Okay. Well, I guess you'll be hearing from me by tomorrow."

"Just call the office and I'll be more than happy to meet you back here with the keys so you can move right on in."

"All right." I nodded, shaking her hand. "Thank you for your time."

"You're welcome. And if you have any questions, please don't hesitate to call me." She concluded by handing me her business card. I took it and proceeded toward the front door.

Carmen and I said our good-byes and then we headed back to the truck. Immediately after we pulled off, Carmen asked, "What did you think about the place?"

I hesitated for a second to collect my thoughts, then said, "It's okay, I guess. But if my circumstances were any different, I would be living in a penthouse somewhere around here."

"And I'd be right there as your roommate," Carmen blurted out, and chuckled as if she were making a joke.

I laughed myself, but not as hard as she did. I glanced over at her, studying her for a moment. I knew she had to have smoked something before I picked her up this morning. There was no way in hell I would ever let her live with me. Her hygiene wasn't up to par for me. Besides that, she wasn't on my level. I was too high-class for her. The only reason I was hanging with her in the first place was because I was in desperate need of a hiding place and she was my family. Aside from that, I would not have had any dealings with her, her mother, or her ghetto-ass sister. But hey, what could I do? Nothing. I was stuck between a rock and a hard place, and there wasn't shit I could do about it.

Later on that evening as we were eating dinner at a restaurant, Carmen got a phone call from her girlfriend saying that there was a shoot-out in Huntersville on Proscher Street and that Rachael's boyfriend may have been involved. Carmen dialed Rachael's cell phone number immediately after she got off the line with her girlfriend, but Rachael's phone went straight to voice mail. She dialed the house number next and when Grandma Hattie answered the phone and told her that Rachael wasn't in, she abruptly hung up and instructed me to drive down Proscher Street before I dropped her back off at Grandma Hattie's house.

"How long ago did your friend say the shoot-out happened?" I asked.

"She said it happened around forty-five minutes ago."

I pressed down on the accelerator and sped up a bit. Luckily we were within blocks of our destination, so the drive to Proscher Street went quickly. When I turned onto the street, I noticed how packed the block was. People were everywhere, but there weren't any policemen or paramedics around. I cruised down the street slowly so Carmen could get a good look and see if she could pick Rachael out of the crowd. It was pretty dark outside and the night lights on the utility poles weren't helping one bit. She finally got frustrated enough to tell me to pull over, so I did.

"I'll be right back," she assured me.

"All right," I replied, and right after she closed the car door behind her, I pressed down on the power lock button to prevent any unwanted passengers from jumping inside and carjacking me.

While Carmen was out sifting through the crowd for Rachael, I looked at my surroundings and instantly thought back on when my life started falling apart and I was out in the rough streets of Miami. I used to score coke from local dealers who looked just like the people on these streets. It felt like I was in a never-ending cycle. What was even crazier was that the palms of my hands had started sweating. This sort of thing happened when I was in this type of element, so I knew it would be only a matter of time before my body started craving for it. All the shit I had going on in my head would be another reason why my body would long for a fix. I had tried to use my family as a tool to keep my mind away from that toxic shit and it had been working so far. But I swore on everything I loved, if I didn't find any peace in my life very soon, I was gonna end up out there getting high just like Aunt Sandra so I could escape all the bad memories I had back in Miami with Sheldon trying to kill me, and my best friend, Maria, and my housekeeper's murders. There's but so much a woman can take.

Thankfully, it didn't take Carmen long to find Rachael. They both walked back to the truck less than five minutes later. After I unlocked the doors, they got inside.

Carmen sounded like she was out of breath. "Girl, you won't believe what happened," she said after she got into the passenger seat. I quickly locked the doors again.

"What happened?" I asked.

"I'll tell her," Rachael blurted out.

"Okay, well, you tell her then," Carmen replied sarcastically.

I took my attention off Carmen and looked through the rearview mirror at Rachael. "First, before you tell me, I need to know if you're all right," I said.

"Yeah, I'm fine."

"Okay, good. What's going on?"

Rachael took a deep breath and said, "A couple of guys from Tidewater Park got robbed last night and they thought my boyfriend, Rodney, had something to do with it. So, when they came out here looking for him and saw him standing out there on the corner with me and a couple of his other boys, they walked up on us and asked him what was up. So, Rodney was like, 'whatcha mean, what's up'? So, they pulled out their guns and shit and asked Rodney if he was the one who sent Bean Bean and Lil Mike to rob their spot. And Rodney was like, nah. He said didn't have anything to do with that shit and that they better get the fuck away from him before some shit caps off. So, when Rodney said that, him and his boys pulled their guns out, too, and I turned around and dove on the ground and crawled underneath a parked car. And the next thing I know, bullets start flying everywhere."

"Oh, my God! Did your boyfriend get shot?" I asked.

"Yeah, he got shot in his side. But he's all right."

"Did anybody get killed?"

"Nah. Everybody ran for cover when the bullets started ringing out."

"Where is Rodney now?" I wanted to know.

"The ambulance people took him to the hospital. But they said he's going to be all right."

My questions continued. "Well, did anyone else get shot besides Rodney?"

"His boy Lil Darren got hit in the arm. But the bullet just grazed him a little bit, so the paramedics bandaged him up in the back of the ambulance and then they sent him on his way."

"Oh, my God, Rachael. You don't need to be hanging out here. It's too dangerous. Do you know you could have gotten shot and killed?" I said.

"I know, I know," she replied, dragging her words.

"Well, if you know this, then why are you putting yourself in harm's way?"

"Because I know my man is going to protect me. He ain't gonna let nobody do shit to me."

"But what if they take him out first? Then what are you going to do?"

"Yoshi, you are wasting your breath," Carmen chimed in. "She is not listening to you."

"Shut up! I am listening to her."

"Well, are you going to stop hanging out here on this damn corner?" Carmen pressed the issue.

"Can you mind your damn business?"

"You are my damn business!" Carmen snapped back.

"No, I'm not."

"All right! All right. There's no need to argue," I interjected.

"I'm not arguing. But she needs to answer your question," Carmen said.

"I don't have to if I don't want to," Rachael snapped back.

"You're right, Rachael, but let me say this," I began, "life will throw you a lot of curveballs and if you just so happen to stand right in the way of one, you will be hit really bad. It's no joke out here. And you see that no one plays by the rules anymore. So, please, just think about yourself for once. Okay?"

"Okay," she said, and then she fell silent.

I looked back at Carmen. "Ready to go?"

"Yeah, let's get out of here," she said. When I pulled away from the curb, a guy dressed in all black walked directly in front of the truck. He stood in the middle of the road until I slowed down. And when I came to a complete stop, he walked over to the passenger side of the car. I couldn't see his face in the dim streetlight.

Carmen recognized who it was, so she rolled down the window. "What's up, Maceo?"

He got straight to the point. "Where your sister at?"

"I'm right here," Rachael announced.

"Yo, I heard what happened earlier. You a'ight?"

"Yeah, I'm cool."

"Well, get out and let me holla at you for a minute," he said.

"All right," she said, opening the door.

"Want us to wait for you?" I asked her.

"Nah, I'm all right. He probably just wants to know exactly what went down since Rodney is like his little brother and he makes moves for him. So, I'll be home right after I finish talking to him."

"Be careful then," I told her.

"I will," she assured me, and then she got out.

After she closed the door behind herself, I let up on the brake and sped off. Since the house was only three blocks over, I made it in front of Grandma Hattie's house in a matter of sixty seconds. I didn't have much to say to Carmen because I felt like I'd said it all to Rachael. But I couldn't leave without asking her if she felt Rachael was all right.

"Yeah, she's fine. She's in good hands with Maceo. He ain't gonna let nothing happen to her. Now, if she was one of his enemies, then we would need to worry, because like I said before, he is crazy. And can't nobody around here do anything to him."

"That's just because he hasn't met his match!"

"Maybe you're right. But ain't nobody out here with enough heart to go up against him. He's too powerful. And what makes him untouchable is that he's got gangs of niggas and policemen who will help him."

"Look, I couldn't care less about all those people he's got in his corner; I still say that he can be taken down."

"Well, let's just say that we probably won't see it in our time." Carmen laughed and then opened the car door. "Thanks for everything," she said.

"No need to thank me," I told her.

After she hugged me, I said good-bye and left.

When I got back to the hotel, I filled out the rental application and then I filled out the money orders I'd purchased earlier from 7-Eleven when I was hanging out with Carmen. All of them added up to one month's deposit and six months' worth of rent. After everything was done, I stuck them in an envelope with the application and placed it on the nightstand next to the bed. A few minutes later, I felt myself drifting off to sleep, so I didn't fight it.

It's Really Official

I elected not to pick up Carmen this morning to ride with me to give the rental agent the application and the money orders. I decided to do this venture on my own; I really needed some me time.

It wasn't hard for me to find my way, considering I had a GPS system in the truck. What a lifesaver! After I met with Cindy and gave her the application and the money orders, she immediately handed me the keys to the property. I was shocked and my facial expression showed it.

"It's official. You are now the occupant of this condo," she said with excitement.

I smiled and said, "Thank you."

"You are most certainly welcome. And if there's anything you need, please don't hesitate to call the office."

"I won't," I assured her.

We exchanged a few more words and then she left. I stayed there at the apartment and wondered what type of furniture I was going to put in there to make it look like home. I knew I couldn't call any of my European designers to hook this place up, because for one, I couldn't afford it with the amount of money I had in my stash, and secondly, I wasn't sure if the Feds had contacted them and advised them to reveal my whereabouts if I ever contacted them. So,

I couldn't take that risk, even if I had the money to spend. I figured my best bet was to go to one of the furniture stores in the area and pick something out and have it delivered. My taste wasn't so bad, so that's the way I'd handle it.

When I stepped back into the truck, I punched the keypad so I could be directed to the nearest furniture store. All of the addresses that popped up were on Virginia Beach Boulevard, so that's where I headed. The first store I went in was Havertys. The furniture they sold was really nice, but a bit pricey for what they were trying to get rid of, so I went to the RoomStore, which was directly across the street, and looked around.

A Black saleswoman helped me pick out everything I needed. I purchased a leather living room sofa with a love seat, a glass coffee table, a small kitchen table with a marble top and chairs to match. I even purchased a bedroom suite with a canopy and a king-size mattress to go with it. The only thing I didn't get while I was there were sheet sets, pots and pans, and curtains for my windows. I had to go to Macy's for those things. Before I left the furniture store, I was told that my things would be delivered in two business days. That time line gave me ample time to get the other things I needed before the big stuff arrived.

After my shopping spree, I stopped by a pay phone and called Carmen. Using a pay phone was kind of foreign to me. I hadn't used a public phone since cellular phones were first invented. And it didn't sit well with me either. I noticed how people looked at me while I was on the phone. I didn't like drawing attention to myself, so as soon as I hooked up with Carmen, I would get her to take me to the nearest wireless store so I could get me a cell phone. I was too cute for this shit! And I had to do something about it.

"Where are you?" I asked Carmen.

"At work."

"What time do you get off?"

"Not until ten o'clock tonight."

"Damn! They got you working some long hours."

"Girl, please. This is norm 'round here at IHOP. Shit, I've got to work like this so I can get them tips."

"Well, handle your business and call me later."

"So what are you about to do now?" Carmen wanted to know.

"I'm getting ready to find me a damn wireless store so I can get me a cell phone. Stopping to use the pay phone isn't working for me."

"I was shocked when I first noticed that you didn't have one."

"Trust me when I tell you I had two BlackBerries and they kept me busy. So I left them back home. I knew that if I had brought them with me, I'd probably cut my vacation short and head on back home."

"My boss just walked by me and saw me on the phone, so I've got to go before he sends my ass home."

"Handle your business, then."

"All right. I'll talk to you later."

"Okay," I said, and hung up.

Back in the truck, I punched in the location of the nearest wireless cellular company and the GPS system highlighted an nTelos cellular phone company on the corner of Newtown Road and Virginia Beach Boulevard in the Check Smart shopping plaza. So, that's where I headed. The parking there was really packed, but I managed to find a space. Inside, I got one of the salesmen to help me pick out a cell phone. He gave me the option to either sign a contract or do a prepay plan. I immediately jumped on the prepay plan because I couldn't let him run my credit. Doing that would've definitely alerted the Feds to my whereabouts. And I couldn't have that. I selected a standard flip phone. It was really cheap looking, but I couldn't care less about the appearance. All I cared about was the actual service. I didn't need all the e-mail and text feature bullshit. I mean, who would I e-mail or text? So, I was fine with what I had.

After I got what I needed, I paid the man and left. Back in the truck, I sat there with my cell phone in hand and had absolutely no one to call. And as I was about to leave, this Benz wagon pulled up right beside me. And out of nowhere this five-foot-eleven guy hops out the car and looks right at me. He took my breath away, and no man has done that in a while. It must have been his caramel-colored skin and masculine build. Our eyes connected, and I tried to turn away and look in the other direction, but I couldn't. This guy had me in a trance. All I could do was smile, and I guess that meant hello because he walked right over to my driver side and introduced himself.

"What's up, beautiful?"

Before I responded, I took one long look at his pearly white teeth and knew instantly that he was up on his hygiene. His skin looked really soft and his voice was deep and smooth like I like it. The only thing that turned me off was the smell of his cologne. It was a bit strong and I knew if I stayed around him a little longer, it would give me a migraine, so I sped up the introduction process and greeted him back by saying, "I'm fine, but my name isn't 'beautiful.'"

"Well, what is your name, then?" he asked.

I hesitated for a moment. Not sure whether or not to answer his question, I just sat there and looked at him.

He pressed this issue. "So, are you going to tell me or not?"

"It's Yoshi," I finally uttered.

"Nice to meet you, Yoshi." He extended his left hand. "My name is Mario."

I took his hand in mine. "Nice to meet you, too, Mario."
I smiled.

"Your hands are really soft," he commented.

"Are they supposed to be any different?"

"You just don't know how many women I have run into
with rough hands."

I chuckled aloud. "I am truly sorry to hear that."

"Don't be. I've got you now," he smiled, getting a little
cocky.

"How old are you?" I cut straight to the chase. He looked
very young and I swear, I hated dealing with babies. I felt
like men who were under the age of thirty tended to be a little immature and I didn't have the time to teach him the
ropes on how to be the man I needed him to be.

"How old do I look?"

"Just answer the question, please."

He smiled. "I'm thirty-eight."

Surprised by his answer, I said, "Really. Oh, my God! I
would have bet money that you were twenty-seven."

"I get that all the time. But I'm thirty-eight," he replied.
"So, what about you?" he continued.

"What about me?" I asked, even though I knew he was
asking me about my age. I had to play the naïve role. Men
like that dumb shit. It made them feel a little more superior
over women. Every so often, I'd get in the game.

"Your age. How old are you?"

"Let's just say that I am in my early thirties."

"Fair enough. So, where is your man?"

"I'm not involved at the moment."

"Why not?"

"Because relationships are a headache and they take a lot
of work on both sides, which always seems to be a problem."

"To me it looks like you've been running into the wrong
cats."

"You might be right."

"So, can I get your number to call you sometime?"

I hesitated for a moment because I wasn't sure about whether or not I wanted to give him my number, but then something inside told me to take a chance. I was a bit lonely and needed some companionship. Shit, who knows? He probably had a ton of money and wouldn't mind spending it on me and might even fuck me to death at the end of the day. I would love that. The thought made me jump at the opportunity, so I gave him my new number.

He programmed my number into his BlackBerry and assured me he would call me later for dinner, if I wasn't busy. I watched him closely as he walked away. His swagger was out of this world and the True Religion jeans he wore fit him perfectly. They weren't too tight or too baggy. He left me imagining how his body looked underneath, not to mention how big his dick was. If all went well, I would sure as hell find out.

Since Carmen was at work, I went back to my hotel room and packed up all my things. After I put all of my belongings into the truck, I checked out of the hotel and headed straight to Grandma Hattie's house to see if Rachael would help me transport some of my things to my new condo. Unfortunately, her little young ass wasn't available. Grandma Hattie told me she had just left with her boyfriend and that she would probably be back within the hour. I elected to stick around and wait for her because I really needed some help. Meanwhile, I sat around and chatted with Grandma while she was watching her soap operas. I couldn't say much until the commercial break.

"You know I found a place."

"That's good, baby. Where?"

"A condominium community called Newpointe."

"Where is that? Is that here in Norfolk?" Grandma asked.

"No, it's in Virginia Beach off Newtown Road."

"So when do you move in?"

"I got the key, so I'm going to move in today."

"How much is your rent?"

"Nine hundred dollars."

"Wow, that's a bit steep, don't cha think?"

"I'll be able to manage," I said, and smiled.

"Well, if you can't, just know that you got a place here."

I started to respond to the ridiculous comment my grand-mother had made, but since I knew it would hurt her feelings, I decided against it. Instead, I smiled and said, "I appreciate the offer."

Thank God her soap opera came back on because whether she knew it or not, she was talking out the side of her neck. I wouldn't dare move into her place. The condition was too wretched and sordid, and roaches were everywhere. I wanted to ask her if she wanted to come live with me so she could get out of this dump once and for all, leave all the has-beens and dope-fiend-ass children behind so that they could deal with their own demons.

After her favorite soaps went off, I convinced her to have lunch with me. We didn't travel too far from her neighbor-hood; as a matter of fact, we ended up eating at a church cafeteria called the House of Prayer. They specialized in soul food and I had to admit that their food was pretty tasty. Grandma Hattie and I ate our poor selves to death and had a good time talking about how much my daddy used to love me. After our lunch date ended, I took Grandma Hattie back home. When we got there I realized that Rachael had not made it back, so I decided that I was going to have to move my things all by myself.

"All right, Grandma, I'm gone," I announced while I sat in the truck. She waved me off and I left.

As I exited her neighborhood, I drove by that guy named Maceo, who always seemed to pop on the scene everywhere you turned. He was talking to a few of the young guys on the block. I figured that they must work for him and he was schooling them on some new and improved shit. I shook my head as he watched me drive by him. He must not have realized that I had a look of disgust on my face, because that moron smiled at me and threw his hands up as if to say, "What's up?"

I completely ignored his hand gesture and kept it moving. I was not about to entertain that clown. He was definitely below my caliber. Not to mention that he'd already fucked my cousin Carmen. I couldn't have that idiot smiling in my face. It would not have worked, so I let his little come-on tactic run right off my shoulder.

I was almost out of the Huntersville section of Norfolk when I drove up on Rachael and her boyfriend, Rodney, standing at the corner of Church Street and Fremont Street. From what I could tell, she was fussing his ass out. There were two other guys standing just a couple of feet away from them, laughing at all the commotion. It didn't take a rocket scientist to figure out that they were friends of Rodney's because they were respecting his space. I pulled over curbside to see if she was all right.

"What's going on, Rachael? Are you okay?" I asked her.

She turned around and said, "Yeah, I'm fine. This nigga right here is trying to play games with me," she complained.

"Ain't nobody playing games with her, ma'am. She just wants to fuss all the time about these fucking chicken heads 'round here," he tried to explain.

"Never mind all of that," I interjected. "Why are you out here in this cold weather when you just got out of the hospital for a gunshot wound?"

"That bullet didn't penetrate nothing. It went straight through me, so the doctors bandaged me up and sent me home that same night."

My questions continued. "How are you feeling?"

"I'm good. But I'll be better if she gets out of my face with that dumb-ass shit!"

Before I uttered another word, I took a good look at this guy Rodney. He was definitely a thug at heart. He was about five-foot-nine, with a medium build. He wasn't cute at all, so I was trying to figure out what was it that Rachael saw in him. His clothes were baggy as hell and his hair was locked up in some very unkept looking dreads. I shook my head in disbelief as she approached me.

Rachael walked up to the driver side door. "Yoshi, I am so sick of him; I don't know what to do. This nigga is always trying to play games with me and lying about these bitches around here. I ain't stupid, I know he was with that bitch Trina last night because my girl Pamela told me she saw him in her face at the club."

"I understand you're mad because you think he's cheating on you and all, but you are not supposed to let a man take you out of your square. Look at his friends over there, laughing at you."

"Fuck them! I don't care. They can get cursed out too, the way I feel right now," she replied, frustrated.

"Sweetie, it's not worth it. Don't let him make a spectacle out of you. People are riding by looking at you and shaking their heads. Don't give them anything to talk about."

"I don't care about these people 'round here. They can kiss my ass!"

I got out of the truck and grabbed Rachael by the hand and pulled her close to me. "I know you're upset. But you've got to get a grip. How do you think a man is going to respect you if you're out here in public arguing with him?"

She sucked her teeth. "This ain't nothing. We do this all the time. But I do know that he better get his fucking shit together before I go off out here."

"But that's not good, honey. You are a lady. And if you want to be treated as such, you are going to have to act the part."

While I was putting some words of wisdom in Rachael's ears, I didn't see an undercover detective car pull up behind my truck. They flashed their lights and hopped out of their vehicle. My heart did a summersault. One of the detectives, dressed in plain clothes, approached me and Rachael, while the other detective walked toward Rodney and his home-boys. When the group saw this, they took off running. All three of them scattered in different directions like roaches. When the detective who was about to approach us saw them run off, he immediately forgot us and switched gears. He took off running directly behind Rodney. Rachael saw this and got upset.

"DT is on your ass, baby. Run!" Rachael yelled as she broke away from my hand. She literally ran behind the officer, who was running behind her boyfriend.

Now how crazy was that? She was just cursing this guy out, now she's helping him get away. If she knew like I knew, she'd better turn her dumb ass around and let that detective do his job before he stopped in his track and arrested her silly ass for interfering with an arrest. I shook my head and hopped back into my truck. I had seen enough and knew that it was time for me to get my ass out of there. I couldn't tell you what the detective was going to say to me, but I am glad he never got the chance to do it.

Before I made my turn on Church Street, I looked in the direction in which everyone ran, and no one was in sight. I guess Rachael wasn't going to let her man go down without a fight. But if it were up to me, I would've let them get him and I would not have said or done shit to stop it. It was evident that Rodney was a piece of shit. He was a block hustler who looked like he needed a makeover and a grown man to show him how to treat a woman. Too bad Rachael had no clue what it was like to be with a man who knew how to love and treat her, because if she did, she wouldn't be subjecting herself to the shit she was going through right now.

Playing a Dangerous Game

It took me at least ten trips back and forth to my truck to get everything into my new place. I had shit piled up all over top of each other until I figured out where everything was going. Tired from all the hustle and bustle, I jumped in the bathtub and took me a hot bubble bath. I sat in that tub for at least an hour, until I noticed that the tips of my fingers had gotten wrinkled. I knew then it was time for me to wash up and get out of there. So I did just that and when I had completely dried myself off with my bath towel, my cellular phone rang. I wrapped the towel around me as tight as I could and raced into the kitchen area of my apartment, where I had my phone charging up.

"Hello," I said immediately after I snatched it up from the countertop and pressed the send button.

"Are you busy?" the familiar voice asked me.

Hearing Mario's voice sent chills down my spine. That man had a sexy voice and I knew if I wanted the dialogue to continue, I had to answer his question.

"I actually just got out the shower."

"So are we on for dinner?" he asked.

"Sure. Where would you like to go?"

"There's a sushi spot off Laskin Road I would love to take you to, if that's okay with you."

"I love sushi. But I'm shocked to hear that you eat it."

"I'm a food connoisseur, so I eat everything."

"Well, what time is dinner?"

"I'm ready now if you are."

"I told you I just got out of the shower so you're gonna have to give me some time to get dressed."

"How much time do you need?"

"Can you give me an hour?"

"Sure I can. Where are we going to meet?"

"I can meet you where I met you earlier today."

"Sounds good. So I guess I'll see you in one hour."

"Okay, see you then," I told him, and then we both hung up.

After I ended our call I raced back into my bedroom and combed through my suitcases looking for something sexy to wear. It was fifty-five degrees outside so I couldn't wear a provocative dress. I settled with another pair of Chip & Pepper jeans and a cute little cashmere sweater. I topped my attire off with a pair of black leather Gucci boots that came up to my knees. I didn't have the black Gucci bag to match so I carried my D&G black leather bag instead. I looked at the time and noticed it was a quarter till seven so I had fifteen minutes left to throw on my coat, grab my keys, and get out the door. I didn't want to give him the impression that I was pressed to see him, so I wasted the entire fifteen minutes sitting in my truck listening to a Keyshia Cole CD. The song "You Complete Me" had my mind going. The words were so deep and to know you have that type of man in your life is a beautiful thing. Who knows, maybe my new friend Mario would be that guy.

Five minutes after seven I decided to leave the parking lot of my building, so it only took me approximately three minutes to get to my destination. When I pulled up I noticed he was parked in the same spot he was in earlier. His windows were slightly tinted so I couldn't see the expression on his face. I knew he was smiling though, because I was cheesing from ear to ear. When I parked my truck directly beside his, he rolled down his window and asked me if I was going to ride with him or follow him.

"I prefer to ride with you if you don't mind."

"Well, come on and get in," he insisted.

Hearing him give me the cue to get into the car with him prompted me to do just that. And when I got into his car, the scent of his Black Ice air freshener hit me like a ton of bricks. He had about eight air fresheners dangling from his rearview mirror and the shit smelled good.

"So, where is this place again?" I asked even though I wouldn't know if he told me. I just wanted to make conversation.

"It's on Laskin Road near the oceanfront."

"What's the name of it?"

"Otani. They got the best sushi and hibachi in town."

"Sounds like you've been there quite a few times."

"I've had my share of visits," he replied as he merged onto the highway.

"I hope we don't run into one of your old girlfriends there."

He laughed and said, "I promise you we won't."

During our entire drive we talked about his last relationship as well as mine, even though I didn't tell the whole truth. My situation with Lance and all the DAs and judges was irrelevant. I didn't want to appear to him as being a ho or a gold digger, so I continued to play the innocent girl role and he accepted just that. When the part of the conversation came up about my occupation, I told a little white lie about how I used to work for a brokerage firm in New York. But since the economy was bad, they had to let me go, which is why I ended up coming to this state. Reluctantly I told him about my family who lived here. I told him that they were kind folk from my father's side and that we weren't really close, but since I was in town I decided to connect with them.

"I would love to meet them," he said anxiously.

"No, you wouldn't. My family is ghetto as hell! They would see you and try to suck all the energy out of you."

Mario laughed. "They can't be that bad."

"Oh yes, they are. Sometimes I wonder why I bothered to reconnect to them after all these years. I mean, it's not like we have a lot in common."

"Where do they live?"

"Some place in Norfolk called Huntersville."

"Oh man! They live in the hood! That place is wild."

"Don't you think I've already witnessed that?" I replied sarcastically, and then I chuckled.

Mario shook his head. "Sweetie, I am going to need you to be careful when you go out there. Cats be getting murdered out there on a regular basis and I would hate for you to get caught up in the cross fire."

"Trust me, when I go out there it's always in the daytime. And I leave right when it's about to get dark."

"Make sure you keep it like that. I would hate to kill somebody behind you," he said, cracking a smile.

"Yeah, right! You wouldn't bust a grape behind me. You would probably forget all about me if something happened to me."

"Well, let something happen to you and you'll see."

I stared at Mario for a good twenty seconds. I looked directly into his eyes to see if I could see the sincerity behind his words. He seemed like he was telling me the truth, but on the other hand, I figured why would he go to the lengths of retaliating if something happened to me? He and I had just met, so what would he gain from doing it? I couldn't figure out what his motive was, so I left it alone and rolled with the program.

When we arrived at the Japanese restaurant, Otani, we were seated at one of the hibachi grills with two other couples. After the waitress took everyone's dinner and drink orders, Mario and I got a little more acquainted. While we engaged in our conversation, I watched his body language. I noticed how he sat straight up in his chair. He wouldn't allow his body to slump over one bit. And the way he held his chopsticks when he ate his food really shocked me. This guy must've been to somebody's etiquette school because he was on point with the way he sipped his hot tea and the whole thing. I wanted to make a comment, but I decided against it.

"So, how far do you live from where you met me?" I asked.

"Are you familiar with the Green Run area?"

"No."

"Well, it's not too far from here. As a matter of fact, it's about a ten-minute drive from where I met you."

"So, do you rent or own?"

"I own," he replied with confidence.

"What is it—a house, condo, or what?"

"I own a three-bedroom home with a one-car garage."

"How long have you been living there?"

"For about four years now."

"What about kids? Do you have any?"

"No."

"Wow! That's a shocker. And you're not married either. Where are you really from?" I asked, smiling.

Mario smiled back, looking just like the actor Idris Elba. The brother was so handsome I wanted to take his ass in the ladies room and fuck the hell out of him that minute. "I'm from Virginia Beach," he said.

"Well, if you're from Virginia Beach, then how is it that you know so much about Huntersville?"

"I used to run out there a few years back."

"Run out there how?" I asked him, even though I kind of knew what it was he was talking about.

"It's a long story, and I really don't want to run you off by saying what kind of guy I used to be."

"You wouldn't run me off," I assured him. But what I really wanted to tell him was that I loved a bad boy. Men who are wrapped up in all sorts of illegal schemes that are getting them rich are my type. I held back though. I didn't want to give him the impression that I was a groupie of some sort.

"So, what do you do for a living?"

"I own a couple of detail and auto body shops."

"What is a couple?"

"Two."

"How is business?"

"Business is fine. As a matter of fact, I'm thinking about finding another location, so I can open up a third."

"In this recession? Your customers must be drug dealers," I replied, chuckling.

"Yeah, some are, but I do have a few customers who are taxpayers, too."

"I'm sure," I said, and took a sip of my mai tai. My questions continued: "So, where are your parents?"

"They are both deceased."

"Oh, I am so sorry to hear that."

"Don't be. We all have to leave here some day."

"What a way to look at it."

"I'm the type of guy who doesn't sit around and dwell on things I cannot control or change. It elevates unnecessary stress in your life so I just go with the flow of things."

"The world would run so much smoother if everyone thought like that."

Mario smiled.

"So, do you have any brothers or sisters?" I asked.

"I have one brother and a stepsister. But she lives in another state."

"And your brother?"

"He lives in Norfolk."

"Are you two close?"

"Not like we used to be. And it's like that because we live two different lifestyles. But we will get together and watch a game every now and then."

"I can understand that," I told him, and continued to enjoy my food.

After dinner we headed to the bar area of the restaurant and had a few more drinks. I must admit that I got drunk as hell and before I knew it, I ended up going back to Mario's house. I couldn't tell you how the interior of his home looked because I was too intoxicated and my focus was blurry, but I wasn't too drunk to notice that he undressed me and placed me in his bed. I wondered if he was going to try to take advantage of me, but when I saw him leave out the room and close the door behind him, I was able to answer my own question.

The next morning he woke me up with a kiss on the forehead and all I could do was smile. I had a slight headache from my hangover, but it was bearable enough for me to sit up in the bed.

"How did you sleep last night?" Mario asked.

"I don't remember," I replied, trying to wipe some of the cold out of my eyes.

"You were pretty drunk last night."

"Don't remind me."

"Are you hungry?"

"No, I'm fine," I told him, even though my stomach was rumbling. And before I could say another word my mouth got watery, so I knew I was about to throw up all over everything around me. Without hesitation, I placed my right hand over my mouth and then I jumped to my feet and ran straight to the bathroom. "Uuuaghhhhhh," was the only sound you could hear as I vomited into the toilet. Mario raced into the bathroom behind me and handed me a hand towel so that I could wipe my mouth.

"I figured that was going to happen," he commented.

With tears in my eyes I looked up at him and mumbled behind the hand towel, "I knew it, too. It seems like I could never hold my liquor."

"Well, I'm going to remind you about that the next time."

Right after I got myself together he picked me up from the floor and carried me in his arms back into the bedroom. He sat me back on the bed and told me to rest. "I wish I could, but I can't. I've got somewhere I need to be."

He placed his hand over my leg and said, "I'm sorry, baby, but I can't let you leave like this. You are in no shape to be driving right now. If you give me a chance to shower and get dressed, I will take you wherever you need to go."

I hesitated for a moment, trying to figure out another way I could convince him to let me leave, but when I couldn't think of anything, I reluctantly accepted his offer. It only took him thirty minutes to shower and get dressed, and five minutes after that we were sitting inside his Benz wagon waiting for it to warm up. Realistically speaking, I didn't have any specific place I needed to be, so what I did was have him take me to Walmart to pick up a few things for my new place and then I had him slide me on over to my grandmother's house.

Thank God my aunt Sandy wasn't around, because she would have embarrassed me to the tenth power. Grandma Hattie wasn't there either. But Rachael and Carmen were there and they rushed outside when I called them from my cell phone and told them that I was out front. Their eyes grew at least an inch in size when they saw Mario's car parked at the curb. Carmen approached the car first.

"Well, well, well, I see it didn't take you long to find a friend," she commented.

"He got a nice car, too," Rachael interjected.

"What's his name?" Carmen wanted to know.

"Mario," I told them.

"Mario," Carmen said, and then she got quiet as if she went into deep thought. Without saying another word, she leaned down into the car window and took a good look at Mario. I looked at her and then at him, and what shocked me was that their facial expressions were the same. And before I could utter a word, Carmen blurted out that she knew him.

"What? You know him or something?" I wondered aloud.

"Yeah, do you know me?" he also wanted to know.

"Didn't you use to hang out here a long time ago?"

"Yeah, it's been about five years or so."

Carmen nodded. "Yeah, that's about right, because I was hanging out here hard in these streets then. And I remember when you used to own that club called Reign. I used to go in there all the time until you sold it."

Mario smiled. "Yeah, those were the days. I was doing really good until I had to shut it down after that guy chased his girlfriend into the women's bathroom and shot her in the head."

"Oh yeah, I remember that! That was sad."

"Tell me about it."

"Whatcha doin' now?" Carmen asked.

"I own a couple of auto body shops now."

"Get that money!" Carmen commented, then focused her attention back on me and smiled.

"What are you smiling for?" I asked her.

"Because I'm happy to see you."

"How was work last night?"

"It was okay. I think I'm coming down with a cold because somebody from the job walked away with my jacket last night so I had to walk home freezing my tail off."

"I told her she needed to quit that dumb job. Those people she works with are ghetto as hell," Rachael blurted out.

I chuckled at Rachael's comment, but then I turned my attention back to Carmen. "Do you have to work today?"

"Yeah, I'm supposed to go in tonight, but I might call in because my throat is starting to feel a little scratchy."

"Have you taken something for it?"

"No, but I drank some hot tea with honey, so that should do the trick."

"How long ago did you do that?"

"Not too long before you pulled up."

"Well, you need to get out of this cold and go and lie down."

"I am."

Mario turned the ignition to his car back on. That gave Carmen and Rachael the cue that we were about to leave. I said my good-byes to both of them. "Tell Grandma I came by to see her," I told them.

"We will," they both said.

As we pulled off, I noticed how Carmen watched Mario and I leave. I looked at her facial expression while he drove off. It was a look of jealousy. So, I wondered, what was going through her mind? Knowing her predicament, she was probably saying to herself, why wasn't it her sitting in the passenger seat of Mario's car since she knew him before I did? Well, if that was indeed what she was thinking, I'm sorry to say it just wasn't meant to be. She was at the wrong place at the wrong time. Not to mention, she was definitely not his type. Judging from how he acted around me, he and Carmen would not have ever clicked. She was too ghetto for his taste in women. Plus they didn't have anything in common. All she would want to talk about was who got shot and what drug dealer got the nicest car, so their conversation would be limited.

The drive out of Huntersville was very interesting. It seemed like every corner we passed, one guy or another knew Mario. "What's up, Mario?" I heard a couple of guys yell from the street corner. Mario would either beep his horn or wave them off. "I see you are a well-known guy."

"You could say that," he replied. And then he immediately changed the subject. "Where do you need to go to now?"

"You can take me back to that shopping center so I can get in my car and go home."

"Why you trying to leave me so soon?"

"Because I need to go home and change clothes."

"Will I be able to see you later?"

"If you'd like to."

"Well then, it's settled. Go home, take care of your business, and call me when you're done so we can hang out."

"All right."

Immediately after we arrived back at the Check Smart shopping plaza, I hopped into my truck.

"Is that a rental you driving?" he asked.

I sighed heavily. "Yes, it is, and I am so sick of it. It's a gas guzzler and they are charging me out the ass for it."

"How long have you had it?"

"For about a week now."

"If you came from New York, then why does the license plate say Texas?"

"Because I flew to Texas to visit a friend and then from there I decided to drive here."

"Damn! That was a long-ass drive. I wouldn't have done it. I would have caught the next flight before I got behind a wheel and drove all those miles."

"It wasn't all that bad. And besides, I enjoyed the scenery along the way."

"Well, when do you have to give the truck back?"

"I have to renew it in a couple of days. But I was wondering if I should give it back and get something different."

"Do you have a car at all?"

"Yes, I do. But it's back in New York."

"We can drive up there and get it if you want."

Hearing this man tell me he would drive me all the way to New York to pick up a car I owned that wasn't even there gave me an instant stomachache. Now, how was I going to get out of this lie? I couldn't tell him that I didn't feel like going up there, because that would cause him to become suspicious about what was really up with me. So I sighed once again and told him my car was in my ex-boyfriend's name and when I broke up with him he confiscated the car from me.

"That was a sucker move," Mario commented. "You mean to tell me there are cats out there who still do dumb shit like that?"

"Yes there are," I replied, putting the truck in reverse. As I backed up to leave, Mario said something in reference to him helping me get another vehicle. He mumbled something about having a 2005 Honda Accord parked at his auto body shop, which he now owned because he did some work on it and the owner never came back and picked it up. I said okay just so I could brush him off and leave. A 2005 Honda Accord was not the type of car I wanted to be driving around town in. I wanted to push that Aston Martin I had back in Florida. Too bad the DEA had already confiscated it—I was shit out of luck. But who knows, maybe if I fucked Mario he'd give me the keys to the Benz he'd been pushing and drive the Honda Accord himself. That's something I would just have to find out.

The Start of Something New

Mario and I had been in each other's presence for the past seventy-two hours. I was thinking he was falling in love or something because he didn't want me out of his sight. Tonight we stayed in and ordered pizza. He pulled out a bottle of Merlot to go with it. We sat around in his living room and ate almost the entire pizza along with the entire bottle of Merlot. I had to admit that I hadn't had that much fun in a while. It seemed like all the problems I had back in Florida had diminished. It felt good to have that weight lifted even if it was just for this moment. After dinner, Mario put in a disk.

"What are we about to watch?" I asked.

"*Scarface*. It's my favorite movie of all time."

"I love that movie, too," I agreed, as he placed the disc inside the Blu-ray player.

As the movie began, I watched Mario as he became engrossed in every scene. I could tell he loved the lifestyle that Al Pacino portrayed in the movie. Whether he knew it or not, I was infatuated with that lifestyle as well, but that was something I needed to keep to myself. So, as the movie played on, I grew tired and told Mario I was going to go lie down and get some rest.

"Go ahead and lie down in the room and I'll be in there to join you in a few minutes."

I got up from the sofa and headed into his bedroom, and within a couple of seconds he was down on my heels. I couldn't believe how fast he turned off that TV and joined me. I lay across the bed sideways and he got behind me in the spooning position. I wanted him to get closer to me but he remained a gentleman and gave me a few inches to breathe. After about a few minutes of him playing the gentleman role, I scooted my body backward into his space. My ass wasn't huge and round like one of those video chicks, but it was plenty for him because when I slid it back into his groin area, his dick erected immediately.

I knew I'd only been in this man's presence for a total of seventy-two hours and it would probably look bad on my part to give him some pussy. But it had been a while since I had a man inside me and I needed to feel that feeling. So, when I leaned my back into his chest, I placed my hand on his leg and massaged it. I looked up into his face and waited for him to kiss me. Three seconds later, he did just that. When his full, soft lips met mine, I almost melted. The connection was so powerful it felt like I was on cloud nine. And before I knew it, he had me undressed with his face buried between my thighs. But what really fucked me up was how gentle he was when he was licking and tugging at my clit.

"Ooooohhhhh!" I began to moan, as the sensation of the feeling got the best of me. "Aaaaaaaaaaaaaaaaahhhhh, yeah, stay right there. Keep licking me right there," I said, coaching him along as he licked me all over my pussy.

"You like this shit, don't cha?" he whispered, his mouth sloppy wet with my juices.

"Yes, baby, you are making me feel so good. Please don't stop!" I begged him as I massaged his head. I grabbed both sides of his head and navigated it in a back and forth motion and the shit felt good as hell. This guy had my fucking toes curled up like I had on clown shoes. I was about to scream out and go crazy, but I couldn't. And before I could even get a grip on myself, I held his head with as much pressure as I could muster up. "Aaaaaaaaaaahhhhhh," I screamed, as I climaxed.

Hearing me scream with passion, Mario slowed down the pace at which he teased me with his tongue. He took licks and then he kissed me smack dab in the puddle of wetness I had brewing in the middle of my vagina. And within moments, he climbed on top of me with his erect dick barricaded behind a Magnum condom and then slid this entire dick inside me. I gasped for air when he filled me up with his eight and a half inches of thick meat. He pumped himself in me for about six seconds before he said, "Damn, your pussy is tight."

I was too engrossed into what we were doing to smile or make a comment, so I grabbed him by the back of his neck and pulled his face toward mine. When his face met mine, I pressed my lips against his and we locked them both together. His kisses were so passionate, I couldn't resist the feeling I was getting. When it was all said and done, he had me down on my knees, inserting himself deep inside me. He was pumping me for dear life. "Oh yeah, right there, baby! Please don't stop!" I moaned.

Fifteen strokes later, he grabbed me by my hips and held on to them tight. I knew he was about to come because his penetration movements got really intense. He started jerking and before I could scream, his dick exploded. "Aaaaaaaaaaaaaagghhhhh!" he screamed, his eyes almost rolling into the back of his head. Soon thereafter, he collapsed right on top of me. I lay there beneath him and didn't say one word. The warmth of his body was like insulation and it felt great.

The very next morning Mario woke me up with another round. He hit me off with a quickie this time and then we both rolled out of bed and took a shower together. It was really nice how he bathed me and I bathed him. Afterward, we got dressed and sat around his kitchen trying to plan out our day. I took a seat at the breakfast table with a cup of hot tea while he stood with his tea. He sipped it a few times and then said, "Want to take a ride with me so you can see my body shops?"

"Sure," I replied.

Immediately after he and I finished our tea, he told me to get my purse so we could ride. It was an early Wednesday morning and the sun was shining bright. The computer-controlled thermometer read fifty-seven degrees outside. It was a bit chilly, but not too much. I had on my D&G bubble goose jacket, so I was fine. I saw a couple of his neighbors on our way down the street and every last one of them seemed to be working class people with families and a dog. I sat back and wondered how I would look living out here among these people. Would I fit in? Or would I stick out like a sore thumb? I probably would never find out, but it sure was nice to daydream about it.

On our way to one of his shops, we stopped by Tropical Smoothie on Holland Road and got a couple of breakfast wraps. They were some kind of good. I devoured my southwestern breakfast wrap. It was like something I had never had before. Mario had an egg and cheese wrap and an energy drink. I guess he was on some type of health kick and that was actually good. Right after our making-out stop, Mario got back on the road and hit highway 264. He sped down this highway at eighty-five miles per hour until we got to the St. Paul's Boulevard exit and then he veered off it. I watched closely as we made a right turn on St. Paul and then we drove about four miles down, passing Twenty-first Street, going through an underpass, and then we went through two lights. After the second light we came to, we immediately made a right turn. His auto body shop was right there on the corner of Monticello Avenue and Twenty-sixth Street. I realized that the shop had just opened because one guy was raising the garage doors while another placed orange cones across the parking lot. Mario and I headed in the shop through the front door. As soon as we entered, he turned on the OPEN sign and walked back to his office. I followed right behind him, passing a ton of brand new tires and chrome rims.

"You sell tires and rims, too?" I asked.

"Of course, that's where the real money comes from," he replied.

"How much are they?"

"The tires can vary from eight to fifteen hundred for four. And the rims could cost you anywhere from two to five grand."

"Wow! That's a lot of money for a set of tires and rims. So, believe me, I will always keep it factory."

Mario laughed.

When we entered into his private domain, I was shocked to see that it wasn't nasty and junkie. He didn't have the executive type of business furniture in there, but the chipped desk he did have was neat. I sat down in one of the chairs placed against the wall while he organized some paperwork he had on his desk. Meanwhile, one of the guys who worked for him knocked on his door.

"Come in," Mario instructed.

Now I had to admit, this guy was even cuter than Mario.

He was kind of on the short side, standing at five foot seven, but he wasn't that bad on the eyes. He could almost pass for the actor Larenz Tate. This guy had the smile and the close haircut. I knew he didn't have any money to back up how fine he was, so I immediately shifted my attention to Mario. He sat behind his desk and waited for this guy to say what it was he came into his office for.

"What's up, T'won? What can I do for you?" Mario asked.

Before T'won answered his question, he looked at me and smiled. "How you doing, ma'am?"

I smiled back. "I'm doing fine. Thanks for asking," I replied.

"No problem," he said, and then he turned his focus to Mario. "Mario, man, my girl got in a car accident yesterday, so she needs to come up here and get her car fixed. But, I need to know—when you do the body estimate, could you give her my discount?"

"Yeah, I can do that. But tell me what's wrong with it."

"Some old man hit her from behind and snatched the bumper off."

"Well, that's not going to be that bad. Just call her and tell her to bring it in today so I can look at it and write up the estimate, and that way she can hand it to the insurance company."

T'won extended his hand for Mario to grab. "A'ight, boss man. Good looking out!" he commented, and then proceeded to leave. But as he was about to walk out, Mario stopped him in his tracks.

"Hey, T'won, hold up a minute."

"What's up?"

"What time did Ryan get here this morning?"

"He was here before I was."

"Why y'all just opening up the shop, then?"

"Because he was sitting in his car fussing with his girl."

"Oh, so he got dropped off this morning?"

"Yeah,"

"Oh, all right," Mario said, and then he dismissed T'won.

I sat back and watched how much respect T'won had for Mario and I was impressed. I was so impressed that right after T'won left, I said, "Hey, boss man, do you think I can get a discount on a kiss right now?"

Mario smiled and stood to his feet. "You can get that for tree," he replied, and then he grabbed me up from the chair and landed a nice wet one on my lips. The sparks I felt were feelings that a young girl gets when she experiences her first kiss.

We hung out at his shop for a couple of hours. While he took care of business with his customers, I got on the phone and called Carmen. She was upset about her mother, Sandra. She said Sandra stole some money from Grandma Hattie, so I was pissed off, too.

"How much money did she take?" I wondered aloud.

"A hundred dollars."

"How did she manage to do that?"

"Grandma always keeps her money hidden inside her bra, but she told me my mother snuck into the bathroom while she was taking a shower and went into the pocket of her house coat and stole her money from it."

"How the hell did she get into the bathroom?"

"She used a fucking butter knife. It ain't that hard to get in these doors around here. That's why all of us put locks on our doors."

"What is Grandma saying about all of this?"

"She was fussing a little bit. But then she said that she ain't gonna worry about it."

"Did your mother need that money for anything?"

"She didn't say, but knowing her, she probably did."

"Where is your mother now?"

"Yoshi, please. Don't nobody know where that bitch is. But

I do know she better stay away from here these next couple of days because if I saw her walking up here, in the frame of mind I'm in right now, I'd probably choke the shit out of her and beat her to death."

"Look, Carmen. I know you're upset. But let somebody else handle her. Trust me, with all the shit she has done to people, she's got a lot of shit coming back to her. It's called the law of reciprocity. What goes around come around."

"Shit, I can't wait that long. She needs her ass kicked right now coming up in here stealing from Grandma, knowing how hard that lady has it. She's been struggling for a very long time. Thank God her house is paid for and all she has to pay is the taxes and her utilities, because she would be shit out of luck with that small SSI check she gets."

"How much does she get?"

"Seven hundred and fifty-three dollars a month. Now just think how she would be able to pay a three-hundred a month gas bill along with a two-hundred a month light bill, pay for her diabetic medication, food for the house and stuff like deodorant, soap, washing powder, and cleaning supplies for the house, plus a mortgage that used to be four hundred a month. It would be impossible because I only bring home two-twenty a week with tips and I have bills of my own. And Rachael doesn't have a job so she can't contribute a thing. So you see, shit is fucked up around here, which means we can't have that stealing shit jumping off. She has to go."

"Why does Grandma keep letting her come into the house?"

"I keep asking her the same damn question. I'm starting to think she likes being taken advantage of."

"Don't say that. She's just torn between emotions, that's all."

"Well, she better get over it because times are hard right now and we need all the pennies we can get."

"It's going to get better. Don't you even sweat it! Hey listen, don't tell Grandma, but I am going to come by there later and give her the money back that was taken from her."

"She ain't gonna accept it."

"Yes, she will."

"All right, we'll see."

"Yes, we sure will," I said. Carmen and I talked for a little while more, until she got another call from her good friend Kimberly. I told her to handle her business and I'd see her later. She said okay and then we hung up.

Immediately after I hung up with Carmen, I put my phone away and left Mario's office to go look for him. He was outside speaking to another customer, so I stood back and watched how he handled his business. What was so cute was that he truly did look like Idris Elba, especially when he played the mechanic guy in the movie *Daddy's Little Girls*. I was being turned on by the second. But what was really odd about this picture was that this was the very first time I ever messed around with a middle-class guy. All the men I'd ever fucked had million-dollar status. I remember saying to myself a while back that I would never fuck with a guy making less than seven figures a year. But look at me now. I guess it's true when they say: "Never say never!"

Getting Things Poppin'

Mario didn't stay at work long. As a matter of fact, he had Ryan take over so we could leave for the rest of the day. I must say that I really enjoyed myself watching him conduct business. Men handling their shit is so masculine to me. I was thinking I might have to stick around this guy for a little while longer, because I saw he was growing on me.

On our way to his car, he got an unexpected visitor. "Go head to the car, I'll be with you in a moment," he said, and then he made a detour toward a brand new, pearl white 5 Series BMW. The windows were slightly tinted so I couldn't see who was behind the wheel. But as soon as the window rolled down, I got a really good look. To my surprise, it was a woman. A beautiful one at that, who looked like she was of Indian descent. She had a caramel complexion with long straight hair. But she didn't look at all happy to see Mario. I got inside his car and watched them from my side mirror. I was struggling to hear what they were saying so I rolled down the passenger side window. "Answer my question, Mario!" I heard her say as soon as I rolled down the window. I think she was talking loud so I could hear her, which I felt was fine in my book.

"I don't have to answer to you," I heard him say. "We aren't together anymore, so get out of here with all that fuck-

ing drama before I call the police and get you for trespass-
ing!"

"You think I give a fuck about the police? Call 'em!" she
snapped as she began to emerge from the car. I saw this and
sat up in the seat, wanting to witness what was about to
happen next.

Mario stepped back from the car as she opened the driver
side door. When she stood completely up, I got a good look
at her. She had to be about one hundred twenty-five pounds,
but she was about two inches shorter than me. Her attire was
very stylish. From what I could tell, she was wearing a pair of
blue denim jeans with a pair of Gucci boots. The heel had
to be at least four and a half inches. And the black leather
jacket she was sporting was very nice as well. If I could say
she reminded me of someone, I would say Meagan Good. And
to be truthful about this situation, I was kind of intimidated
that she looked better than I did. The only thing I had over
her was that I had more class and I was an attorney who
made millions fighting for my clients in court. I couldn't tell
you what she did for a living, but whatever it was, it couldn't
be much because anybody with a thirty thousand or more a
year salary could buy a 5 Series BMW. I could buy a BMW
dealership if I wanted to.

"Selina, you better get back in your car," he warned her.

"Not until I find out who this chick is you got in your
car," she said, rushing past him.

Hearing her say that she was about to come and find out
who I was threw me for a loop. I was shocked as hell. Speechless more or less, I held my cool and rolled the window back
up so they wouldn't notice that I was eavesdropping on
their conversation.

As she marched over toward the passenger side of his car,
he followed behind her. I pretended I was doing something

when she knocked on the window. I looked up and rolled the window back down.

"Yes," I said.

"Are you fucking Mario?" She went straight to the point.

Caught off guard by her question, I looked at her like she was crazy and said, "Did you ask Mario?"

She put both of her hands on her hips and said, "Yes, I sure did."

"And what did he tell you?" I threw the question back at her.

"He wouldn't answer me."

"Well, there you go," I replied nonchalantly, and continued to look at her.

Now I could tell that she was not at all pleased by my response because she was turning pink and purple in the face. I didn't know what this woman was capable of doing, so I leaned forward and rolled my damn window back up.

"Yeah, bitch! You better roll that window up if you know what's good for you," she commented. Ryan and T'won both ran outside to see what the commotion was all about.

By this time, Mario had jumped in the driver seat of the car. He sounded like he was out of breath. "That chick is crazy! Please ignore her," he said, turning the ignition on.

When she heard him start up the engine, she ran her crazy ass around the front of the car to prevent him from driving off. "Nigga, you ain't going nowhere until you tell me who she is."

"Selina, get from in front of my car before I run your ass over."

"Do it, Mario! And watch and see if I don't get your dumb ass locked the fuck up!" She placed her hands on the hood.

I looked over at him and he had the most frustrated expression on his face. He looked like he was about to blow

his top. I honestly didn't know what to say to him for fear
that he might snap on me. So, I just sat back and waited to
see what he was going to do. Several seconds later, he pulled
out his BlackBerry.

"What are you getting ready to do?" I asked.

"I'm getting ready to call the police. I can't keep dealing
with her bullshit. She's a fucking stalker and I just can't seem
to get rid of her crazy ass for nothing in the world."

Hearing the word *police* scared me to death. I couldn't
let him call the police like that. That was definitely a bad idea,
so I grabbed the phone out of his hand. "What are you
doing?" he wondered aloud.

"Don't call the police. You don't need all that negative
attention up here at your place of business. Just get out of
the car and talk to her," I tried to reason.

"That shit ain't gonna work. She's fucking crazy! And
knowing how crazy she is, she's bound to swing on me."

"Not if you talk to her nicely."

"You can't talk to her nice. That chick doesn't like reason. She likes a lot of fucking drama. That's all she knows."

I didn't know what else to say to Mario. It seemed as
though his mind was made up. So when he reached for his
phone, I had no choice but to hand it to him. And as soon
as he dialed 911 on the keypad and put the phone to his ear,
he started talking. My heart began racing because I knew
that it would be only a matter of a few minutes before the
police arrived. I sat back in the seat and wondered what in
the hell I was going to do. I was so afraid I almost pissed on
myself. Lucky for me, when Mario started giving the police
dispatcher information about what was going on and who
was the cause of the problem, Selina heard him and it seemed
like she was having second thoughts about sticking around.
He was very loud when he spoke to the dispatcher. Especially when he was giving out her description and the type

of car she was driving. Several seconds later, Selina punched down on the hood with her fist and stormed off. "Fuck you, you coward!" she spat out of her mouth.

Mario ignored her antics and continued to speak to the dispatcher. "She's leaving and getting in her car right now," he said.

"You said she's leaving?" I heard the dispatcher ask.

"Yes, ma'am. She just got into her car and now she's pulling off."

"All right, then stay on the phone with me until she's completely gone," she instructed.

"She's gone now," he announced a moment later.

"Okay, feel free to call again if she comes back on the premises. But in the meantime, you're gonna have to go to the magistrate and take out a restraining order on her."

"I will. Thank you," he said, and then they both hung up.

After he hung up with the dispatcher, he didn't hesitate to get out of there. I sat back in the seat and didn't say a word. Half a mile from the shop, he broke the silence by asking me, "Are you all right?"

"Yes, I'm fine," I told him.

He began to apologize. "I am so sorry you had to see that."

I rubbed him on the leg and said, "You don't have to apologize. But tell me, why was she acting out like that? Women only act like that when the man has been leading them on or giving them false hopes. So, which one did you do?"

Mario sighed and said, "Selina and I were together for about three years and we just broke up about a month ago because I found out she was stealing from me."

"Are you kidding me?"

"No, I am not."

"How much did she take?"

"I can't put a dollar amount on it. But it seemed like every time I looked in my stash a couple of hundred dollars would come up missing. I thought I was just miscounting my money, but when I came home one day and saw her in the act, I told her she had to go."

"You actually caught her stealing your money?"

"Yep, I sure did."

"What did she do?"

"She couldn't do shit. She just stood there and looked stupid."

"I'm sorry to hear that."

"Nah, it's okay. I'm just glad I caught her stabbing me in the back before I married her silly ass."

Shocked by his response, I said, "Oh, so you and she were going to get married?"

"Yep. We had set the date for October seventeenth of this year, but those plans are null and void now."

"What was so significant about October seventeenth?"

"Nothing. That's just a date she picked."

"Damn, that's a bummer."

"No, that's actually good on my part. See, I can't have a woman in my life I can't trust. I need to know that you're gonna be faithful and honest with me. So, if I require that, then I damn sure ain't gonna have you stealing from me. In my book, stealing from me is like lying, and I can't deal with it."

Knowing that Mario was serious as hell about what he was saying got me to wondering how much longer I was going to keep up my lies. I wanted so desperately to open up to him and let him know who I was and what I was really about, but then I figured it was too late. He probably wouldn't believe me, and on top of that, he might turn my ass over to the police. I would be devastated for sure. So, I guessed the best thing for me to do would be to keep quiet.

Later That Night

I went over to Grandma Hattie's house like I had promised. She was in the den area watching television when I walked in the house. Carmen, of course, wasn't there, but Rachael was. She was standing outside on the front porch talking to Rodney. They seemed like they were being civilized to each other, so I just spoke and kept it moving. My main concern was my grandmother anyway so, when I approached her sitting in her favorite chair, I leaned over and hugged her. She smiled and asked me what I was up to.

I took a seat next to her. "I came here to see you," I told her.

"Oh, that's so sweet. You are such a sweetheart."

"Never mind about me. What's going on with you?"

"Oh, nothing. Just sitting around watching my regular programs."

"Carmen called me and told me Aunt Sandra stole one hundred dollars from you."

Grandma Hattie sighed heavily. "Yeah, she found a way to sneak in the bathroom and steal my money when I was taking a shower. But, that's gon' be the last time I slip up and let her get me like that."

I reached into my pocket and pulled out two one-hundred-dollar bills and handed them both to her. Grandma was a little hesitant to take the money from me at first, but when I expressed to her how it would make me feel if she accepted it, she went ahead and took it.

"I'm gon' hide this money right here in a good spot. Ain't nobody gon' find it this time," she assured me, and stuffed the money inside her bra.

I smiled at her as she tucked her money away. "Have you seen Aunt Sandra since she took your money?"

"No, baby. I probably won't see her for the next couple of days. Every time she manages to steal money from me she always go in hiding for two or three days, until her money runs out. And then she come back in here smiling like she ain't did nothing wrong."

"Does she have a key to the house?"

"No, she doesn't have one. But she always finds a way to get in here, even when no one is here."

"Why don't you get a restraining order against her? She doesn't deserve to be around you. She is bringing you and everyone in this house down."

"I know, I know. But she's still my daughter and I can't turn my back on her."

"I understand all of that, but she needs some serious help. And she's not gonna be able to get any while you are enabling her."

"You're right. But, I just don't know what else to do."

"You gotta put your foot down, Grandma."

"I have, but it didn't work."

"You gotta stay firm and let her know who's the boss around here."

"Baby, I don't have the energy for all that. I'm just gonna let God deal with it. He ain't brought me this far to leave me now."

I sat there and looked at the sincerity in her face. It was

apparent that she wanted me to leave the situation alone, so I did.

"Where's Uncle Reginald? I haven't seen him since I've been here."

"He's fine. He was around here earlier fixing my plumbing problem."

"Does Uncle Reginald know that Aunt Sandra steals from you?"

"I told him a couple of times."

"How does he feel about that?"

"He doesn't say much anymore, but he used to fuss about it."

"How do you feel about Rachael's boyfriend?"

"Rodney is fine. I just don't like it when she stays out with him all night."

"Have you told her how you felt?"

Grandma laughed. "Rachael doesn't listen to me. She doesn't listen to anyone in this house, for that matter."

"Well, she needs to listen to somebody because Rodney is no good for her. Do you know I witnessed her running down behind the police when they started a foot pursuit for her little boyfriend? I couldn't believe how she put her life in jeopardy for that boy."

"That ain't nothing new. She'll do anything for that boy. I wouldn't be shocked if she turned against me for him."

"He got her wrapped around his fingers like that?"

"Yes, he sure does."

"That's not healthy. That little boy is bad news. And I can see it just as clear as day."

"Ain't no need for you to get all worked up behind Rachael and her mess. She doesn't listen to nobody and I don't think she ever will."

Hearing Grandma Hattie tell me yet another member of

the family isn't going to change made me shut all communication down. It was fruitless to continue going over and over how she could influence them to do better. Unfortunately, she wouldn't listen, so I threw up my hands. I sat there a little while longer and then told her I had to go. She wanted to know why I was always in a rush to leave her. "You never stay here more than thirty minutes."

"That's not true, Grandma. I've been here longer than that."

"I can't recall when you have."

I stood to my feet. "All right. The next time I come over here, I promise I will stay longer."

She stood up beside me. "I guess I'll walk you to the door."

"Thanks," I said, heading toward the front door.

"I heard you got a man in your life. So, all I am going to tell you is to be careful. Because the men around these parts will sweet-talk you right out cha draws and act like they don't know you the next morning."

"I ran into a few of those type of men in my younger days."

"Well then, you know what I'm talking about."

I smiled at her and said, "Yes, ma'am. I do."

"You keep your eyes and ears open and come back and see me when you get a chance. But call me first so I can cook you something special."

"Okay, I will," I promised.

When I walked outside, Rachael and Rodney had already left. I wanted to say good-bye to Rachael but I guessed she had something else on her agenda. I kissed my grandmother on the cheek and told her I loved her. And she told me she loved me back as quickly as I can turn my head.

When I was leaving the neighborhood, I accidently ran across Sandra standing at the corner of Church Street and Washington Avenue. She was leaning over into the passenger side window of an old model Volvo. She looked a hot mess trying to solicit sex to that White man. From what I could see, he looked like an old-ass man. I figured maybe he couldn't get a piece of ass from home so he had to resort to tricking with a dope fiend. "Times must be extremely bad for you to stoop to that level," I murmured to Sandra, though she couldn't hear. I rode by them and shook my head.

I wanted to surprise Carmen, so I elected to ride past her job. I used the GPS system in the truck to get the directions to IHOP and when I programmed my exact location, it took me straight there.

When I arrived, she was taking care of a couple at their table. She was juggling their food entrées and their condiments while she held a smile on her face. I walked in and had the hostess seat me at a table. "Your waitress will be with you shortly," she told me.

"Thank you," I replied, and focused my attention back on Carmen.

Right after she handed the couple their food, she went over to another table and took the orders of two women and one man. They were all young and Black. They looked like they were around the ages of twenty-one to twenty-five. I assumed that they were college kids. But when one of them opened up her mouth, I knew they were straight out of the ghetto. "Do you know that we have been sitting here for about ten minutes waiting for you to take our order?" she said sarcastically.

The other woman laughed. The guy didn't say a word, but he did try to hush his friend up. "Shhhh," he said, trying to cover up her mouth.

"Don't be trying to cover up my mouth. I am grown. I can say anything I want," she griped.

"I am sorry about the wait, ma'am. But I was held up by trying to handle someone else's table."

"I don't care about that shit! That's not my problem. I just need someone who's not going to make me wait a long time and who will give me good service."

"I know it's not your problem. But like I said, I had another table I had to handle first."

"Look, I am not trying to hear that shit! Where is your manager?" she snapped.

"He's in the back. Would you like to speak with him?"

"I sure will. Because you are in the fucking way."

Now I had to admit, Carmen really handled herself well. If it were me, I would have cursed that ghetto-ass bitch out. And I would have spit in her fucking face and dared her to get up from the table. I could truly tell that it was hard trying to service the public. Everybody had fucking issues and their attitudes were crazy. I couldn't deal with it because I would either end up in jail or beat up one.

While Carmen walked away to get the manager, I heard all three of those idiots laughing behind her back. I was getting angrier by the second. I wanted to go and confront the one who was rude to Carmen, but I did not want to cause a scene, because it would have been one. Thank God for common sense, because if I didn't have any, I would be over there pronto.

About thirty seconds later, Carmen and her manager both walked back to the table. She finally recognized that I was there when she returned to the dining area. I winked at her and signaled for her to come by my table when she was done handling her business. Now when the manager, who was in fact a Black man, approached the hostile customer and her friends, he asked them what the problem was, even though Carmen had already prepped him in the back.

"What is your name?" the customer asked.

"It's Derrick," he replied.

"Well, Derrick, the problem is we have been sitting here

for about fifteen minutes now and we haven't gotten our order taken or anything. Everybody else around us got something to drink or their food order and we don't have anything. And we are extremely upset about that."

"I am sorry that you are upset. But unfortunately tonight we are short-staffed. Carmen here has to wait on four more tables than she normally works, so if you bear with her, I'm sure she will get your food out as soon as she can."

"Well, since we waited so long, can we get a discount or something?"

The manager smiled and said, "Yes, you can. Just have Carmen bring your check to me and I will adjust it for you."

"All right, thank you," she said.

After Carmen's manager calmed the lady down, he left Carmen behind to take their orders. Immediately after she did so, she prepared their drink orders and handed their food ticket to the chef. Right after she served them their drinks she raced over to my table with pen and pad in hand. "Can I take your order?"

I smiled. "I am so proud of you. You truly handled yourself well."

"You heard her?"

"I'm sure everybody heard her, as loud as she was."

Carmen sighed heavily. "Yoshi, if we were in the streets, I would have beat that bitch down."

"I'm sure. Because I wanted to come over there and yank her ass out of that chair myself. She was really acting a damn fool over there."

"Tell me about it. But you know what? I get that shit all the time. Sometimes I let it roll off my back. Other times I be wanting to go upside their head, but I can't afford to lose my job. And not only that, people are crazy and they'll try to pull out a gun on your ass and kill you on the fucking spot, and I don't have time for that."

"What time do you get off?"

"Two hours from now. Why?"

"I just asked."

"What are you doing here? Are you trying to order something?"

"No, I just wanted to stop by and see you."

"Well, you see how I'm doing. The question is, how are you doing? You and your man got married yet?"

I smiled. "Now what kind of question is that? You know I am not into that commitment stuff. He's all right, though. I am enjoying myself."

"I bet you are." Carmen smiled back. "Did you get a chance to stop by the house and see Grandma?"

"Yes, I did."

"Did you talk to her about the money situation?"

"Yes, and when I gave her the money she hesitated to take it but I shoved it right into her hands. I told her that I wanted her to have it because I didn't want to see her without."

"And what did she say?"

"She didn't say much. We got on the subject of your mother, but you know, she shied away from it. It seems like she doesn't want to turn her back on your mother. I told her that she's gonna have to let that situation go because it is tearing her down."

"Yoshi, you can talk to her until your face turns blue. She ain't gonna listen to you. She would rather for my mother to sneak into her house and steal her blind than for her to lock her ass out so she can be on the streets. It's crazy and I don't even say anything to her about it anymore. I do curse my mother's ass out when she gets out of pocket. But other than that, I just leave it alone. I've got problems of my own, so I will not let no one stress me out about theirs."

"You can say that again," I agreed, then changed the subject. "What's up with your manager? Is he cool?"

"Yeah, he's all right."

"Is he cool to work with?"

"Sometimes, when he ain't on his period."

I burst into laughter. "What do you mean by that?" I asked.

"I know you noticed that he was gay."

Shocked, I said, "No, I didn't."

"Yeah, girl, he is flaming. So when he has had a good night with his man, he'll come in and let us do anything we want. But as soon as his man act like a damn fool and does something stupid, he comes in here and starts scratching everybody's eyes out."

I chuckled. "Girl, you are so funny." I took my attention off her because two men came into the restaurant.

The hostess escorted them to their seat, so Carmen looked at me and said, "I'll be right back. That's my section they're in."

"Okay, take care of your business," I told her.

I sat back and watched her as she strutted her stuff on over to their table. Both men looked really appealing to the eye—one of them a chocolate color and the other one a light brown. They had to be at least six feet even and from what I could tell they looked like they had nice bodies. I've got a real good eye when it comes to sizing a man up while he's in his clothing. I mastered that technique a while back. They looked to be brothers. And when they spoke to give Carmen their order, I almost melted.

"Can I get the T-bone steak and scrambled eggs?" the chocolate brother asked.

"And what will you have?" Carmen asked the other.

"Give me the steak and cheese omelet with a side of hash browns."

"Is that it?" She looked at both of them.

"Yes, it is," they said in unison.

When she walked away from the table, they looked straight at her ass and glued their eyes to it. I laughed to myself because they were being typical men. But what really tickled me was when they smiled while they were talking about her. So, it was evident that they were saying something good. Once Carmen was done with putting their orders in, she grabbed her other customers' food and took it to their table. They weren't acting like damn fools this time. I guess they were happy to finally be able to eat. Afterward, she walked back to my table.

I leaned over and pinched her in her side and said, "I don't know what those men were saying about you when you walked away from them, but they were watching your big ol' bootie until you got out of sight."

Carmen smiled. "That doesn't surprise me. My butt is kind of phat back there," she joked.

"Yes, it is. So, you better keep it on lock and key. Remember, these guys around here need to appreciate and treat you good first before you go all out and give up the ass. They need to work for it. So, don't go back over there and let one of them whisper some bullshit in your ear so he can get your number."

"I won't. I don't have time for a man right now."

"Good! Keep it that way unless I say different."

She gave me a high five and said, "That's right, cousin. I knew you would have my back."

"You better remember that, too," I told her, and stood up from the table. "Well, let me get out of here."

"Where are you about to go?"

"I'm going back over Mario's house and hang out with him. We might go out and get a bite to eat or something."

"Well, call me later."

"I will, sweetheart. Now, you take care," I told her. I gave her a hug and then exited the restaurant.

I got Mario on the phone and told him that I was on my way.

"Where are you?" he asked.

"I just got on the highway."

"Have you eaten yet?"

"No, I haven't. Why?"

"Because I'm at the house whipping you up something special."

I smiled to myself. "What is it?" I wondered aloud.

"It's a little something my mother taught me how to cook a long time ago."

"And what was that?"

"Have you ever had Chicken Oscar?"

"No, not that I can recall. What is it?"

"It's a broiled chicken breast stuffed with lump crabmeat and a hollandaise sauce poured on top."

"Whoa, that sounds real good. What time is dinner?"

"As soon as you get here."

"What else did you cook with it?"

"Do you like asparagus?"

"Yes, I love asparagus."

"Well, I steamed some and now I got it in a bowl of sautéed butter sauce. And for dessert, I am going to put you on a silver platter and spread whipped cream all over you and stick a cherry smack dab in the middle of your stomach. Now how does that sound?"

"It sounds delicious. Too bad I won't be able to eat any," I replied with a chuckle.

"You can have some of me."

"I can't wait," I told him. "Do you need me to pick up anything while I'm out?" I continued.

"You know what? You can pick up a bottle of champagne if you like."

"What kind?"

"I don't know, sweetie. Get whatever you like."

"What about a white wine? Is that okay?"

"Sure, baby, get whatever you like. Tonight it's about you."

"It's about you, too."

"Okay, well, it's about us then. Now hurry up and get your ass here. You've been gone too long."

"Mario, I've only been gone for two hours. Good grief."

"That's two hours too long. And I miss you, so get your butt back here."

I laughed at his comedic way and assured him that I'd be there right after I left the liquor store.

Playing the Wifey Role

After the great dinner and staying up late last night, this morning I decided to show Mario I could do a little something in the kitchen too. I wasn't as good a cook as him, but I'd employed a few chefs to work in my home, so I knew a few culinary treats.

While he was asleep, I ran to the store and picked up a dozen eggs, a pack of American cheese, a pack of Colby, and a pack of cheddar. I also picked up a pound of raw, jumbo shrimp, a half pound of scallops, and a pound of crabmeat. All that was left for me to do was pick up an onion, minced garlic, and a red bell pepper, so I did that before I went through the checkout. When I returned to the house he was still asleep, so I went into the kitchen and started heating things up. By the time he woke up around noon, I had cooked him a sizzling three-cheese seafood omelet with a hint of garlic. I ran to the bedroom and literally dragged him into the kitchen to eat. I didn't even give him time to brush his teeth. I wanted him to have his meal when it was piping hot! And that's exactly how he got it. I also poured him a glass of cold pineapple juice, since I had forgotten to pick up a carton of orange juice from the store.

After breakfast, he and I both hopped into the shower and got a quickie in there. If I kept the sex thing going on, I was going to end up pregnant again, and I couldn't have that, especially at that time. God knows I can't bring a baby into this world while my life is upside down. Mario seemed like he was a little more stable than I was. But he could have been putting up a facade, like me. Time would tell, though. I just hoped sooner than later.

I jumped back in the bed since he told me he was going to chill inside. The weather wasn't too pretty outdoors. Although it was mid afternoon, the gloomy sky made it seem later. A lot of people called it baby-making weather. I called it sleep time, since that's what I did. I slept kind of light, so when I heard Mario talking on his BlackBerry from the living room, I was able to tune in without straining myself. He tried to talk very low and be a little discreet, but I was born with the ears of a dog, so I can hear a pin drop from miles away.

"What time you want to meet up?" I heard him say. "Dino, now you know that's not a good spot. Too many police be coming through there all times of the night," he continued. And then I heard him say, "Nah, man, you are trying to get me locked up talking like that. You know I don't get down like that, so call me back when you learn how to conduct business," he said, and then he fell silent.

Now, I can't tell you what that call was about. But I do know that whatever it was, it was dealing with something illegal. I lay back in the bed and wondered what it was he was talking about. Drugs came to my mind first. And then I thought maybe he could be buying illegal guns. But whatever it was, it didn't sound right. And since I didn't want to wrack my brain with it, I turned over and dozed back off.

While I was asleep, I got a call from Carmen. I tried to ignore it, but she continued to call me back to back until I picked up. I was really agitated when I finally answered it. "What is it now?" I asked.

"Yoshi, I am so sorry to bother you, but I am sick as a dog right now and I need medicine bad."

"Well, take some."

"We ain't got shit in this house to take other than Grandma's hot tea with honey and that shit ain't gonna help me. I need something stronger, like NyQuil or Tylenol Cold and Flu medicine."

"Well, get Rachael to go out and get it for you."

"She's not even here."

"Where is she?"

"She's somewhere in those streets running down behind her fucking boyfriend. And even if she was here, that tramp wouldn't go to the front door for me."

"Where is Grandma?"

"She's downstairs watching TV."

"What time is it?"

"It's a little after eight."

"So, what do you want me to do? Because I'm in bed right now."

Carmen started coughing uncontrollably. "Look, Yoshi, you know I wouldn't bother you if I really didn't need that medicine," she said between coughs. "But my head is killing me and my throat is sore as hell. I think I've got a fever because I'm burning up in this fucking bed."

"It sounds like you got the flu."

"It feels like it, too."

"Okay, well look, give me about thirty minutes and I'll be over there."

"All right," she replied, still coughing and gagging.

I hurried up and disconnected that call. I couldn't take listening to all the irritating noise, so I shook my head and my arms like I had something on me and then I slid out of the bed and headed out of the room. I walked down the hallway toward the living room and when I looked around the corner, I realized that Mario was nowhere to be found. I turned around and looked into the kitchen and when I saw that he wasn't in there, I knew that he had to be gone.

"Where in the hell could he be?" I asked myself as I picked up the house phone and dialed his number. He answered on the third ring.

"What's up, baby?"

"Where are you?"

"In Hampton taking care of some business."

"What time are you coming back?"

"I'm not sure. Why?"

"Because I need to run out to Huntersville. My cousin Carmen is sick as a dog and she needs some medicine like right now."

"I know you want to go out there, but it's too late for you to be in the streets this time of night. I would go crazy if something happened to you."

"Calm down, because nothing is going to happen to me. I am a big girl, so I can handle myself."

"Not in these streets. I know a handful of niggas who would randomly kill a woman at the drop of a hat. So don't tell me you'd be able to handle them."

"Stop being so overprotective."

"I'm not. I just know how niggas out here are. They don't play fair. And if they saw you roaming around here all by yourself, they'll try you and you won't be able to do shit about it."

"But, Mario, she sounded really bad on the phone. I can't leave her hanging like that. That's family and plus, I already told her I was coming."

"Well, call her back and tell her to get somebody else to do it."

"That's the thing, she doesn't have anyone else she can count on."

"She doesn't have a man?"

"No."

"Well, she needs to get one, because I can't have you running out there this time of night every time one of your family members needs something."

"Mario, I understand everything you're saying but I got to do this for her just this once. She's counting on me. I can't just let her sit there when I gave her my word that I would be there."

Mario fell silent. It was apparent he wasn't trying to hear what I had to say. He was very adamant about me not going to Huntersville, but I still had a duty to fulfill and I couldn't let him stop me. "Are you still there?" I asked.

"Yeah, I'm here."

"Well, why did you get quiet?"

"Because I don't want to talk about it anymore. You know where I stand with this, but I see you are the type of woman who is going to do whatever she wants to do, so I am going to sit back and let you do you."

"Come on, Mario. It's not that serious."

"It may not be for you. But it means a big deal for me because I am a man, and if my woman is in the street this time of the night and something happens to her while I am not around, that shit will fuck with me."

"Listen, I'll tell you what. This is the last time I am going to go out this time of the night without you. And while I am out, I promise I will be very careful."

"Yeah, a'ight," he replied nonchalantly.

"And what does that mean?"

"It means, all right," he replied sarcastically.

"Okay, Mario, I am going to say bye now because I see that you aren't going to let this go."

"I'm done."

"Okay, well, I'll see you when I get back."

"All right," he said.

When I got off the phone with Mario, I leaned against the countertop in the kitchen and wondered what was going through his mind. I didn't want him to be upset with me because I went against his wishes. I just hoped he didn't hold grudges long, because I sure could. And two people who do that and are a couple won't last very long.

See No Evil

As much as I didn't want to go out this time of the night, I had to go over to my grandmother's house to check up on Carmen. Mario was against me leaving his house, but I had to go after I heard how badly she sounded over the phone. I knew that if he was home and not in the streets taking care of business, he would have either stopped me from leaving or he would have driven me out to Huntersville himself. Since Rachael wasn't around to go out and Carmen needed medicine to get over this bad cold she had, I elected to play good Samaritan and do it myself.

Carmen looked like shit when I walked into her bedroom. I immediately took a seat beside her on the edge of the bed. Covered up in pink flannel pajamas, a flower-printed satin head scarf, and an old-looking wool blanket, I told her she looked really bad. She tried desperately to laugh but it wouldn't come out. So I rubbed her across her leg and told her to take it easy.

"What do you normally take for this type cold?" I asked.

"I usually take lemon and honey TheraFlu. It comes in a blue and yellow box and the box has about six or seven packs of the powder medicine in it. You can also get me a half gallon of orange juice."

"Any particular brand?"

"Simply Orange or Tropicana is fine."

"Okay, you got it," I said, standing up.

"What store are you going to?"

"I was going to that Thomas Market place on the next block."

"Oh, that's cool. They should have what I asked for."

"Okay," I said, and left.

When I exited the house, I looked up the street and then at my truck parked directly in front of the house. The distance between where I was standing and the store was only two blocks, so I figured that it might not be so bad if I walked instead of driving.

As I started making my way in the direction of the little convenience store, I realized that there wasn't a lot of foot traffic outside. It was only a few minutes after ten o'clock, so that was unusual for this time of the night. The few days I'd been in town, I noticed how busy these streets could get when the junkies and the crackheads beat the pavement down to get their next high. It got so bad, it looked like a circus. At times, I thought I was watching a fucking drug convention. But for some reason, the streets weren't jumping this night. I figured maybe the police came through and ran a lot of the freaks to the other side of the neighborhood. Who knows, maybe all the drug dealers ran out of dope and left to go re-up. But whatever the reason, it felt good to walk down the block and not have to say "excuse me" every five to ten seconds.

This was my second time going to this little convenience store, so I remembered where the orange juice was. And I had a female store employee point me in the direction of the cold medicine. After I picked up the brand Carmen wanted, I paid for my items and turned around to leave. But before I took the first step, I looked back at the woman behind the counter and asked, "Where is everybody?"

"Who are you talking about?" she asked.

"I'm talking about the people outside. It looks like a fucking ghost town out there. There's not a drug dealer or a dope fiend in sight."

She laughed at me. "If the streets are that clean, then that means that either the police done been through here and did a sweep or the drug boys ran out and left so they can get some more. Just count your lucky stars that you don't have to walk through all that garbage tonight."

"You got a point," I replied, and then I left.

Again when I was back on the streets, it still seemed very odd that I wasn't being bombarded with a slew of fiends. I felt a bit strange, but the woman did say that I needed to count my lucky stars, so that's what I did, walking back in the direction in which I came. This time around the walk seemed longer for some apparent reason. I had to pass a row of houses and then cross a dark alley that smelled like nothing else but urine. When I passed by it the first time, I had almost regurgitated the couple slices of pizza I had eaten earlier. And since I knew my stomach wouldn't tolerate that unbearable stench this time, I held my breath, put my head down, and tried to walk by it as quickly as possible.

Before I got past the alley, I was startled by a shout down at the end of it. I immediately turned my head in that direction and noticed that there was a bit of commotion going on. I stopped in my tracks to zoom in on what was happening down the alley, and that's when I realized that two men had guns pointed directly at the head of another man. They had him surrounded like they were the predator and he was the prey. I could tell the man was pleading for his life.

"Maceo," he said. "Man, I wouldn't ever snitch on you. Whoever told you that shit is a motherfucking liar! You can take me to them so we can straighten this shit out now!"

"Nigga, shut the fuck up! And stop acting like a fucking pussy!" Maceo roared.

"Yeah, nigga, shut the fuck up and take this shit like a man!" the other man added.

Witnessing all this mayhem scared the hell out of me, so I put one foot in front of the other and started making my way back to my destination. I refused to be a witness to anyone's murder, but fate dealt me a different hand, because as soon as I took the second step, I heard four gunshots fire, one after the other. Panic-stricken, I dove down on the ground, crawled to a nearby Dumpster, and hid behind it. I scraped my knees up underneath my three-hundred-dollar denim jeans. I damaged my jacket, too, but I couldn't have cared less. My life was more important, and I wasn't going to risk it for an outfit. I could replace clothes, but I can't say the same for my life.

Two seconds later, Maceo and the other guy ran out of the alley, toting their guns in hand, and hopped into a black 2009 Expedition truck with tinted windows. Not once did they look back, so there was no doubt in my mind that they didn't see me. I let out a big sigh of relief after they sped off and made a right turn onto the next street.

Before I stood up to my feet, I looked back down the alley and saw the man's lifeless body lying face down on the ground. His head was lying in a huge pool of blood. The sight of it began to turn my stomach inside out, so I stood up to get out of there. I made sure the coast was clear, and when I felt I was no longer in harm's way, I ran like hell. While I was running back toward Grandma Hattie's house, I couldn't do anything else but think about that guy who was just shot to death. And then I began to wonder whether or not he was dead. I mean, what if he wasn't? I probably could have saved him. But then again, I figured he had to be dead because they shot him four times. There was no way he could be helped. Panting, I finally arrived in front of my grandmother's house. And it didn't shock me to see her standing at the front door awaiting my arrival.

"Oh, my God! I heard the gunshots. Are you all right, child?" she asked as she stormed out onto the porch.

"Yes, ma'am. I'm fine," I assured her, and collapsed on the old sofa she had placed there for outdoor decor. Yes, the same sofa I swore I'd never sit on.

"Thank you, Jesus. I thought you got caught up in a drive-by," she said.

And as bad as I wanted to respond, I couldn't. Instead, I held my hand over my heart, closed my eyes and began to thank the Lord in a quiet prayer for watching over me.

"Well, did you see where the shooting was coming from?" she wondered aloud.

I really wasn't in the mood to revisit that nightmare. So, I lied, "No, Grandma. I didn't see a thing."

Her questions continued. "Well, I wonder if anybody got shot."

"Grandma, I can't answer any of those questions because as soon as I heard the first gunshot, I started running and didn't look back."

She shook her head in dismay. "These young people out here are going to kill each other before it's all over with." She headed back into her house. She stood there in the doorway and waited for me to follow her, but I handed her the bag that contained Carmen's medicine and orange juice and told her I would see them in the morning. She gave me a hug and told me to be careful.

By the time I arrived back at Mario's place, I was a fucking nervous wreck. All I could think about was that guy getting shot up in the back of that alley. I immediately turned on the television to see if the local news station had any information about the shooting. But when I turned it to one of the news channels, there was only regularly scheduled programming. I looked down at my watch and realized that it was five minutes till eleven. Frustrated, I flopped down onto the edge of the bed. "Come on now, cut this bullshit!" I snapped.

I sat there and waited patiently for the next five minutes to roll around and it finally did. And just like I had thought, the local news station had one of their field journalists on the scene, broadcasting the story live. The Black female reporter didn't have much information, but she did indicate that the man found in a dark alley in the rough neighborhood of Huntersville was pronounced dead when the police arrived. The reporter also indicated that it wasn't clear why he'd been shot four times, but the authorities did believe that it was drug related and that the identity of the murder victim would be revealed after his family had been notified. "If you have any information about this murder, please contact Norfolk Police Department at 1-800-LOCK-U-UP," the woman urged.

"Oh shit! He is dead!" I said, my hand covering my mouth as I turned away from the television.

I sat there on the edge of the bed with the remote in my hand and turned the volume down. My heart was racing at the speed of lightning. I honestly couldn't believe what I had just heard. I mean, it was a no-brainer that the guy was dead. Maceo and his partner put four slugs in his body. I turned back to the television and saw the news station flashed the one-eight-hundred number across the screen once again. One part of me wanted to make an anonymous call, but then I had to remind myself that if I made the call from Mario's house, it could be traced. It would be fucked-up around the board, especially if they somehow found out I was a fucking fugitive. That alone made me go to plan B, which meant I needed to keep my mouth closed.

After the news went off, I took a cold shower. For the moment, it took my mind off the murder. But when I got into bed, my mind weighed heavily on how the guy's family must have felt after the police gave them the bad news. I also wondered if he had left any children behind. That would really be fucked-up, if that was the case. I tossed and turned for at least an hour before I fell asleep.

I woke up when I heard Mario come in through the front door.

"Hey, baby," he yelled, "you up?" I heard him make his way down the hallway toward the bedroom.

I sat up in the bed when he turned on the bedroom light. "Yes, I'm up. But what time is it?" I asked him, squinting my eyes from the bright light coming from the lamp.

He smiled. "It's two o'clock, baby. Get up."

"For what?" I whined. "I'm tired, Mario, and it's late."

"Baby, I picked us up some breakfast from Denny's, so come in the kitchen and eat with me."

"I'm sorry, but I don't even have an appetite right now," I told him. "So, put it in the microwave and I'll eat it in the morning when I get up," I assured him.

Seeing the exhausted look on my face, Mario left me alone. "All right, I'ma let you go back to bed for now, but you better eat this food as soon as you get up."

I smiled. "I will, sweetheart. You don't have to worry about that," I told him, and then I lay back down. Immediately after he turned the lights back off, I began to think about the murder that happened hours earlier. The weight of it felt like a ton of bricks on my shoulders. I wanted so badly to walk in the other room and tell Mario what I had experienced, but I couldn't because I didn't know whether or not I could trust him. He was well-known in this area and especially in Huntersville, so it wouldn't surprise me if he knew the guy who was killed as well as the shooter. I lay there in the bed and began to weigh my options about whether or not I should talk to Mario. I mean, I needed someone to talk to so I could lift this burden. But, for some reason, my intuition spoke louder and told me to keep my mouth closed. I was a stranger and I was in unfamiliar territory—two good reasons for me to listen to my mind instead of my heart.

After thirty minutes of mulling over how I was going to come to terms with this ordeal, I still came up with nothing. I figured the nightmare would go away one day and I would be all right, so I turned over and forced myself to go back to sleep.

I Didn't See
This Shit Coming

The constant ringing of my cell phone woke me in the morning. I knew it was Carmen calling me, so I reached over to the nightstand and picked it up.

"Hello," I said, sounding groggy.

"Girl, get up. It's eleven o'clock in the morning."

"Carmen, what do you want?"

"I was calling to see if you were all right. Grandma told me you were outside when that boy got killed last night."

"Yeah, I'm fine," I told her, even though I was lying.

"Well, girl, it's been a mess out here. The homicide detectives been knocking on everybody's door trying to find out if they saw anything."

"Did they knock on your door?" I asked, and then my heart started beating uncontrollably as I waited for Carmen to answer me.

"Yeah, they came to our door this morning, but Grandma told them she ain't seen shit. Then she sent them right on their way."

"Do you think they're coming back?"

Carmen sucked her teeth. "Hell nah, those crackers ain't coming back. They got the message when she told them she didn't see shit the first time."

"Did you know the guy who got killed?" I asked her.

"Yeah, I knew Lil D. He was working for that guy Maceo I showed you at the restaurant that night. But word has it he was a snitch, so it wouldn't surprise me if I found out Maceo had him killed."

Knowing Carmen had an idea that Maceo could have had something to do with Lil D's murder gave me chills all over my body. I wanted to tell her everything I saw. But I knew the telephone was the worst device to talk on when you're saying something incriminating. So again, I elected to keep my mouth shut. She and I talked for a few more minutes until I ushered her off the phone. I had to use the bathroom really bad, so I told her I would call her back.

"Am I gonna be able to see you today?" she yelled through the phone before I pressed the end button.

I sighed heavily and told her, "Give me a couple of hours. I'll let you know."

"You just don't want to leave Mario's side," she spat back.

"What are you talking about, Carmen? Mario doesn't have anything to do with this. I just got a few things I need to take care of. And if I have enough time, I'll call you and let you know."

"Yeah, right! You know that nigga ain't trying to let you out of his sight. It wouldn't surprise me if he got your ass on lockdown. It's been about a week now since you had your spot out there in Newpointe and I bet you haven't slept there one night. Have you?"

"No, I haven't," I replied.

"Well damn, have you been there long enough for the furniture people to bring you your furniture?"

"Yes, I have, smart ass!" I replied sarcastically.

"You mean to tell me he let you out of his sight long enough for you to do that?"

"Mario doesn't have ties on me like that, so mind your damn business, please."

"Don't worry, I will. But remember you just met that nigga, so don't get all caught up in his world. I know you're used to living the big life and fucking with niggas with money, but Mario ain't the type of nigga you need to be selling yourself to. Between me and you, he used to sell plenty of drugs out here in Huntersville. Mad niggas know and respect him because he made a lot of money out here. Now, I don't expect you to drop him like a bad cold, but you need to be careful."

"First of all, I am not naïve, so don't talk to me like I am. Remember, I have built my life around being an aggressive attorney, so I know bullshit when I see it. As far as Mario is concerned, I don't care what type of lifestyle he had before we met. He and I are just friends, so if he told me to get out of his house today, there won't be any love lost. So, I'm gonna tell you this only once: I am a big girl and I don't get caught up in the lives of men I deal with. I know how to disconnect my feelings when I'm fucking them. And I know how to separate business from pleasure, which is something a lot of women don't know how to do. So if I tell you I got my end covered, believe me."

Instead of commenting, Carmen remained silent, as if she was speechless.

"Are you still there?"

"Yeah, I'm here."

"So, you don't have anything to say?"

"No."

"All right. Well, like I said earlier, I'll give you a call later to let you know whether or not I'd be able to stop by."

"Okay," she said, and then we both hung up.

Immediately after I rolled out of bed, I went into the bathroom because I had to piss really bad. After I washed my hands, I washed my face and brushed my teeth. I knew Mario was in the living room, probably watching TV, so I wasn't about to let him run up on me with my breath smelling like shit. I exited the bathroom dressed in a pair of his plaid, cotton boxer shorts and a white tee and walked straight down the hallway toward the living room. The closer I got, I started hearing voices. They were voices of two men talking but they sounded like they were mumbling. I didn't want to startle Mario and his guest, so before I went further, I yelled out, "Baby, where you at?"

The talking stopped immediately. "I'm in the living room," he yelled back.

Without saying another word, I turned into the living room and my eyes damn near popped out of my head. Mario noticed my reaction and asked what was wrong. I stood there motionless as my eyes stared directly into Maceo's face.

Maceo smiled at me and said, "Don't I know you from somewhere?"

I didn't know whether or not this was a trick question, so I played the dumb role and said, "I'm not from here, so I don't see why you should."

"You probably saw her out in Huntersville because she's got family out there," Mario supplied.

"Who you related to out there?" Maceo asked me.

"Carmen and Rachael. They live a couple of blocks away from that little convenience store on the corner."

"I know who you talking about. I use to fuck with Carmen a long time ago, but she ain't tell me she had family that look like you."

Mario looked at Maceo like he was crazy. "Nigga, you trying to holla at my girl?"

Maceo chuckled. "C'mon now, dawg. We family. You know I wouldn't do no shit like that."

Mario looked at Maceo like he didn't believe him, then he said, "Yeah, nigga. Right."

By the time Mario and Maceo had finished exchanging

words, I had taken a seat directly beside Mario. I didn't know whether or not to embrace him from the fear of being in the presence of Maceo or run for my life because these two were related. What a small world.

Mario placed his hand on my thigh and asked me if I was hungry.

"No, I haven't gotten an appetite yet, but I'm sure it'll resurface in the next few hours."

He placed the back of his hand against my forehead. "Are you all right?" he asked.

"Yes, baby. I'm fine. I'm just not in the mood to eat right now."

"Damn, nigga, you got homegirl calling you 'baby' already. What, y'all getting ready to tie the knot?" Maceo blurted out.

"Negro, can you please mind your own business and let me handle this over here?"

Maceo threw both of his hands up as if to say he surrendered. "No problem, dawg. You got it."

Hearing Maceo's voice made me cringe. And I knew if I looked him in his face, I would've gotten sick to my stomach, so I tried everything within my power to avoid looking at him. Thank God he got a phone call on his cell.

"Excuse me, y'all, I gotta take this call outside," he announced, then he made his exit.

Immediately after Maceo went outside, I told Mario I had to leave.

"Where you got to go?" he asked me.

"I got to run a couple of errands," I lied.

"Sweetheart, I can take you wherever you gotta go."

"No, I'm fine. You got company, so stay here and entertain him."

"C'mon, now. Maceo is my brother and he has a key to my spot, so I can jet out on him anytime I need to."

Oh, my God! Did Mario just tell me Maceo is his brother and he had a key to his house? What the fuck was going on? I couldn't be around this man, or in this house for that matter, knowing that Maceo had access to it. I had to find a way to break it off with Mario before I got myself in some shit I couldn't get out of.

I stood up and said, "You are such a sweet man. There are some things that I need to do on my own. I have been with you every day since I met you, which means I haven't spent the night in my own house."

"So, what you saying? You need some time to yourself?" he asked, indignant.

I placed my hand over his shoulder and said, "You know what? That's exactly what I need." Then I walked back in the bedroom to gather up my things.

When I was in the room packing my things, Mario came in and tried to convince me to stay. He did everything but get on his knees and even that wouldn't have made me stay. I truly feared for my life, so I got the hell out of there.

Mario escorted me to my truck. And while I was placing my things in the backseat, he said, "So when are you taking the truck back to the rental place?"

"I'm supposed to do it tomorrow."

"What are you going to do about transportation? Because if you want me to bring that Honda back to the house, I could," he reminded me.

"I'll call you and let you know," I replied, and then I got into the truck.

While I was talking to Mario from the driver seat, I looked through the rearview mirror to see where Maceo was. Unfortunately, he was still hanging outside near the end of the driveway talking on his cell phone. Whoever he was speaking to really had him in an uproar. He made a lot of hand gestures as if to express his frustrations. I couldn't take being in Maceo's presence any longer, so I gave Mario a quick peck on the lips and put the truck in drive.

"Don't forget to call me," he reminded me as I began to turn the truck around in the middle of the street. Mario lived in the middle of a cul-de-sac, and I didn't want to drive all the way down to the dead end and then turn around. When I finally turned the truck completely around, I could see Maceo's expression through my peripheral vision. It wasn't an expression of cruelty or anything of that nature. It was an expression of invincibility. It was like he wanted me and the rest of the world to know that he was the man and he couldn't be touched. I avoided eye contact with him as I drove past him. I used to have that same attitude and it got me exactly where I was. This was a situation I didn't care too much for, so I knew I needed to do something, and do it fast.

Nowhere to Turn

I went back to my place in Newpointe. Even though I had a house filled with furniture, it still didn't feel like home. I collapsed down on my sofa and wondered to myself what I needed to do with my life to get out of this slump. Here I was in the state of Virginia and I was all alone. I had family and a new male companion, but it still felt like I was here all by myself. I knew I couldn't go to them with all the problems I had going on. They wouldn't understand that I was a fugitive and that I had run from the DEA. Not to mention, I had witnessed a fucking murder last night and I knew who the gunman was. I had too much shit on my shoulders and if I didn't release it soon, I knew I would be headed for a psych ward. I laid my head down against the armrest of the sofa and stared off into the ceiling of my apartment. I felt a headache coming on so this was the best remedy, since I had not one aspirin in my entire house. I lay there for about thirty minutes in complete silence until my cell phone rang. I started to ignore it, but then I said "what the hell" and answered it.

"Hello," I said, even though I knew it was Carmen.

"Whatcha doing?" she asked.

"Lying down on my sofa."

"You at home?"

I sighed. "Yes."

"Damn, I just talked to you not too long ago while you were at Mario's house."

"I left his house like twenty minutes after I got off the phone with you," I replied, and then I fell silent.

"I hope you didn't leave on my account," Carmen chimed in.

"No, I left because I needed to come home."

"You sure?" she pressed the issue.

"Yes, I am sure."

"Come on now, be honest. You ain't got to front with me. I know you feeling Mario because you wouldn't have been staying over his house as long as you stayed. So, for you to just get up and haul ass right after you get off the phone with me sends me a clear message that my conversation must've had an effect on you."

"I am sorry, but you are wrong. I told you I needed to come home and that's about the size of it," I said, even though that wasn't the whole truth. I sensed Carmen saw through my story. I guess it wasn't adding up in her book. If I looked at it from her perspective, I would've probably thought the same way. I sighed once again. "So, what's going on?"

"Well, I called you back to tell you that I was sorry for earlier and that I wanted to make it up to you by taking you out for lunch today, if you got time."

"You know what? I've got plenty of time, so I would like that very much. What time do you want to go?"

"I'm ready now if you are."

"Give me about an hour to get myself together and then I'll pick you up."

"Okay. See you then."

"All right."

* * *

I called Carmen on her cell phone to let her know I was in her neighborhood and that I wanted her to meet me outside. But she wouldn't answer her phone. I called her four times back to back and still I got no answer. So reluctantly I had to get out of my truck and go up to the front door and knock. Grandma Hattie answered the door.

After we hugged, I stepped across the doorway and moved out of the way so she could close the front door behind us. "Where is Carmen?" I asked.

"She's upstairs trying to prevent her mama from wearing her clothes. Go ahead on up there," Grandma replied.

I looked up at the flight of stairs before me and began to dread even climbing one of them. They looked so fragile and weak, it was pathetic. I feared that I might fall right through the board of one of them if I pressed hard enough.

"Whatcha waiting for? Go ahead on up there," she urged.

"Can you call her for me?"

"Child, she ain't gon' hear me 'cause she got her door closed. So, go on up there."

"All right," I said, and put my right foot on the bottom step. I took my time to climb each and every step but I made it to the top. And when I made it to the top, I rushed over toward Carmen's bedroom door and knocked on it.

"Who is it?" Carmen yelled from the other side of the door.

"It's Yoshi," I replied.

The door opened immediately after I announced who I was. Carmen had a smile on her face that brightened up the entire house. "Girl, come on in," she said.

Although I was in her room the other night, somehow I missed noticing it looked like a messy locker room. Her bed was in disarray with clothes thrown all over it. She even had clothes thrown across her floor with shoes mixed throughout it. I saw a cup and a plate in her drawer with food residue lingering around the fork left in the middle of the plate.

I frowned my face up and said, "Girl, you need to clean this room up. How can you sleep in all this mess?"

Carmen chuckled. "My room ain't that bad," she replied, trying to downplay it, and then she grabbed me by the arm.

I showed a little resistance. "I am ready to go."

"Okay, well, let me get my mama out of my closet so I can lock my door."

"She's in your closet?" I asked, as I peered around the bedroom door into her walk-in closet. Aunt Sandra had her back to me, so I couldn't see her face. It appeared she was busy trying to find something to wear.

Carmen sighed. "Yeah, and she needs to come on."

"Where is your cell phone? I tried to call you four times," I said, still standing in the same spot. I was not about to move another inch. I just wanted Carmen to get her mother together so we could leave. The faster I got out of this roach-infested bedroom, the better off I would be.

"It's downstairs in the living room, charging up."

"Well, can you get your mother to hurry up? I'm ready to go."

"I'm ready," Aunt Sandra said after she turned around holding a pair of denim jeans and a black shirt in her hands.

"Ma, you can wear that shirt, but you can't wear those jeans. How many times we gon' go through this?" Carmen whined.

"Come on, Carm. You know I'ma take care of your stuff," she pleaded as she walked toward Carmen.

"Ma, I'm not trying to hear that. I told you, you can wear the shirt but I'm not gonna let my jeans walk out of here."

"So, whatcha gon' let me wear then? I need to get out of here."

"You can say that again," I added.

Aunt Sandra walked a couple more steps toward Carmen.

"Carm, please let me wear them. I promise I'ma take care of 'em."

Before Carmen could speak, I interjected. "Please let her wear the damn jeans. I'll buy you another pair if you like."

"See, your rich cousin here is going to buy you another pair. So, you gotta let me have 'em now," Aunt Sandra said.

Frustrated, Carmen sighed heavily. "All right, take 'em, Ma. But don't come back and ask me for anything else. I'm tired of letting you wear my clothes and you don't take care of them."

I grabbed Carmen by the shoulder. "Stop whining and let her go, because I am trying to get out of here."

"Yes, stop whining and let me go so you and Miss Prissy over here can go and handle y'all business," Aunt Sandra commented sarcastically.

I ignored her antics. It was clear that she was below my caliber. Any dope fiend who walks around town in two-week old clothes with personal hygiene issues and gets high off drugs day in and day out is merely a lost cause. I turned my nose up to her and acted like she didn't exist.

"I see you turning your nose up at me. I don't stink!" she commented as she walked out of the room.

"I beg to differ," I responded while I kept my back to her.

"Yeah, whatever," she mumbled underneath her breath, and went into the bathroom.

Carmen looked at me. "Girl, don't pay my mama no mind. She's crazy!"

"Don't you think I already know that?" I replied.

Carmen laughed. "Give me a second and let me grab my coat and lock my bedroom door," she said.

"I'll be outside waiting in my truck," I told her, and left.

A few minutes later, Carmen met me outside. She hopped in the truck with me and then we got out of there. It was her idea for us to eat Mexican, so we went to this spot off Granby

Street. I had to admit that the food was delicious and I enjoyed Carmen's company. She was very pleasant this trip. She wasn't acting ghetto like she normally does, so I was pleased with her.

"Whatcha want to do next?" she asked me after she paid for the tab.

"I'm up for anything. Just don't take me back to Grandma's house."

"All right. We can go to the mall by my house if you like."

"Okay, that's cool," I said, and that's where we headed.

It was a Saturday afternoon, so we knew MacArthur mall would be packed. We entered from Dillard's department store entrance and browsed a bit. We did, however, stop in Sunglass Hut. I picked myself up a hot pair of Salvatore Ferragamo sunshades. Carmen looked at me like I was crazy when I shelled over three hundred fifty for my shades.

"Girl, please. There's nothing like rocking a hot pair of shades," I told her, and walked out of the store.

On my way into the next store, my cell phone rang. I knew who it was before I even looked at the caller ID. Carmen looked back at me and smiled. "Don't front. You know it ain't nobody but Mario."

"He can leave a voice mail message," I told her.

Shocked by my response, Carmen stopped in her tracks, grabbed a hold of my arm, and said, "Something is wrong. And you gon' tell me what it is," she demanded.

"Nothing is wrong," I tried to convince her. "I just don't feel like talking to him right now."

"Yoshi, you ain't holding back on me, are you?"

I politely removed my arm from Carmen's hand and said, "No, I am not." And before I could say another word, my cell phone rang again. I looked back at the caller ID.

"It's him again, ain't it?"

I nodded.

"Want me to answer it?" She held out her hand for me to give her my phone.

"No, I got it," I assured her, and then I pressed down on the send button. "Hello," I said.

"I just called you a minute ago. Did you get a missed call?" he asked.

"I heard my phone ringing. I just couldn't pick it up at the time because I had some bags in my hand," I lied.

"Where are you?"

"I'm at the mall."

"Which one?"

"MacArthur mall."

"How long have you been up there?"

"For about an hour or so."

His questions continued. "Who you up there with?"

"I'm with my cousin Carmen."

"Damn, he's sho' asking you a lot of questions!" Carmen mumbled underneath her breath, but it was loud enough for me to hear her.

I placed my finger over my mouth and said, "Shhhh!"

"Am I going to see you later?" he asked.

"I'm not sure yet. But I'll let you know."

"What's up with you, Yoshi? Did I do or say anything wrong?"

"No, Mario. You haven't done anything. I told you I just need to go home and handle a few things. That's it."

"Well, have you decided if you need the Honda or not?"

"I'll let you know by tomorrow."

"So when am I going to hear from you?"

"I'll call you as soon as I get home," I assured him.

"All right," he said, and then we both hung up.

Right after I hung up with Mario, Carmen started running her mouth fifty miles per minute. I tried to tune her out but it didn't work. She strutted down behind me to probe me for information. "Why is that nigga being worrisome?" she asked. "He acts like y'all are married or something."

"He was not acting like we were married."

"That's a damn lie! That nigga was asking you questions like he got papers on you."

"You are being so dramatic!" I said as I continued to walk down the mall concourse.

Following on my heels, she said, "You can call it what you want, but I know when I see a nigga getting all possessive. You better watch his ass! Him and his fucking brother, Maceo, ain't wrapped too tight. They are fucking insane."

"Now you tell me," I mumbled.

"Whatcha say?" she asked.

"I didn't say a word."

"Yes, you did. You're holding back on me." She pressed the issue.

I stopped in my tracks. "Look, Carmen, I don't know why you're so fixated on my relationship with Mario. There's nothing going on between him and me. I'm not mad with him and he's not mad with me."

"He may not be mad at you, but you sure got something going on."

"I just needed to get away so I could have some me time and that's about the size of it," I repeated.

Carmen sucked her teeth. "Yeah, right. Remember you're talking to a woman who has been through it all. I can tell when another woman is having some type of drama in her life. You and Mario were fine when I talked to you earlier on the phone and now all of a sudden, you don't want to be bothered with the man. Something ain't right, and I ain't gonna let you convince me otherwise. Now you can walk around here and tell me anything if you want to, but I know better."

"Why is it so important for you to know what's going on in my life?"

"Because you are family. We are blood. And not only that, you're here all by yourself, so I ain't gon' let no nigga come into your space and fuck it up just like that. Shit, I just want you to be able to come to me if you have any problem with any of these cats around here. Who knows, I may be able to help you sort some of your problems out since I know most of the games these niggas 'round here be playing."

Hearing the sincerity in Carmen's voice made me want to fall into her arms and tell her everything. She was right—I was her family. We were blood related, so I should have been able to go to her and tell her anything. Who knows, she probably could have helped me with all of the burden I had on my shoulders. I needed somebody to help me carry this load. But then something inside of me told me to hold back. This burden was too big for her, so it wasn't wise for me to let her get involved. And then again, who knows, she probably could handle it.

Deep down inside, I was playing the game of tug-of-war and I didn't know which way to go. So, I looked into Carmen's eyes and said, "Cousin, I really appreciate your love for me. But I'm a big girl, so I can handle Mario's shit as well as any other man's shit that comes my way. And if there comes a time where I can't, then I'll let you know."

"Yeah, okay," she replied, and then she walked off toward the store called Forever 21.

I went in another direction. I elected to take a seat in one of the massage chairs placed in front of Forever 21. I sat there and thought about all the events that had taken place in my life. Over the last few months, so much had happened to me. I was at the top of my game in Miami before my past addiction resurfaced. I went from almost being a partner at my law firm to being a suspect for the murder of my best friend,

Maria, who was a DEA agent and an informant for me. I thought about the package that was sent to my house by who-ever was setting me up. It contained Maria's badge and the videotape of her being murdered in my home. I was horri-fied.

La La, aka Lance, the multiplatinum rapper from Hous-ton whom I'd successfully defended for murder and con-spiracy charges, helped me get away from the chaos once I got out of jail on a three-million-dollar bail. But soon after La La and I hooked up and he let me get away on his yacht, he was shot coming out of a nightclub. I knew that the people who were after me killed Lance and Maria, and the thought of losing two people that I loved made me feel so angry in-side.

I wanted justice for them, but I knew I wasn't in a posi-tion to get it for them. So, I had to live with it, which was something I wasn't ready to do. And then to come here to the state of Virginia, only to go through another episode of being a part of someone else's murder, had truly taken a toll on me. My mind was racing for answers and couldn't come up with anything. I sat there in that massage chair and watched Carmen as she browsed through the entire store. Even though I knew she made a lot of bad decisions in her life, she dealt with them and she looked like she was han-dling it. I wanted to have that same carefree spirit she had and I vowed to myself that I would get it.

When our little shopping trip was over, Carmen and I each got a soft pretzel from the pretzel stand and exited the mall. It was around four o'clock in the evening when we ar-rived back at Grandma Hattie's house. She was in the kitchen making a pot of chicken soup when we walked in. From the very second I walked through the door, I announced that I couldn't stay long. I had to give her heads-up so she wouldn't make me stay any longer than I wanted to. Carmen headed upstairs to put her purse away while I stayed in the kitchen and talked to Grandma Hattie.

"You got somewhere you got to be?" she questioned me.

"Yes, ma'am," I lied.

"Where you gotta be this time of the evening?"

"I have a date," I lied once more.

"Be careful, baby. These men out here aren't what they appear to be."

"Trust me, I always got my eyes and ears open."

"You'd better. Because you don't want to end up like your Aunt Sandra, 'round here all strung out on drugs behind a man. I remember back when she met this guy named Patrick McCall. Rachael was only two years old. And this guy came from out of nowhere promising her the world, so you know she wanted to jump at the chance of happiness, because she had just broken up with Rachael's father. Now this Patrick fellow was a clean-cut guy. He worked for the Ford plant and he came from a good family. He said and did all the right things in the beginning. But when he got Sandra where he wanted her, he started acting like a pure fool. He became mentally abusive and then he started cheating on her with every woman who walked cross his path. Sandra went through seven years of that mess. And I guess when she felt like she couldn't deal with it anymore, she drifted out on those streets and started using drugs."

"Has she ever said she wanted to get off drugs?"

"All the time. But as soon as she's faced with some other problems, she'll run right back out in those streets. I keep telling her that those drugs aren't the answer. She's gonna first have to get some help. And the help starts at home with your family. Whether she knows it or not, we are all she has. When the tough times hit we are the only people who will bail her out. What I am saying is, your family is all you got. Now I know we ain't got the money or the big fancy house, but we are here if you ever need to talk. Sharing your problems takes years of stress off your life. So, don't you ever forget that." She squeezed my shoulder.

I thought long and hard about what she had just said, as I watched her walk back over to her pot of chicken soup. And what was so crazy was the fact that she was right. Your family is all you have. And since my mother was thousands of miles away in her Florida retirement home, the family I had here was all I had left. The murder incident began to weigh down on me again. And the fact that I was involved with the murderer's brother had become taxing. I couldn't go another day carrying this load all by myself. I needed someone I could talk to and Grandma Hattie seemed like the perfect person. But then again, she was a very old woman and I didn't think she would be able to handle that type of information.

Carmen, on the other hand, I felt would be the perfect person to talk to. She'd hung out on those streets for a lot of years, I was told, so she would definitely know how I should handle this problem. But before I told her, I just needed her to assure me that she wouldn't tell anyone else. She had to keep this secret to her heart like I'd done because it was a matter of life and death. And if she could grasp the importance of that, the better I would feel.

So after I thought about my situation a little more, I finally got up the gumption to go to Carmen. She was coming out of the bathroom when I arrived at the top of the staircase.

She smiled at me. "If you got to use the bathroom, you better wait at least thirty minutes, because I blew that bad boy up," she advised me.

I didn't crack a smile. Instead, I grabbed her by the arm and pulled her into her bedroom. "I need to talk to you," I told her.

"What's the matter?" she asked.

When we stepped into her bedroom and took a seat on the edge of her bed, I noticed Aunt Sandra was walking upstairs toward us. Aggravated by her presence, I asked Carmen to close the door. So, when she stood up to do so, Aunt Sandra rushed toward the bedroom door. "Now, I know you see me coming," she roared as she pushed back on the door.

"Ma, we are trying to talk," Carmen explained.

"Well, talk then," she replied sarcastically. "I just need to get a pair of socks out your drawer."

"All my socks are dirty. Go on in Rachael's room and get a pair of hers," Carmen said as she pushed back on the door.

"You know Rachael's bedroom is locked."

"Well, whatcha want me to do? I don't have a key to get in there."

"Don't be acting all funny 'cause you got Miss Rich Girl in there," Aunt Sandra yelled through the door while Carmen was closing it.

"I ain't trying to act funny. So stop tripping and go on back downstairs with Grandma and see if she'll give you a pair of her socks."

Aunt Sandra hit the door with her fist. "Fuck both of y'all!" she yelled.

"Yeah, all right, Ma. Go on 'bout cha business."

I heard Aunt Sandra walk away from the door and head back downstairs, so I felt like the coast was clear and began to open up to Carmen.

"What I'm about to tell you, you gotta promise me that you will not tell a soul. You can't tell anyone. I'm talking about your mama, Grandma Hattie, your boyfriend, or Rachael. This has to stay between me and you."

With a sincere expression, Carmen said, "So, what is it?"

"First you have to promise me that what I'm about to tell you won't leave this room."

Carmen sighed. "I promise, I promise."

I looked into Carmen's eyes and took a deep breath, and before I realized it, I was running everything down to her. You should've seen her facial expression when I told her I witnessed the entire murder and that Maceo along with another guy were the killers.

Her mouth flew wide open. "Oh, my God! You saw the whole thing," she said.

I nodded my head.

"Why didn't you say something to me that night?" Carmen wondered aloud.

"I was too distraught to tell anybody. All I wanted to do was get the hell out of here before anybody saw me."

"Where exactly were you standing when you saw Lil D get murdered?"

"I was walking by the alley where he got shot at."

Carmen shook her head in disbelief. "Oh, my God, this is crazy," she said. "If Cynthia knew Maceo was the one who killed her baby daddy, she would go off. She would have her whole family looking for Maceo and that other nigga who was with him."

"You aren't going to tell her, are you?"

"Hell nah, I ain't going to tell her. Do you know how serious this shit is? I don't want to be associated with this in no shape, form, or fashion. I don't even want my name coming up when people start talking about it." Carmen stood up from the bed. She paced back and forth around her bedroom like she was trying to come up with a solution.

"What are you thinking about?" I asked.

"I'm just trying to figure out why Maceo had to kill Lil D like that. They were tight like brothers."

"Remember you mentioned to me over the phone earlier you heard a rumor that Lil D was snitching? Well, that rumor must've been correct because right before Maceo and the other guy shot him, they tormented him and called him a snitch."

"Oh shit! So what people were saying was true," she said, stopping in her tracks.

I sat there and stared at Carmen, wondering where she was going with this. She knew Maceo and Lil D, so she knew the history behind them both. I just sat there in limbo and waited for her to draw her own conclusion—and in the process, advise me on how to handle my part in this matter. I had been through one murder after the other and my head couldn't keep taking all of this psychological bullshit. So, I interrupted her train of thought and told her I was in the company of Maceo this morning.

Her eyes and mouth grew at least two inches in size. "Oh, so that's why you left Mario's house all of a sudden?" she guessed.

"You damn right. My skin was crawling the whole time I was around him and I couldn't take the feeling, so I got out of there as quickly as I could."

"Did Maceo say something to you?" she asked.

"When I initially walked in the living room and saw him sitting there, he asked me where he knew me from. And Mario told him he probably saw me out here in Huntersville because I had family who lived out here."

"Did my name come up?"

"Yeah, when he asked me who I was related to, I told him."

"And what did he say?"

"He didn't say anything."

"Well, what are you going to do about Mario? Because you know nine times out of ten, you are going to see Maceo when you are in Mario's company. Maceo is his only brother and they are close. I've heard that Maceo looks up to Mario because he is the older brother."

I shook my head. "I don't know what I'm going to do. I've been trying to figure out a way to tell him that I don't want to see him anymore."

"Just tell him that the relationship is going too fast, so you want to take a few steps back."

"He is a very aggressive guy. Do you think that's going to work?"

"It's gonna have to."

"I don't know, Carmen," I said, and then I fell silent because of a cracking noise I heard from the other side of the door. I immediately jumped to my feet and grabbed a hold of the doorknob, and when I snatched it open I looked into the hallway to see who was there.

"Who is it?" Carmen whispered.

"I don't see anyone," I whispered back.

"Is Rachael's door closed?"

"Yes, and it still has the lock on it, too," I replied.

"Wait a minute, I'ma go and check the bathroom," she said, and then stepped out of the room and proceeded down the hall. I stood there at the entrance of her bedroom door and waited for her to do her investigative work. My heart began to pound hard with each step she took. And when she grabbed hold of the doorknob to the bathroom to turn it and it wouldn't move, my heart stopped.

Carmen started banging on the door. "Who's in there?" she demanded.

"It's your mama, girl. Whatcha want? I'm trying to take a shit in peace," Sandra replied.

"Do you think she heard our conversation?" I whispered loud enough for Carmen to hear me.

She shrugged her shoulders as if to say she didn't know.

"Ask her," I continued to whisper.

"Ma, were you just standing by my door?" Carmen asked her.

"No, I wasn't," she replied defensively.

Carmen pressed the issue. "You sure you weren't trying to ear hustle?"

Aunt Sandra cracked the door open good enough for her to peep out at Carmen. "Girl, get your ass away from this door so I can use the bathroom in peace. I ain't got time for your bullshit!" she snapped.

"You sure you're using the bathroom?" Carmen continued as she tried to peer into the bathroom.

Aunt Sandra refused to answer her question and slammed the door in her face. Carmen walked away from the door and reentered her bedroom.

I looked at her nervously. "Do you think she was standing by the door listening to us?" I asked.

"It's kind of hard to tell."

"What if she did?"

"Whatcha mean?" Carmen asked as she closed the door to her bedroom.

"What if she did hear us? Do you think she would say something?"

"Who would she say something to?" Carmen shook her head. "Nah, she ain't like that," Carmen assured me. "She'll talk shit to all of us around the house, but she wouldn't dare sell out on us."

Carmen's effort to convince me that her mother wouldn't run her mouth didn't fly with me. I knew Sandra didn't like me and that alone made me wary. As far as I could see it, I didn't mean shit to her. I was a liability, so if she had any clue that I was on the run from the DEA, she would turn my ass in for sure and spend all the reward money on heroin. My life would be over and there wouldn't be shit I could do about it.

I stood around Carmen's bedroom for another couple minutes and then I decided to leave. I felt like I was an alien there. The very feeling I had when I was in Mario's house crept over me and I had to shake it, so I left without hesitation. Grandma Hattie and Carmen both walked me out to the truck. I hugged them both and assured them that I would call them to let them know I got home safe.

Mind Games

Mario called me at least five times before I answered his call. It was a few minutes after nine when he finally got a chance to hear my voice. I could tell he was really frustrated so I played the apologetic role just to see if his mood would change.

"What have you been doing all this time? And why have I got to call you ten times before you answer my call?" he whined.

"Mario, you didn't call me ten times. You called me four before this last time," I corrected him.

"Look, that's beside the point. What's up with you?"

"Nothing is up."

"Where are you?"

"I'm at home."

"So, whatcha gonna do? Are you gonna let me see you tonight or what?"

I sighed. "Mario, I would love to see you but I've got a lot of things on my mind and I would not be good company right now."

"Come on now, be straight up with me! What's really going on?"

"Look, Mario, I'm just having some personal issues right now and it's nothing you need to concern yourself with."

"I understand all of that. But what do you expect me to do in the meantime? Just sit around and wait for you to collect your thoughts?" he replied sarcastically.

"Mario, I'm really not in the mood to argue with you tonight."

"I'm not trying to argue with you either. All I want to know is why the sudden change in your mood this morning? Since you left I've been trying to figure out what I've done to make you run out on me like you did."

"You haven't done anything! So stop worrying yourself about it."

"Why the fuck you keep telling me not to worry when you are still leaving me with nothing to go on?"

I exhaled loudly. "Look, this isn't going anywhere, so I'll talk to you tomorrow after you cool down."

"So it's like that?"

"It's not like anything, Mario. I just want to get some rest and who knows, I may feel better tomorrow morning."

Irritated, he said, "Yeah, a'ight!" and then abruptly disconnected the call.

Instead of getting upset behind his antics, I placed my phone down on my coffee table and lay down on the sofa. At that very moment I didn't have the strength to pick the phone back up to call my family to let them know I made it home safely. I just wanted to be alone and not hear another sound. I got that very wish and without even realizing it, I dozed off.

The very next morning I was awakened by the sunlight beaming through my mini-blinds. I tried to block it with my hands but the light was too bright, so I got up and started my day. After realizing that it was only a few minutes after eight o'clock, I made myself a cup of hot tea, drank every ounce of it, and then I jumped into the shower. Right after I hopped out of the shower, I lotioned myself down from head to toe and then I slipped on a light blue Puma sweat suit and a pair of all white Puma sneakers. My hair looked a hot mess. I couldn't do shit with it because it needed to be washed and treated by a professional, so I brushed it back in yet another one of my famous ponytails and called it a day. Not too long after that, I blocked my number and called the rental car company. As soon as the representative got on the phone, I lied and told her that I was in Maryland and I wanted to drop the car off to them.

"What part of Maryland are you in?" the woman asked.

"Baltimore," I replied, since that would have been the most popular answer.

"What is your name so I can look up your account?"

It seemed like as soon as I uttered my name, she became weird, and I knew it wasn't a figment of my imagination. So, I got a little leery and asked a few questions. "Do you have my account up?" was my first question.

"Yes, ma'am."

"Well, what are you doing? Is there something wrong?"

"No, ma'am, nothing is wrong. But would you be able to wait a couple of seconds while I put you on hold?" she wanted to know.

And at that point, I knew something wasn't right. Fear overpowered my entire body so I immediately disconnected my call. "Oh shit! What the fuck am I going to do?" I said aloud after my panic button went off.

Not knowing what to do next, I paced around the living room and dining room area of my condo. I even looked out the window a few times to see if my place was under surveillance. But every time I looked outside I noticed every car that was parked in my neighborhood was empty, so I felt one percent better. "Oh, my God, what am I going to do?"

I asked myself again. I couldn't come up with a solution. However, I did know that I had to get rid of that truck. The rental car company assumed that I was in the Baltimore area of Maryland, so they were going to have every policeman there on the lookout for me. And who knows, they may have even spread their territory out more and had state troopers on every highway surrounding Maryland on the lookout as well. Shit, they could even call the authorities here and advise them to look out for me, too, which would be fucked-up on my part, so I had to make a move and make it quick.

I got back on the horn and called Mario. I really didn't want to be bothered with him, but I had nowhere else to turn. I had to get rid of that truck and there was no doubt in my mind that he would have the connections to get the job done. Immediately after he answered the phone, I asked him was he up and had he gotten dressed yet?

"Yeah, why?" he wondered aloud.

"Because I need to see you."

"Are you all right?"

"Not really."

"What's wrong?"

"I don't want to talk about it over the phone, so can you come by my place?"

"You know you never showed me where you lived."

"I'm not too far from that Check Smart plaza where we met."

"Where are you exactly?"

"I live in this community called Newpointe."

"Oh yeah, I know where you are," he told me. "Give me about fifteen minutes and I'll be there."

"Okay," I replied, and then the phone went silent.

Fifteen minutes went by in an instant and just like Mario had promised, he was at my front door before his time limit expired. I had never been so happy to see him. When I opened the door, I fell into his arms like he was my savior.

"What's going on?"

I pulled him inside my place and closed the door behind him. "I can't take that rental back to the company," I told him.

"Why not? What's the matter?"

"My ex-boyfriend reported it stolen," I lied. That was the only excuse I could come up with. I couldn't tell him I was a fucking fugitive. He probably would have gotten away from me as far as he could.

"You bullshitting!"

I didn't crack a smile. I gave him the most sincere expression I could muster up. "I am dead serious," I said.

"Well, how do you know this?"

"I just got off the phone with the rental agency and the lady told me," I continued, knowing damn well I didn't give that woman a chance to say a word.

"So, whatcha want to do?" he asked me, standing over top of me looking like a giant.

I looked up into his eyes and said, "I want you to get rid of it."

"Get rid of it how?"

"Get somebody to destroy it."

Mario looked at me strange. "Why would you want to destroy it?"

"So the company won't be able to find it. I don't want him to know where I am," I replied, getting aggravated.

Mario grabbed me by both my shoulders to keep me still. "Look, Yoshi, that'll be a bad move. All we need to do is take the truck across state lines and let a state trooper find it. He'll get in touch with the rental car company so they can come pick it up and you won't even be around to take the heat."

"You sure that'll be a good idea?"

"Hell yeah! You don't want to destroy those people's shit! They would get your ass for grand theft auto and some more shit."

"All right, so when are we going to make this thing happen?"

"Now," he said. "Give me a minute and let me make a quick phone call," he continued, and backed away from me.

He stepped outside onto the patio and made a two-minute call. When he returned to the house, he told me to hand him the keys to the truck. I grabbed the keys off the countertop in my kitchen and handed them to him. "What's getting ready to happen now?" I asked him.

"I've got someone coming to get the truck right after we leave."

"Where are we going?"

"I'm gonna take you back to my house because I don't want you to be around when my boys come out here to handle that situation."

Putting up some resistance, I stood there and didn't move.

"What's wrong now?" he asked.

"Can we go somewhere other than your house?"

"What's wrong with my house?"

"Nothing. I just want to go somewhere else."

"Where do you want to go?"

"It doesn't matter. Just take me somewhere. I need to get out and get some air so I can clear my head."

"Have you eaten?"

"No."

"Are you hungry?"

"I can eat something small."

"Okay, well, get your purse so I can take you to this little spot on Holland Road."

Mario and I headed outside to his car, but before he got in he opened up the truck and left the keys inside of it. While we were driving away I took one last look at the truck because I knew that I wouldn't see it again.

I felt really funny riding in Mario's car knowing what I knew about him and his brother, Maceo. I knew I was treading on thin ice, but I had nowhere else to turn. My family would not have been able to help me with my situation, but I knew Mario would, so I had no choice but to call him. I just hoped that when his boys did pick up the truck, they didn't fuck around and get caught with it.

The little spot on Holland Road turned out to be a place called Mom's Kitchen. It was a cozy diner type of atmosphere and the waitresses there were really nice. I ordered the breakfast combination, which consisted of turkey sausage links, two eggs, a side of fried potatoes with onions, and two slices of toast. Mario ordered the T-bone steak, two eggs, and a side of grits. While we were enjoying our meal we were interrupted by his telephone. He immediately got up from the table to avoid speaking around me. I knew it couldn't be nobody but his brother or the guys who were given the task to get rid of the truck, so I sat back patiently and waited for him to return to the table. When he finally did, he had this bizarre look on his face and it scared the hell out of me. I was fear stricken until he opened up his mouth.

"I just got a phone call from the nigga following the asshole driving your truck, telling me that he had to call the other driver twice about how reckless he was driving down the fucking highway."

My mouth fell wide open. "Are you serious?"

"You damn right I'm serious. So after I got off the phone

with my peoples, I called the idiot driving your truck and cursed his ass out!"

"What did he say?"

"The nigga couldn't say shit because I told him to shut the fuck up as soon as he tried to open up his mouth. I swear I don't need the fucking aggravation! All I need is his ass to do the job and get back here safely. That's it!"

"How far are they?"

"They don't have too much farther to go. They should be back in this area in the next hour and a half."

I exhaled. "Good," I said, and then I went back to eating.

Immediately after we left out of there, we got back into his car and headed back toward the beach. I wanted to stay a little longer at the beach, but it got a little too cool, so there was nothing left for us to do but drive back down the highway.

Now, I had not heard from Carmen all day so I got on my phone to call her. She answered her line after the second ring.

"Girl, you are going to live a long time because I was just thinking about calling you," she said.

"Where are you?"

"I just walked in from work not too long ago."

"I kinda figured you were at work because I hadn't heard from you."

"Yeah, I had to do my eight-hour shift so you know I'm tired as hell, but I'll bounce back after I take me a long hot shower."

"That sounds good right about now."

"It's going to feel good, too." Carmen chuckled. "So where are you?" she continued.

"I'm with Mario."

"Oh shit, you with him?"

"Yes I am," I replied nonchalantly.

"You better be careful. I told you he ain't to be played with."

"I remember what you told me," I assured her.

"Have you run into Maceo again?" Carmen asked.

"No, I haven't."

"Yoshi, please be careful."

"Trust me, I got everything under control. So, please, let's talk about this later 'cause now is not the time." I said this because she was talking pretty loud on the other end and I wasn't sure if Mario could hear her or not.

Carmen's questions continued. "Is he dropping you off at home?"

"We haven't talked about it yet."

"Well, you better tell him now before he ends up taking you back to his house and I know you don't want that."

"No, I don't," I agreed. "So let me call you back when we get to where we going because I'm not getting good reception right now. You keep breaking up."

"You better call me back," Carmen demanded.

"I will," I told her, and then we both hung up.

After I disconnected the call, I tried to avoid looking in Mario's direction. I looked out the passenger window at the trees we were driving by and all I could think about was what excuse I was going to use to convince him I needed to be home. When he saw me staring off into space, he rubbed me on my thigh to get my attention. "What you thinking about?" he asked.

"Nothing," I lied. "I was just looking at the birds flying around in the sky and wished that I could fly."

He laughed and said, "Damn, that's funny! Whenever I got in trouble when I was a kid, I wished I could fly, too. You know, so I could run away from my problems. But I don't think too much about it now."

I turned around and looked at Mario and asked him if he had ever been incarcerated.

"I spent six months in a detention center when I was sixteen. But I haven't been to the big house since I became an adult. Why did you ask?"

"I was just being curious."

"Have you ever been locked up?"

I hesitated for a second before I answered his question. There was no point in giving him too much information about my life, since I knew we weren't going to last.

"Yes, I have. But it was only for DUI and reckless driving."

Mario burst into laughter. "You better slow your roll around here because Virginia police are petty as hell. They will give you a ticket for petty shit, like changing a lane without using a signal light."

"Trust me. I've heard some of the stories," I told him. Then I noticed that we were about to come up on Newtown Road.

"Would you like to go home?" Mario asked. I could tell from his tone that he didn't want me to go home, but I didn't want to go to his house and chance seeing Maceo.

"Yes, please," I responded softly, hoping my answer wouldn't lead to an argument.

He immediately got off on my exit and drove me straight home. I could tell he was a little upset, but he was a grown man, so he'd get over it really fast. Before I got out of the car I thanked him for taking care of the situation with the rental truck.

"No problem," he said, and then he leaned toward me to get a kiss.

I leaned forward and kissed him even though I really didn't want to. But at this point, I felt obligated to do it. Right after I exited his car, I walked around to the driver side.

"How are you going to get around now?" he asked.

"That's a good question," I replied.

"I told you if you wanted me to get you that Honda Accord from my body shop, I would."

I thought for a second and then I said, "Okay, that would be fine, but I only want to use it until I can get myself another vehicle."

"Yoshi, you don't have to go out and get another car. You can drive that one as long as you want."

"Look, Mario, I appreciate the gesture but I've got to be able to get my own transportation."

"Are you looking to buy?"

"Yes, of course."

"How much are you willing to pay?"

"I'm not sure. I guess it all depends on how well the car looks and drives."

"Well, I'll tell you what. Let me bring the Honda Accord around here tomorrow so you can test-drive it. And if you like it, you can buy it. Now how does that sound?"

"Sounds good," I replied.

While he and I said our good-byes, one of my female neighbors pulled up in her car. She wasn't pushing anything glamorous, it was only a gold 2007 Acura TL. She had her music blasting like she was at a nightclub. I cringed at the sound of it. And when she got out of her car, she made it her business to walk right by Mario's Benz. She was an attractive woman with a light complexion. Her hair was styled in micro braids and they were pulled back in a ponytail, which draped down her back. She must have had at least twenty inches of hair on her head and she swung it back and forth with each step she took. I could tell she had just come home from work because of her uniform. The front label on her shirt read "Firestone," and her name, which was Karen, was engraved directly below it.

She smiled as she passed us and then she made a 180-degree turn to see Mario's face. Her expression lit up instantly. "Oh, shit. Is that you, Mario?" she asked.

He smiled back at her. "Yeah, what's up, Karen?" he said, extending his hand so she could shake it. "How you doing?" he continued.

"I'm doing good. Just getting off work, and now I've got to go in the house and do a little of laundry," she replied, showing off a gold crown on the side of her top teeth. She redirected the question back to him. "But how are you doing?"

"I'm doing great. I'm still in business for myself and things are good considering this recession we're in," he told her. "But let me introduce you to Yoshi. She's my friend and she lives here, too."

Karen turned her attention to me and said hello. I did the same and then we both turned our attention right back to Mario. "Well, let me get inside." She sighed.

"Take it easy," he told her.

"I will. And it was nice seeing you after all this time."

"Same here."

"It was nice meeting you, too," she said to me, and then she walked off. I turned and watched her go. I was curious to know exactly where she resided. As she walked toward her residence I couldn't help but look at her hourglass figure. She was definitely eye candy. Her waist had to be twenty-six inches and her ass at least thirty-eight inches. She had the shape of Buffie the Body, but the only difference was that she was light skinned. After I saw where she lived, I turned my attention back to Mario.

"You know a lot of people, don't you?" I asked.

"Not really," he replied modestly.

"You can talk your ass off, but I know the deal."

He chuckled. "You are so funny!"

"No, you are. I bet you've been with at least two hundred women or better."

"Oh no, I've never been that type of man."

"Have you ever slept with her?" I asked him, looking directly into his face to see any signs that he was lying.

He hesitated for a second and then said, "Nope."

"That's hard to believe."

"Go and ask her if you don't believe me," he insisted.

"Hmm, how well do you two know each other?"

"I used to go out with her cousin a few years back. But now she's married and moved down to Atlanta."

"How long ago was that?"

"Tina and I broke up about four years ago. But I think she got married and moved to Atlanta about a year ago."

"Why did you two break up?"

"Because we just couldn't get along."

"What kinds of problems did you two have that you didn't get along?"

"We used to argue about a lot of stupid issues and I couldn't take it. So I told her I had to bounce."

"Oh, so you broke up with her?"

"It wasn't a thing of who broke up with who. I'm a practical man and I'm very easy to get along with. Now, if I'm out here beating down the pavement to bring home the money so I can get the bills paid, then you shouldn't be stressing me out about dumb shit."

"What do you consider dumb shit?"

"It's a long story."

"Well, I'm gonna let you slide this time. But when I ask you again, make sure you have an answer for me."

"You got it," he assured me.

"What time can I expect you tomorrow?" I asked as I began to walk away from his car.

"Well, I got to do a few things in the morning, but as soon as I'm done I'll bring you the Accord."

"Do you have any idea what time that would be?"

"Give me until around noon."

"Okay," I said, and then I stepped completely away from him. He sat there in his car and watched me until I walked inside my house. I waved him off as soon as I crossed the door seal. And when I saw him begin to drive away, I closed my door and locked it.

Two Days Later

Mario brought me the Honda just like he promised. It was a 2005 model and was very clean. I drove around in it all day yesterday so I could get used to it. I stopped at Grandma Hattie's house to see if she needed me to run some errands for her, but she told me no, so I told her I'd be back over there today since it was the first of March and I knew she would need to go to the bank to cash her Social Security check. She was standing outside when I pulled up in front of her house. I knew she was waiting for the mailman, so I smiled at her as I exited the car.

"Up bright and early I see," I commented.

"And so are you," she replied.

"How long have you been waiting outside?"

"About ten minutes. But he shouldn't be much longer because I just saw him go on the next block."

"Is Carmen here?" I asked as I stepped up on the porch.

"No, she just went up the street. I think she said she was going over her friend's house. I can't remember which one she told me because all their names sound so crazy."

I laughed. "Where is Rachael?"

"She didn't come home last night. So she's probably with that little thug she messes around with."

"Have you eaten breakfast?"

"Yes, honey, I had myself a nice cup of tea and a bowl of oatmeal," she told me. "What about yourself? Did you put anything in your stomach?" she continued.

"I had a cup of coffee. But that's it. I'll probably get me a bite to eat as soon as I leave here."

"Nonsense! Go on in that house and get you a bowl of that oatmeal."

"No, Grandma, I'm fine."

"You sure?"

"Yes, ma'am, I'm sure. I don't want anything heavy right now. So, I'll probably stop at one of those sub shops and get me a wrap or something."

While we were talking back and forth, my cell phone started ringing. I looked down at the caller ID and noticed it was Carmen. "Speaking of the devil, that's Carmen now," I said aloud.

"Tell her you're here at the house so she can get her butt back here," Grandma Hattie said.

"Hey, girl. What's up?" I asked.

"Where are you?" she asked. Her voice sounded weary.

"I'm standing in front of the house talking to Grandma."

"You're at Grandma's house?" she asked, her voice becoming more strange. "Get out of there right now!" she screamed.

Alarmed by the urgency in Carmen's voice, fear consumed my entire body. I didn't know whether to jump into my car or run into Grandma Hattie's house. "What's wrong?" I panicked.

"Maceo knows you saw him kill Lil D," she screeched.

"But how?"

"It had to be my mama because I didn't breathe a word to anyone."

"I knew it!" I screamed, and Grandma Hattie looked right at me.

"What's wrong, darling?" she asked.

"I got to go, Grandma. But I'll call you," I told her, scrambling back into the car.

"Carmen, where are you?" I asked her immediately after I locked the car door.

"I just left my girlfriend Pam's house. I'm walking up B Avenue right now. So, ride around here and pick me up."

"Wait! Stay on the phone until I see you."

"Okay," Carmen said, and fell silent.

Worried, I said, "Are you still there?"

"Yeah, I'm just thinking about where my mama could be. I need to find her ass right now so she can tell us what the fuck is going on."

Breathing like I had just run the fifty-yard dash, I said, "I'm coming down B Avenue now. Where are you?"

"I'm right here on the left by the yellow house. So slow down as soon as you pass that red van parked on the right side."

"All right," I said, and did just as Carmen had instructed me.

When she approached the car her face looked flushed. I could tell that this whole situation had affected her as much as me. I reached over to unlock the passenger side door, so she could get in.

She hopped in the car immediately after I pushed open the door. "When you get to the next block, turn right, so we can get out of here," she instructed me as she looked straight ahead.

"Where are we going?" I asked.

"I don't know. But we're going to have to figure out something," she replied.

Before I could make a rebuttal to Carmen's lame-ass plan, my cell phone started ringing. I looked down at the caller ID and when I noticed that it was Mario, my heart fell to the pit of my stomach. I didn't know whether to answer it or not. So, I looked to Carmen for her guidance.

"Oh, my God! It's Mario!" I said.

"Don't answer it," Carmen whispered.

I held the phone in my hand, not sure about whether or not I should listen to Carmen. I didn't want to go against her because I knew at the end of the day she would be the only one to have my back. But by the same token, I didn't want it to appear to Mario that I was avoiding him. I figured if he knew about the situation involving me seeing his brother murder Lil D, he would either make mention of it to me or try some funny business to lure me to him. I wanted to know either way where his head was, so I went against Carmen.

"Hello," I said, but it was barely audible.

"Hey, baby, where you at?" he asked me.

Knowing that he wanted to know my whereabouts gave me an uneasy feeling in my heart. There was no doubt I was scared, so I looked at Carmen. She only shook her head as if to say she was disappointed with my actions.

"I'm in Virginia Beach. Why?" I replied.

"Whatcha 'bout to get into?"

"I don't know, why?"

"Because I want to see you," he said calmly.

"You just saw me not too long ago," I said with a giggle. I had to play the role so he wouldn't know that I was on to his fucking schemes.

He pressed the issue. "I know, but I miss you."

"I miss you, too," I lied, my stomach turning inside out.

"Well, meet me at the house in about thirty minutes," he insisted.

"I can't meet you there that soon."

"Why not?"

"Because I'm in the middle of something."

"Like what?"

"I'm taking care of something for my grandmother," I lied once again.

"How long is that going to take?"

"I'm not sure. But give me about an hour and I'll call you back," I told him.

"All right, call me back."

"Okay," I said, and then I hung up.

"What did he say?" Carmen asked me immediately after I disconnected the call.

"He wants me to meet him at his house."

Carmen looked at me like she saw a ghost. "You're not going, are you?"

"No."

"Why did you answer your phone?"

"Because I wanted to talk to him so I could feel him out. I needed to hear the tone of his voice to figure out whether or not he knew what was going on."

"Fuck all that! You didn't have to hear his voice. That nigga knows that you saw his brother kill Lil D, so now he trying to get you to meet him so he can kill your ass."

Hearing Carmen tell me that Mario's only motive to get me to meet him was so that he could kill me really stung me in the heart. Here I was again, on the fucking run for my life. I thought I was coming to Virginia to live a peaceful and quiet life but that all went down the drain after I fucked around and ended up at the wrong place at the wrong time. What the fuck was I going to do, run away again? Where in the hell would I go? My father was dead and I wasn't on good terms with my mother. I had no siblings, and I didn't have family anywhere else. And my money wouldn't last long enough for me to be traveling from state to state. I had about 160 grand left to my name and I didn't have any resources to replenish it either. So, whatever plans I needed to make had to be mapped out very carefully and most importantly in a timely fashion.

Carmen guided me down a lot of back streets to avoid running into Maceo or any of his homeboys. We ended up on highway 64 going in the direction of Chesapeake. Carmen told me she had a friend by the name of Kimberly who lived out there. She said Kim was cool and that she'd let us camp out over there for the time being until we figured out what to do next.

"You aren't gonna tell her about the Maceo situation, are you?"

"Hell nah, are you crazy?"

"So, what are you going to tell her?"

"I'm just gonna tell her that you're trying to get away from an abusive-ass husband and could we crash at her house for a few days."

When we arrived at her friend's place, Kimberly welcomed us with open arms. She lived in a very small apartment. I overheard her tell Carmen that her section eight voucher was about to be cut off due to some lies she told, which they found out about. Her three bedroom was very small, but I did notice it was clean. Her three children were from the ages of five to seven and they all were one year apart. Kimberly was an average-looking woman, and I guessed one hundred pounds soaking wet. She wore a head filled with weave extensions and it looked like she needed them replaced. Not to mention it looked like she needed a relaxer around her edges, too. Nevertheless, she seemed like a nice person. She might not have had money to buy designer brands like I'm used to, but she did wear the clothes she could afford in a very neat fashion. Her hospitality was extraordinary. She baked a cheesy lasagna for Carmen and me. It was mouthwatering. And I must admit that her beautiful spirit took my mind off what I had going on outside her house. While

everyone was eating and talking, my cell phone started ringing again. Kimberly continued to talk, but Carmen got quiet.
She looked at me to see if I was going to answer it or not. It
only took Kimberly two seconds to take notice that I had
fear in my eyes. She became concerned at that instant.

"Is that him?" she asked.

I nodded my head.

"Give me your phone. I'll give that nigga a piece of my
mind."

"Oh no, you don't have to do that," I said.

"Yeah, that won't be necessary," Carmen interjected.

"So, what are you going to do, just let him continue to
walk all over you? Fuck that! Stand your ground and show
him that he has no power over you!" Kimberly continued.

As soon as my cell phone stopped ringing, I looked at
Kimberly and said, "He doesn't have any power over me. I
just don't want to make this situation any worse," I lied.

"Have you called the police on his ass?"

"Yes, I have. But it didn't work."

"Why not?" She continued.

"Because he's a police officer himself." I lied once more.
Every time she asked me a question, I found myself falling
deeper and deeper into more lies. I had honestly felt bad
about the lies I told her. But at this juncture I couldn't tell
her what was really going on. I realized that I had opened
my mouth enough as it was, so I wasn't about to sell my
soul again.

During the course of the night, Mario called me at least
twenty times. He even left voice mail messages telling me
that he was worried and he needed me to call him as soon
as I got his message. In another one of his messages, he said
that he loved me and that I wasn't treating him right. His
message sounded so sincere, but I knew it was a front, so I
deleted it and went straight to the next message. When I

had finished listening to every single message I had in my voice mail box, I turned my phone off. I couldn't bear the agonizing feeling I kept getting every time my phone rang.

Not even twenty minutes after I turned off my phone, Carmen's phone started ringing. My heart jumped and so did Carmen's, because her phone hadn't rung all day long. She looked down at the caller ID. She didn't recognize the number so she didn't answer it. And about six rings later, it stopped. But as soon as we exhaled, her phone started ringing again. She looked back down at the caller ID. "It's the same number," she whispered to me while we sat on the living room sofa.

It was a few minutes after midnight, so everyone in the house was asleep except for me and Carmen. "Who do you think it is?" I wondered aloud.

"I don't know. But whoever it is, they want to talk to me real bad," she said, and then the phone stopped ringing.

"Why don't cha block your number and call that phone number back so you can find out who called you," I suggested.

"Nah, if they want to talk to me, they'll leave a message."

"What if it's Maceo?" I asked.

"It can't be, because he doesn't have my number."

"Do you think that was Mario?"

"How would he get my number if Maceo doesn't have it?"

"Do you think your sister could've given it to them?"

"Oh shit, Rachael," Carmen replied, as if she had just thought of something. "I haven't called her all day. I need to find out if she's all right," she continued, then called Rachael.

Rachael did not answer. Carmen let the phone ring seven times and then she hung up. "Damn, I wonder where she's at."

"She might be asleep," I said.

"Not on a Saturday night. Rachael hangs out on the block with her little boyfriend until about one o'clock. And not only that, she always answers her phone, so something ain't right."

Vibrating and ringing once again, Carmen's phone started jumping in her hands. She looked down at the caller ID once more and said, "It's that same number again. You think I should answer it?"

I hesitated for a bit and then I said, "What if it's them?"

"What if it ain't?"

"I don't know, Carmen. Answering it may not be a good idea."

Without saying another word, Carmen pressed the send button on her phone and said, "Hello."

Before the caller spoke, Carmen grabbed me by the arm and pulled me close to her, shoulder beside shoulder, and placed her cell phone to both of our ears.

"Carmen," Sandra screamed through the phone. "They gon' kill me if you don't tell them where Yoshi is," she sobbed.

Anxiety and terror filled my heart when I heard the fear in her voice. "Ma, where you at?" Carmen asked in a low tone to prevent Kimberly from hearing her.

"I don't know." She began to sob uncontrollably.

"Don't worry about where she's at!" a man's voice interjected. "Just tell me where your cousin is and I'll let your dope-fiend-ass mama go," he continued, his voice low and stern.

I quickly removed the phone from my ear. Hearing his voice scared the shit out of me and gave me the creeps. "That's Maceo, isn't it?" I whispered.

Carmen nodded, as her eyes became watery.

"Where is your cousin?" he asked once again.

"I don't know," Carmen lied.

"Stop lying, bitch! You know where she's at."

"I swear, Maceo, I don't," Carmen whined.

"Shut the fuck up, bitch! I ain't trying to hear that bullshit! Just tell me where she's at!" he demanded.

"I don't know."

"A'ight, since you wanna play games, I'm letting you know right now that I'm getting ready to hang up. But I'm gon' call your ass back in thirty minutes and when I do, you better tell me where your cousin is. And if you don't, I'm gon' kill your mama," he warned, then hung up.

Right after Maceo hung up, Carmen sat there on the edge of the sofa with a panicked expression on her face. Tears fell from her eyes and for the first time since I got here, I actually saw the love she had for her mother.

"What are we going to do?" I asked. I couldn't take any more.

"If I don't tell him where you are by the time he calls me back, he is going to kill my mama." Carmen repeated Maceo's words, her body motionless. She acted as if she couldn't believe what was going on herself.

"Do you believe him?" I asked.

"Yeah, I believe him." She looked like a zombie in the face, except for the tears that fell one after the other.

I asked again, "What are we going to do?"

"I don't know."

"Do you think we could stall him for longer than thirty more minutes, until we think of something?"

"No, that's not going to work."

"What are we going to do then?"

Coming back to life, she snapped out, "I don't know, Yoshi!" She then stood up from the sofa. I watched her walk over toward the living room window; she pulled the curtains back and peered out of it. After she closed the curtains, she turned back around and looked at me. She didn't say a word, but I knew her mind was going one hundred miles per minute. I was afraid to ask her another question for fear that she would just lose it, so I sat there quietly and waited for her to say something to me first.

Before she uttered another word, I swear fifteen minutes went by. But when she started talking, I couldn't stop her. "If we called the police, it ain't gon' do no good because Maceo got so many of them on his fucking payroll, you wouldn't know who to trust. All them motherfuckers are crooked as hell! There aren't any more good cops out there because all their asses are underpaid and overworked; that's why their greed for street money has gotten out of control. I wished all their asses would burn!" she snapped once again.

I looked down at my watch. "We only got five minutes left before he calls you back so we better come up with something," I warned her.

She stopped in her tracks. "I don't know what to tell him. I mean, we can't give you up." She began to sob once again.

Hearing Carmen's loyalty as she sided with me touched my heart. The last person I had a special bond with like that was Maria. She was the only person who had my back until I fucked up our relationship behind my greed. I will never forget how she saved me on more than one occasion. I stood up from the sofa and embraced Carmen. Whether she knew it or not, she made me feel alive again. I felt like I wasn't in this world alone anymore and that Maria had sent Carmen to be my guardian angel. When I hugged her, I held her as tight as I could. And when I let her go, I stepped back just enough so I could be within a few inches of her face. I used my hands to wipe away the tears from her face and said, "You know what? I've always felt like a loner and that I didn't have anybody in my corner. But you showed me different by that comment you just made."

"And I meant that. I can't give you up." Her tears came down harder and faster.

"Stop crying, Carmen. We're going to figure something out," I told her, even though I hadn't the slightest idea what we were going to do. My back was up against the wall just like hers. But I was grateful that she wouldn't give me up to Maceo to set her mother free. I guess she felt like my life meant more than her own mother's. Whatever her reasons were, I'm just glad that we were on the same page.

I sat back down on the sofa and watched Carmen as she continued to pace the floor. And then out of the blue, her phone rang and vibrated again. I jumped back to my feet, while Carmen snatched her cell phone from the holster attached to her jeans. She flipped it open and stuttered the word hello. I rushed to her side and leaned my head forward so I could hear what he had to say.

"You ready to tell me where your cousin is?" he asked.

"I told you I didn't know."

"Why you playing games with me, Carmen? Bitch, do you know I will kill you and your whole motherfucking family?"

"I'm not playing games with you. I called her cell phone five times and it kept going straight to voice mail."

"You know what this means, right?"

"No," she said, barely audible.

"Listen then," he said, and then Carmen and I heard a loud scream echoed in the background. We both knew it was her mother screaming for her life but there was nothing we could do. And before Carmen could utter another word, the phone went completely dead. Then all of a sudden Carmen's body fell limp against me, and I realized that she'd fainted.

I carefully lowered her to the floor and cradled her head. "Carmen," I whispered urgently in her ear. "Wake up. Come on, girl. We can get through this."

She blinked her eyes several times, and after a few more moments, she finally said, "Okay, I'm all right. I think."

"Girl, don't you ever scare me like that again." I tried to smile, but couldn't. Sandra was dead, and Maceo still wanted to get at me. "Please try to warn me the next time, okay?"

I helped Carmen to her feet and escorted her to the sofa. I took a seat beside her and laid my head back on the headrest. I had no idea what we were going to do. We desperately needed a plan.

As the night went on, nothing else happened out of the norm. Carmen's cell phone didn't ring anymore and she didn't have any more fainting spells. I believed we stayed up for another two hours until our bodies couldn't take the exhaustion anymore. We tried desperately to keep one another up, but it didn't happen. We fell asleep about three hours before the sun came up.

Eight Hours Later

Carmen and I got up this morning around ten-thirty. Kimberly was already up, fixing breakfast for us and her children; then she got everybody dressed and headed out into the streets. She told me and Carmen that today was her boyfriend's visiting day at Indian Creek prison. She told us she was going to be there all day and then she was going to go to her mother's house afterward because she was cooking a big dinner.

Carmen and I stayed inside. There was nothing for us to do around the house but turn on the television. She sifted through all the cable channels Kimberly had, but we couldn't find anything to watch that interested us. I wanted to look at the news to see if it was reported that Aunt Sandra's body was found in a ditch somewhere, but nothing like that was mentioned. We decided to go out to the local Walmart store since it was only a half mile from Kimberly's apartment. Carmen and I both needed a change of undergarments really bad. We also needed some toiletries and a change of clothes, so as soon as we stepped foot into the store, I headed straight to the lingerie department and picked up a few panty and bra sets. Then I went to the women's section. They didn't have much to choose from and I hadn't worn clothing this cheap since I was a kid. After Carmen got a few lingerie pieces, she came over to the women's section and helped me pick out something to lounge in until we were able to get something more suitable. I ended up purchasing two off-brand sweat suits. One of them was all gray and the other one was black and white. Carmen picked up a pair of generic denim jeans and a sweatshirt to wear with them.

On our way out of the store, Carmen's cell phone vibrated and rang. This time she had it in her pocket so she quickly retrieved it. Right after she checked the caller ID, she looked at me and said, "It's Rachael."

"Answer it," I insisted.

"Hello," she said.

"You called me last night?" she asked calmly.

"Yeah, where were you?"

"Me and Rodney went to a party. And I didn't hear my phone ring because the music was so loud."

"Have you been home yet?" Carmen wanted to know.

"Nah, why?"

"Have you seen Mama or talked to Grandma?"

"Nah, and why are you asking me so many questions?"

"Look, Rachael, I ain't trying to get into all that with you. I just needed to know if you talked to Mama or Grandma?"

"And I told you, nah."

"When you going home?"

"In a few minutes. Why?"

"Well, when you get home can you call me?"

She sucked her teeth. "I'll think about it," she replied sarcastically.

"Come on now, Rachael. This is serious. Stop acting childish!"

"Yeah, whatever!" she said, and then she hung up.

Frustrated by the fruitless conversation she had just had with Rachael, Carmen slammed her cell phone shut. "She is one stupid little bitch!" she screamed. "She just will not cooperate for nothing in the world."

"What did she say?" I asked her while we were putting our bags in the car.

"First of all, her ass stayed out last night, so she hasn't been home yet. And when I told her to call me when she got there, she wants to ask me a bunch of damn questions."

"Come on, get in the car. She'll call you back when she hears something," I told her.

After we climbed inside, her cell phone rang again, so she looked down at the caller ID. The number didn't appear. The word *private* came across the screen. Carmen looked at me. "You think I should answer it?" she asked me.

I honestly didn't know what to tell her, so I shrugged my shoulders.

Her phone rang at least six times until it stopped. And right before we exhaled, it rang again. At this point I couldn't take it anymore, so I snatched the cell phone out of her hand and answered it.

"Hello," I roared through the receiver. But I got no response. So, I yelled hello again.

This time I got a response. "Is this Yoshi?" the voice asked. It was barely audible.

My heart fell into the pit of my stomach. "Who is this?" I snapped.

"It's Mario," he replied in a low tone.

I almost dropped the phone when I heard Mario say his name. I looked for the end button to disconnect the call, but I pressed the speaker phone button instead. "It's Mario. How do you hang it up?" I whispered as panic filled my heart.

"Wait! Don't hang up!" he pleaded. But I didn't listen to him. Carmen took the phone out of my hand and disconnected the call. When the screen went completely dead, I exhaled a sigh of relief.

"Come on. We got to get out of here," I insisted.

"Yeah, let's go," she agreed as she turned her phone off.

I started the car and headed out of the parking lot of Walmart. I pressed down on the accelerator and hauled ass back to Kimberly's house. It was around six-thirty in the evening when we returned, so it was kind of dark outside. Kimberly wasn't home as of yet, so we used the key she left us to get in and out of the house with. Carmen hopped out of the car first.

I followed right behind her after I reached in the back-seat to retrieve my bags. As soon as I closed the driver side door behind me, I turned around to walk toward the front door and got the surprise of my life. I almost fainted when I saw through my peripheral vision the silhouettes of two men walking toward me. I turned to my right and locked my eyes on the one I instantly recognized. My body became numb and I couldn't open my mouth to scream for help. Carmen had already gone inside the apartment, so I was left to fight off these two goons by myself.

Mario approached me first while the guy followed closely behind him. I didn't know what to do.

"I need to talk to you," Mario said calmly.

I don't know how I did it, but I got up the willpower to scream at the top of my lungs. And within a flash Carmen dashed back outside. Mario rushed toward me. "Hey, calm down. I just want to talk to you."

I didn't respond. I was too frantic. So I just stood there with my hands barricading my face, awaiting the evitable.

Meanwhile, Carmen leaped in the air and dove right on Mario's back. She started pounding on him with both of her fists. "Get away from her and leave her alone!" she screamed.

Her little punches didn't penetrate him at all. "I only want to talk to her," he replied irritably. He and his friend struggled a bit, but they got her off his back. And even after they managed to get her away from Mario, she tried to run up on him again.

"You are a fucking liar! And what did y'all do with my mother?" she screamed as she raced toward him.

Mario held his hand out toward Carmen to prevent her from swinging on him again. "Hey, Carmen. Can you calm the fuck down, please? I came here to help y'all."

"I don't want to hear that shit! Tell me what y'all did to my mother! Where is she?"

"Maceo had her killed."

"Oh, my God! I am going to kill y'all!" she screamed, as she rushed to attack Mario again.

I looked around for help, but it seemed that no one was home.

"Can you get her, please?" Mario instructed the guy.

And just like that, the guy grabbed Carmen and lifted her in the air.

"Put me down!" she screamed.

"Not until you calm down," the guy told her. His voice was deep like Barry White. His stature was like Shaq O'Neal, so Carmen couldn't do shit with him. I wanted to help her but my body was still numb and I honestly could not move. Shit, I didn't know if he had a gun or not.

"Yoshi, can you please tell your cousin to calm down? We are not here to hurt y'all. We are actually here to save your lives," he explained.

I looked up at Carmen dangling in the air and something told me that I needed to defuse the situation right away, so I opened up my mouth and said, "Carmen, calm down so we can hear what he has to say."

"Fuck that! These niggas killed my mama!" she yelled back.

"Please, Carmen, let's hear what he has to say," I begged. At this point, I wanted all the commotion to stop.

Carmen kicked a little bit more, but when I looked at her one last time, she settled down, so the guy placed her back on her feet. She slumped down to the ground and had the saddest expression as tears poured from her eyes. I wanted to rush to her side but I didn't want to make any sudden moves. So, I turned toward Mario and asked, "How did you find me?"

"There's a GPS tracker installed on the car you're driving."

My mouth fell wide open. "Oh, my God! So you knew where I was the whole time?"

"Yep. I couldn't come out here last night because I couldn't get away from Maceo. He was acting like a madman last night and believe me, I tried everything in my power to prevent him from killing her mother. But he wouldn't listen to me."

"What did he do to her?" Carmen cried out.

"I'm sorry but I can't say," he said, obviously holding back.

"Tell me! I want to know," she demanded in another loud scream.

Mario looked at me for an okay. When I nodded my head and gave him the go-ahead, he looked back at Carmen and said, "He had his boys gag her and tie her up and dump her in a bathtub of acid."

Carmen screamed louder. "Oh, my God! They tortured her!"

I couldn't stand seeing her in this shape, so I rushed over to her and embraced her. I rubbed her head and told her to let it out. And while I was holding her in my arms, Mario stepped over to where we were and told me that Maceo was looking for me and that he wasn't going to stop at anything until I was found. He also told me that Maceo knew that I was driving the Honda, so he had people, including a couple of police detectives from the city of Norfolk, on the lookout for me.

"But why do all of that?" I asked. "I wasn't gonna rat him out," I explained.

"To him that doesn't matter. His thing is you saw him murder somebody so you've got to go. Point blank."

I stood there in shock as Mario broke everything down for me. I couldn't believe what I was hearing. "I came out here to get you so I can take you somewhere safe."

"Why go through the trouble? I mean, I'm someone you just met. What would you be getting out of this?"

"Yoshi, you may not believe this, but I fell in love with you the very first night we spent together. I love being around you and I don't want to lose that feeling."

"I'm sorry, but I don't believe you. You are going against your own flesh and blood for me. That's insane."

"Yoshi, it's true! I love you and I swear I can't let anything happen to you. Maceo is a nutcase and he has medical records to prove it. See, I'm not down with all that murdering shit! I've never been like him. I just want to live a simple life, make my businesses succeed, and stay alive long enough to have a few kids and see them grow up. But it seems like every time I found someone to share my life with, Maceo would always find a way to come between us. It's like he never wanted me to be happy."

"All that sounds sweet," I said, then asked, "When did Carmen's mom tell him about me witnessing him murder that guy?"

"She didn't tell him."

"Well, how did he find out that she knew about it?"

"She made an anonymous call to the 1-800-LOCK-U-UP hotline from a friend's house without blocking the number, so that information was passed along to a homicide detective who happens to work for Maceo. When it was time for her to pick up her reward money, the detective sent her straight to Maceo."

With a look of despair, I dropped my head. "And I thought she purposely went to him and told him."

"Nah. She denied knowing anything at first. But when he had her tied up and began to torture her, she told him everything she knew then."

Carmen heard every word Mario said. She seemed even more distraught than she did last night. I began to rub her back. "It's going to be all right," I told her, even though I had my doubts.

Mario continued to convince me that he wanted to help me and that he never had intentions of hurting me. He told me Maceo came to him and asked him to call me and tell me to meet him, but Mario told Maceo that he didn't know where I was because I was mad with him and had turned my phone off. I listened to him very closely and wondered to myself whether or not this guy was being sincere. I wanted to believe him since I'd run out of options and had no other place to run.

"So, what's going to happen now?"

"If you allow me to take you out of here, I will put you somewhere safe until I can iron out all this shit."

"Where would you take me?"

"I was thinking about driving you to Edenton, North Carolina, and putting you in a hotel for a couple of days."

"Why there? I mean, I can go back to my place."

"That won't be a good idea because one of the guys who moved your truck works for Maceo, so now Maceo knows where you live."

"What are we going to do with Carmen? I can't leave her."

With a sincere look on his face, he said, "I was going to take her with us."

"Okay, well, how can we trust you that you won't take us to Maceo?"

"I don't know. All I got is my word. And I truly do love you, Yoshi, so that should be enough."

I looked at Mario for at least twenty seconds before I gave him an answer. I tried desperately to follow my mind, but my heart took control. "All right," I finally said. "We'll go with you."

I grabbed Carmen by the arm and pulled her to her feet. I could tell she was a little apprehensive by her body language and facial expression, but when I whispered in her ear that we were going to be all right over a dozen times, she then told me that she was putting her life in my hands. I hugged her and told her I would be able to handle it.

Mario let her call Kimberly to let her know that we were leaving and that we would call her after we got settled. Kimberly said okay and told us not to be strangers. Carmen assured her that we wouldn't.

Before we left Kimberly's place, Carmen begged Mario to let her go to her house to check up on Rachael and Grandma Hattie. He was hesitant about it at first, but when she stressed to him the importance of how much her family meant to her, he felt obligated to grant her wish. "I will let you go under one condition," he said.

"What is that?" Carmen asked, while she wiped the tears from her face.

"You got to let my man here drive you there."

"Can Yoshi ride with us?" Carmen asked.

"Yes, I want to ride with her," I interjected.

"I swear to you that that will not be a good idea. Maceo has his men on the lookout for you, Yoshi, and if they see you, my man here ain't gonna be able to fight all them niggas off," he explained.

I wasn't trying to hear what he was saying and my expression showed it. So, he said, "Look, sweetheart, you are going to have to trust me on this. Please just let my man here take Carmen out to Huntersville really quick so they can come back and meet us. The quicker I can get you out of this area, the better off you are."

Carmen stepped up and said, "He's probably right, Yoshi. You probably won't be safe going back to my house, so go with Mario and I'll meet up with you later."

I hesitated for a second, and then said, "All right."

Not too long after Carmen and I agreed to go separate ways, we all departed. I jumped in Mario's Benz wagon and the guy Mario brought with him drove away the Honda with Carmen in it. Before they pulled off, I hugged her and told her to be careful. I also told her I'd turned my phone back on so she needed to call me as soon as she got there and right before she left. She assured me that she would.

The Ride of My Life

I rode in complete silence for the first fifteen minutes of the drive. Mario reiterated a few times about how much he loved me and that he didn't want to lose me. I listened to him but I really wasn't moved. My emotions were too tied up in what had happened to Aunt Sandra. I was also thinking about the well-being of Carmen, Rachael, and Grandma Hattie. I would truly be devastated if I lost them, too. It seemed like every time I came in contact with someone I loved, something ended up happening to them.

I looked at Mario and said, "Do you think Carmen and that guy are going to be all right?"

"Gene can take care of himself. Believe me, he got the right ammo with him just in case something funny jumps off."

"Has your brother threatened to do anything at all to my other relatives?'

"No, he hasn't. He just wants you," Mario told me. His tone was low but what he said was clear to me.

"Remember last night when you called me and told me that you missed me and that you wanted me to meet you at your house?"

"Yeah."

"Did you mean that? Or were you trying to set me up?"

"I meant it. But if I would've told you I knew what was

going on and that I wanted to help you by saving your life, so meet me somewhere, you wouldn't have believed me. So, I tried to use reverse psychology even though it didn't work—you hung up on me anyway."

I didn't respond to his comment. I just turned back around and gazed out the window.

The drive to our destination probably took us about an hour if not more. It was very peaceful and I had to admit that I was beginning to feel at ease. When we arrived in Edenton, he drove to the downtown area. I could see that it was a small town; every business looked like it was family owned and run. I could probably count the number of businesses that sat across from each other on both of my hands. The town kind of reminded me of the show on TV called *Mayberry RFD* that only had one sheriff and one deputy. Not too far from the family-owned businesses the town had a Walmart and a Marriott hotel, so we stopped at the Marriott hotel and got us a nice suite. He paid for one whole week and tipped the desk clerk an extra three hundred dollars with specific instructions not to register his real name in their log. She said, "No problem," and handed him the key cards to his room.

As soon as we got to the ninth floor, where our suite was located, we rushed into our room and began to unwind. I headed for the shower, while Mario turned on the television. I believe I stayed in the shower for at least twenty minutes, letting the hot water relax me. And once again, I had time to reflect back on my life and where I went wrong. The first thing that popped in my head was how, finally achieving success as an attorney, I let greed come into my life and tear it apart. I did not have to make all those bribes to win my cases. I was smart, so I could have climbed to the top without all the rigamarole of paying off judges and DAs or even fucking them, for that matter. And on top of that, I even resorted to snorting cocaine again. How idiotic was that? I couldn't take the blinders off to see how I was ruining my fucking life. I remember when Maria told me I needed to slow my life down because I was about to get into a head-on collision. And you know what? She was right. Look at me, hiding out from the Feds, the DEA, Sheldon and his crew, and a fucking local psycho named Maceo. They all wanted a piece of me, and I couldn't oblige. I just wished that they would leave me alone.

When I finally decided to soap up, the water got cold, so I did a rush job with the soap and washcloth and then got out of there. Right after I grabbed the towel from the towel rack, I exited the bathroom. When I entered the bedroom where Mario was, he was sitting at the edge of the bed watching television with his back facing me. He didn't know I was standing behind him, so I looked over his shoulder to see what he was watching.

My heart dropped when I saw a picture of me plastered on *America's Most Wanted*. I wanted so desperately to run, but where was I going to go? I knew then I had to stay where I was and face the music.

I stood there the entire time listening to the broadcast. The host revealed everything there is to know about me, so I knew I had some explaining to do when Mario turned around and popped the first question. The segment about me didn't last very long. But it lasted long enough for Mario to find out that I used to be a successful, high-profile attorney. And that I was a millionaire, living in a $5.2 million, split-level penthouse located on Collins Avenue in the heart of Miami, Florida. He also found out that I too had had a team of important officials on my payroll to assist me in winning my cases, until authorities from a different side brought the whole operation down.

I couldn't see Mario's face, but I knew he was tuned in to

what he had heard. At one point he shook his head in disbelief. I couldn't stand it anymore. My heart couldn't take it, so I walked up to him and said, "I know you're shocked by what you just heard, but not all of what that man said is true."

He turned around and looked at me with the most confused expression he could muster up. I knew he didn't know what to say, because he wouldn't open his mouth to comment.

I took another step and said, "Yes, I lied to you about who I was and where I was from. But I did not kill my best friend or my housekeeper. I was set up."

Mario got up from the bed and took two steps backward. "How long were you going to keep this shit away from me?"

"Mario, I wanted to tell you but I was afraid you would act like you're acting right now."

Again he shook his head in disbelief. "I know now we aren't going to be able to spend the rest of our lives together."

"Don't talk like that. I did not commit those murders, so I can fight those charges with the right attorney. I just don't know anyone from Miami who would help."

"Why is that?"

"Because I shitted on a lot of them and the ones I didn't shit on, I turned my nose up at. So I had a lot of enemies who were waiting patiently for my demise. And when I finally fell on my face, I was the laughingstock of Miami. Do you know how humiliating it is to have all the power in your hands one day and then lose it the next?"

"Yes."

"No, you don't!" I snapped, tears beginning to fall from my eyes. "I was a very powerful attorney and a junior partner at my firm. No one could touch my acquittal rate. No one! I was the best and I had millions of dollars to prove it.

I even had clients who were my friends. They loved me. They showered me with expensive gifts like diamond bezel Chopard and Rolex watches. I even got an Aston Martin a few months back. You see, I was well respected and I couldn't be touched."

"Somebody touched you," he interjected.

"That's because I left myself open. I became vulnerable and too consumed with money and the fame."

"Well, it's over now."

I stood there with a blank expression on my face. I didn't know how to react to Mario's statement. Holding my bath towel up with my hands, I said, "What's going to happen now?"

"I don't know. You tell me," he said flatly.

"I want to turn myself in so I can get this mess behind me and get on with my life, but I'm afraid."

"What are you afraid of?"

"The Feds and the DEA aren't the only people looking for me."

Puzzled, he shrugged his shoulders and shook his head. "Well, who else is looking for you?"

I took a deep breath and then I said, "I was representing a client named Sheldon Chisholm. He was the boss of a Haitian mafia down in Miami with murder and drug charges pending against him. Well, after he gave me a hefty retainer, I promised him that I would be able to get him an acquittal, since I had the right people in place to make his evidence disappear. When we parted on good terms, he was happy and so was I. Well, shortly thereafter, my inside operation within the justice system was sabotaged, so the acquittal I promised my client went right out the window. And when I went to him and told him that things might not work in his favor, he threatened my life. So, here I am."

"Ahh man! You got a lot of heavy shit going on in your life!" he commented.

"I know, and that's why when I came here and saw how peaceful life was, I wanted to be a part of that. But I also knew that it wouldn't be long before my situation back in Miami would rear its ugly head and I'd have to deal with it."

"I don't know, Yoshi. This is some serious shit!" He turned his back to walk over to the window. He peeped behind the curtains and then he pulled them back. When he turned around to look at me, I had taken a seat on the edge of the bed.

"I don't know what you're thinking, but I can't let you turn me in if—"

"That's not what I'm about, Yoshi. I don't do shit like that. But at the same time, I'm trying to figure out how I would fit into your life with all that shit you got going on."

"All I need is a good attorney and I'll turn myself in."

"But I don't know any attorneys around here who would want to pick up a case like yours. That shit you're in is probably too high-profile for them. I mean, how would they defend you in a case riddled with murder and corruption? It would be next to impossible."

"My case isn't that complicated. All you have to do is point in the direction of the most qualified attorney in Virginia, and I would stand beside him and assist him."

"I don't know that any attorneys are on your level."

"I'm sure you know someone. Just take your time and think about it."

He fell silent for a second, deep in thought. About five seconds later, he scratched his head and said, "Maybe I can call Saks or Brocoletti and see if either has a license to practice down in Florida."

"How long have they been practicing law?"

"Brocoletti has been on the scene for at least fifteen to twenty years. And Saks is a three-generation law firm."

"Well, call Saks first and see what they say. And if they

can't defend me, then call that Brocoletti guy, because I'm ready to get my life back on track," I replied, getting to my feet.

Mario reached for his BlackBerry. But before he grabbed a hold of it, I threw my arms around him and buried my face into his chest. "Please don't leave me. I need you."

He rubbed his hand across my back. "I won't," he assured me. "You don't need to worry."

While we were embracing, Mario's BlackBerry started ringing. He pulled his phone from his holster and answered it. "Yo, what's good?"

"You got that bitch wit cha, don't cha?" I heard Maceo's menacing voice echo through the phone.

I pulled back from Mario. I wanted to give him enough room to say whatever it was he needed to say. "I don't know what cha talking about," he said calmly.

"Nigga, stop playing games with me. I got your boy Gene and Carmen right here and they told me you got the ol' girl with you."

I couldn't have heard that right. I squeezed Mario's hand, my question in my eyes.

Before Mario said another word to Maceo, he looked at me and muffled the phone. "I'm sorry, baby, but he's got your cousin," he whispered.

I damn near screamed when Mario told me Maceo had Carmen. At that very moment, I wanted to rip Maceo's fucking head off. The ruthless Yoshi was trying to rear her ugly head. I wanted so badly to snatch the phone out of Mario's hand, but I held my composure and allowed him to handle the situation, while I made a plan of attack on my own.

"Where are they now?" Mario asked Maceo.

"Nigga, don't worry about them. They are in good hands. You just need to bring me that bitch and do it like right now," he demanded.

Maceo started yelling like his fucking mind was going bad. Mario started to hang up on him, but I begged him not to do it. My cousin Carmen's life was on the line and I wanted to know what price I needed to pay to get her back. "Lil bro, won't cha just let Gene and the girl go? She ain't done shit to you."

"Nigga, I ain't your bro. You a traitor, nigga! I got shit for you," Maceo roared through the phone.

"Come on now, Mace. I ain't never turned my back on you and I ain't gon' start that shit now."

"Nigga, fuck you! You hiding that bitch out so I can't find her. I'll tell you what, if you don't bring her to me by nightfall, I'ma kill her cousin and Gene right here on the spot," he threatened.

Maceo muffled the phone again. "He told me that if I don't bring you to him by nightfall, he is going to kill my man Gene and your cousin."

Fear consumed me that instant. Here I was trying to re-group so I could get my life back on track, but then I was faced with a decision. Do I save my own life and haul ass back to Florida where Sheldon wants me dead? Or do I stay here and fight Carmen's battle? I knew I had to make a de-cision right then because Maceo was on the other end and he wanted an answer. I thought about what Carmen had added to my life since I'd been in town. And I thought about if the shoe was on Carmen's foot how she wouldn't hesitate to give her life in exchange for mine. That's just the type of woman she was, and I respected the hell out of her for it.

Without thinking about it another second, I said, "Tell him you're gonna bring me to him but he cannot lay one finger on her."

Mario got back on the phone and relayed the message. From there Maceo gave him specific instructions on where and what time to meet him. But before Maceo hung up his phone, Mario said, "Why don't you let Gene go right now. He ain't got shit to do with none of this."

"A'ight, you got it!" Maceo replied and then we heard a loud shot. BOOM! Mario and I both jumped. The loud gunshot magnified through the receiver and almost shattered both of our eardrums. "You heard that shit, nigga? I just shot your right-hand man in the motherfucking head. I told you I ain't playing with none of y'all! So you better bring that bitch to me before her cousin be next," he yelled. And then the call was disconnected.

I sat back in a daze because I just heard this fucking maniac shoot Mario's friend Gene in the head. How cold-blooded can he be?

"Are you sure you want to do this?" Mario asked me.

"I have to," I said.

"Look, I know that you want to save Carmen's life, but I know my brother and he is not going to let her go."

"But I'm going to give him my life for hers."

"It's not going to matter. He wants both of y'all dead. And it wouldn't surprise me if he wants to take my life, too."

"Can we do something about it? I mean, why isn't he locked up somewhere?"

"I told you Maceo is a mental health case. He is a schizophrenic and he is supposed to take his medicine on a daily basis but he doesn't. He did a ten-year sentence at Central State Hospital about five years ago for killing our stepfather. It doesn't matter what he does to people, he will never be put behind bars for it."

"What does your mother say about his behavior?"

"She died of heart complications about two years before Maceo snapped out on our stepfather and killed him."

"Does he have children?"

"Nah, he doesn't have any. He never had a woman long enough to get her pregnant."

I sat there and laid my face in my hands. I was speechless and had no clue about what I was getting myself into. I did know that I didn't want to die and I didn't want Carmen's life taken either, so I had to come up with a plan and do it quickly.

I looked back up at Mario. "What are you thinking about?" he asked.

"I'm trying to figure out how we can get Carmen back without handing my life over into your brother's hands."

Mario thought for a minute and then said, "We're just gonna have to play it by ear. But one thing is for certain, and that is when we make the trade, you're going to have to stay by my side."

"What if he starts shooting at the both of us?"

"He's not going to do that."

"But what if he does?"

"He's not going to do that," he repeated himself.

It was clear that he didn't want to face the music. To my understanding, he didn't have any answers for me, so he brushed it off. I could live with that. "Can you fire a gun?" he continued.

"No."

"Why not?"

"Never got around to shooting lessons."

"Well, don't worry about it. I'll have my burner with me so I'm gon' make sure you'll be all right," he assured me.

He and I continued to discuss our plans while I got dressed. I slipped on the sweat suit I purchased earlier at Walmart. Mario looked at it funny but he didn't make a comment about it either way. Now wasn't the time. Several minutes later he grabbed his car keys and told me to come with him. My heart was beating rapidly. I swear if I had to take a shit I would've done it right then and there. I noticed with each step I took, my stomach started doing flips. I grabbed hold

of Mario's hand and held it the entire way down to the car.
I swear I didn't want to let it go for nothing in the world. I
looked at him one last time before we got into the car. "I'm
putting my life in your hands," I said solemnly.

"Don't worry. I got it," he replied, and then he kissed me
on the forehead.

Blood Is Thicker
than Water

"Where are we going again?" I asked.

"We're going back across state lines."

"I know that, but where?"

"We're going to this old house we had in Hickory. It's abandoned now but we use to used it for a stash house. It's way in the boonies, surrounded by four acres of cornfields. Nobody ain't gonna be able to see us back there because it's dark as hell throughout the whole place."

"Why couldn't we meet him somewhere else?"

"Because that's his spot. He's known for going back there when he wants to get rid of bodies."

Hearing Mario tell me that Maceo got rid of the bodies he killed out there made me want to throw up. Right then and there I knew I didn't have a chance to get out of this shit I was about to get myself in. There was no way God was going to save me from this. I figured that maybe it was my time to leave this earth. Who knew? I would probably be better off. Without further hesitation, I pulled out my cell phone and made a quick call to Grandma Hattie. She answered her phone on the second ring.

"Hello," she said.

"Hey, Grandma. How are you?" I asked her, trying my best to sound as cheerful as possible.

"I'm fine, baby. Where you been? I've been worried about you."

"I'm fine, Grandma. I just had to leave because something came up."

"Is Carmen with you? Because she hasn't been home. And the manager from IHOP called this evening looking for her to see why she ain't come to work."

I got choked up behind her question. I honestly didn't know how to answer it. If I told her what was going on, I know her heart wouldn't be able to take it. But if I lied to her, my heart wouldn't be able to take it. I was literally stuck between a rock and a hard place and I had no idea how to come out of it. I hesitated for another second and then I said, "She's not with me now. But I'm on my way to see her."

"Well, when you do, you make sure you tell her that her boss is not happy that she didn't show up to work this evening. So, she better call 'em and give 'em a good reason why she was a no-show."

"I sure will."

"Don't be nice when you tell her because she thinks life is a joke. It's hard out here and I keep telling her that she's one of the lucky ones who has a job. I also asked her why can't she be a big-time lawyer like you. I mean, she was smart in school just like you were, but for the life of me, I can't tell you what happened to her. She thinks it's easy out here. Folks are getting laid off every time you turn around. So, you tell her I said she better get her act together before they fire her butt."

"I will, Grandma. Don't you worry."

"Whatcha doing, anyway, hanging out with some men? That why y'all didn't bring y'all butts back over here?"

"No, ma'am. We just had a few things to take care of."

"Well, y'all be careful because there are some crazy folks out here."

"We will."

"All right, sweetie, now you take care of yourself. And don't forget to talk some sense into your cousin's head when you see her."

"I won't."

"I love you."

"I love you, too, Grandma, and don't you ever forget it."

"Believe me, I won't," she assured me.

Immediately after I hung up with her I sat back and sank deeply into depression. I wished like hell I could've told her to rescue me. Or for that matter, pray for me. I knew she had a direct connection with the man upstairs so he would have heard her prayer loud and clear. I saw Mario looking at me through my peripheral vision, so I turned my head and looked at him.

"Are you all right?" he wondered aloud.

"No, not really. My grandmother made me feel so guilty on the phone just now. I felt like I lied to her."

"What do you mean?"

"She still thinks that I am some big-time attorney and that my life is so peachy. She has no idea that I screwed up everything I accomplished. And if she knew that I was on the run from the Feds, she would be so disappointed."

"I don't think she would. Just when you think a person would react one way, they do the exact opposite."

"Not her. She thinks so highly of me. If she knew that I was a fraud, it would hurt her poor heart."

"Stop beating yourself up. It's going to be all right."

"I hope you're right," I said, and then I turned my head to look back out the window.

It was pitch black outside. We rode by thousands of trees and miles of fields with crops growing on them. The farmland here was massive, it was unreal. And even though it was really dark outside, I could see the silhouette of an old scarecrow hung up on a wooden cross stuck inside the ground in the middle of the field. It looked really creepy.

"We're almost there," he announced.

I swear I wished he would not have told me that. I was already a nervous wreck, but I was becoming a real basket case now. "How much farther we got to go?" I couldn't help but ask. I mean, he did open the door for that question.

"We got about ten more miles to go. So, if you're having second thoughts, I'll turn the car around right now."

"No, I'm fine," I lied.

"You sure, Yoshi?"

"Yes, I'm sure, Mario. Remember—I am not doing this for me. I am doing this for Carmen."

He sighed heavily. "What if you can't help her because she's already dead?"

"Don't talk like that. He said he wouldn't kill her unless I didn't show up."

"I heard what he said, Yoshi. But I know my brother and I just don't trust him."

I fell silent and thought about what Mario had just said. What if she was already dead? My going out to meet Maceo would be in vain. But what proof did I have that he would keep her alive? I guess I had nothing to go on but his word, so that's what I intended to hold on to.

The rest of the drive Mario grabbed my hand and held it. It felt good to know that he was by my side. I just hoped that we were the last ones standing.

Making the Switch

I was nervous as hell the entire drive to the place where Maceo wanted to make the switch. Mario kept running the plan over and over to me so I wouldn't forget what to do. I tried to prepare myself mentally, but I swear it wasn't working. All I could think about was what if something went wrong and I ended up dead. I also thought about Carmen's well-being, too. I had to do this for her. And if nothing else, I had to make sure she would come out of this alive. I knew she would have done it for me without any questions.

The closer we got to our destination, the worse off my stomach felt. I was consumed with fear and doubt about me not coming out of this situation alive. But, at this point, I knew that I had to leave everything in God's hands, so that's what I intended to do.

Mario drove down this long, dark road. There were no streetlights in sight to navigate us down this dirt road. I figured the road had to be at least four miles in distance before ending at the main road. That alone was scary. And by the time we reached the raggedy old house, we noticed that it looked deserted. The white paint on it was chipped away and two of the windows were boarded up. A withered cornfield surrounded the old house.

"I'm gonna park right here," Mario said, as he pulled onto the grass near the beginning of the dirt road. He turned the car completely around so he could dash out of there if he had to. We sat there in the dark with the headlights on and waited for Maceo to appear with Carmen. My heart raced out of control and I couldn't contain it. "Where is he?" I wondered aloud. "I thought he was going to be here!"

"I don't know. But he should be here any minute now," Mario assured me, though his voice sounded a little doubtful.

"Look, I know that I'm coming out of left field with this, but I'm going to need you to be honest with me," I said.

"What is it?"

"Remember the other morning when I got back into bed after I fixed you that seafood omelet?" I asked.

"Yes."

"Okay, and do you remember me getting in your bed to take a nap right after we got out of the shower?"

"Yes . . . ?"

"Okay, well, while I was in the bed I overheard you talking on the phone about meeting someone concerning something you wanted to get from them, but you weren't too happy about where he wanted to meet you. And then I heard you say something to the effect that when he wants to do business the right way, give you a call. So, I was wondering what that was all about. Where you trying to buy drugs from the guy on the phone? Or are you into something else? Because the way I took that conversation, you were getting ready to get into something illegal."

Mario took one long look at me, like he was trying to think of a lie, so I said, "Do you have to think about it?"

"No."

"Well, answer my question. I need you to clarify this thing for me just in case something happens to me tonight."

"Nothing is going to happen to you. Stop talking like that."

"Mario, please answer the question. What are you into? Because I know now that those businesses you have are a front. If we come out of this and stay together, then I don't want to be in the dark about what's going on with you."

He hesitated for a second and then he said, "To answer your question, no, I am not into selling drugs. I used to be in that lifestyle but now I'm strictly trying to do business the right way so I don't have to be looking over my shoulder every time I turn around. Now, as far as that conversation is concerned, I was talking about tires and rims. I've got this guy who works for the company I get my merchandise from and every now and then he'd come across some inventory that the company overstocked. And what he would do is rig up a fake invoice and call with a location of where to meet me. Sometimes we'll meet up in the back of an alley and other times we'll meet up in the back of my stores. It's been kind of hot lately with the police roaming around the Park Place area, which is around the corner from where my store is, so I don't want to arouse anyone's suspicion and have them tear me off behind some stolen goods. No sir, I would rather wait when the time is good than take a chance and end up in jail behind being stupid."

"Do you have to do that?"

"No, I don't. But let me say that when I do get that extra inventory from that guy, it brings me an extra ten grand a week in sales profits. And that's money I can put in my pocket."

"Would it hurt you if you stopped?"

"No."

"Well, has it ever crossed your mind to stop? I mean, you've got so much to lose and I would hate for you to lose it behind something so frivolous."

"It's funny that you asked me that because just this morning I told the guy that I wanted to chill out for a while."

"That's good. I am proud of you."

He smiled and said, "When all of this is over, you and I are going to have a serious talk about our future together."

"I thought we already did that back at the hotel."

"No, we didn't talk about everything."

"What did we leave out?"

"We'll get into that later. Right now, we need to be more concerned about me getting you and me out of here alive. My brother probably has a lot of shit up his sleeves, so we need to be focused on him. You feel me?"

I nodded my head and then I sat back in the seat and said a silent prayer. I knew there had been a lapse in time since I last talked to God, but I needed him. He was the only one I knew who could bring me out of this mess alive. Mario talked a good game on the way here but I sensed fear in his heart. Yeah, he was older than Maceo and bigger in stature, but the underlining issue was that Maceo was a mental case and Mario knew it. When Mario told me how Maceo spent time in a psychiatric institution for his mental illness, I was completely blown away. Why he was still on the street and not in a padded room with a straitjacket strapped to him was beyond me. Let Mario tell it, he can handle Maceo, but his actions showed me something different. So, as we continued to wait, an uneasy feeling came over me. It felt like we were being watched. My peripheral vision was working overtime and I grew restless looking over my shoulder. My nerves were so rattled I probably would've jumped out of my skin if somebody came behind me and said boo!

During the next ten minutes, Mario kept looking at his Rolex watch. He saw how the time kept slipping by while Maceo was a no-show. But before he got restless to the point of backing out of this meeting, a car started driving down the dirt road toward us. My heart started racing uncontrollably as I watched the car travel in our direction. I could see four heads in the car from where I was sitting, and Mario made mention of it. "That nigga lied and said he was only bringing one nigga with him. It looks like he's got two bodies in there along with your cousin."

"Oh, my God, Mario, what are we going to do?" I panicked.

He grabbed hold of my hand. "Calm down. I'm not gonna let anything happen to you."

I laid my hand over top of his and squeezed it tightly. "You promise?"

He looked me in my eyes. "Yes, I promise. Ain't shit gonna happen to you," he assured me, and then he released my hand to grab his gun. He'd driven with it on his lap. He placed his hand around the handle of the semiautomatic pistol and pulled back on the slide. "You ready?" he asked me.

I took a deep breath and then I exhaled. "Yes," I finally answered him.

"Well, remember not to get out the car until I open the door," he instructed me.

"I got it."

Two seconds later he got out of the car and walked around to my side and grabbed a hold of the door handle. My heart stopped beating that instant. Crazy thoughts of me getting shot up behind this dried-up cornfield intruded on my brain. This was not the way I planned my life to end. But then I figured at least I didn't die in the hands of Sheldon and his Haitian henchmen.

"What's the holdup? Get your ass out that car!" I heard Maceo yell. He stood beside his car, which was parked only twenty feet away.

"I'll let her out as soon as you let her cousin out."

"Don't try any funny shit!" Maceo warned Mario.

"How the fuck I'm gonna try some funny shit when you got two of your boys with you?"

Maceo ignored Mario's question and signaled the guy in the backseat to bring Carmen out of the car. I watched closely as the guy climbed out the backseat and walked around to the other side. He pulled on the door handle to open up the door and then leaned into the car to grab her. My eyes were fixated on every move he made, so when he looked like he was struggling to remove her from the car, I got a bit nervous. I sat up in the seat to zoom in a little closer.

"What's the holdup?" Mario yelled from where he was standing.

"Shut the fuck up, nigga! He got her!" Maceo roared.

My heart started beating once again after I heard the thunder in Maceo's voice. I knew he was there for the purpose of killing me, so it was only a matter of time before he would unleash his venom on me. I couldn't see his eyes because of how dark it was in these backwoods, but I could see his facial expression and it wasn't a pretty sight.

"Yeah, a'ight! Well, tell him to hurry up then," Mario stated, his voice as stern as Maceo's. From the outside, it appeared that Mario tried to stand his ground with his brother because he didn't want to seem like he was afraid. But, it didn't take a rocket scientist to see that he was on the brink of running out on me, so he could save his own life. Shit! That's what I would've have done. He had not been messing with me long enough to put his life on the line for me. In my eyes, I was just another piece of pussy; that came a dime a dozen. So, I could've been replaced on the spot. I knew any other man would've done that in a heartbeat.

Finally the guy who struggled to bring Carmen from the car managed to get her out. But when I looked at his body language a little closer, I noticed that something was not right. I tried to get a zoom in on her but the headlights from

Maceo's car prevented me from doing it. But as soon as he stood straight up and threw Carmen's body down on the ground, I realized that her face was covered with a pillowcase and that she was either unconscious or dead.

"What's wrong with her? Why the fuck she ain't moving?" Mario yelled.

"Cause she's dead, nigga!"

Maceo's words hit me like a ton of bricks. My heart pounded so rapidly in my chest cavity, I thought it was going to burst out. Carmen's body just lay there lifeless on the ground and my heart couldn't take it. Tears poured from my eyes as I grabbed the door and pushed it open.

"You killed my fucking cousin!" I screamed as loud as I could. The rage in my voice commanded some attention and I got it. The force of my weight on the door pushed Mario out of the way, so he staggered a bit. He was caught off guard by my reaction and tried to regain control of the situation. But it was too late. Because as soon as I stepped out of the car, Maceo and his other two men pulled out their arsenal of machinery and started firing away. Bullets were flying everywhere. Maceo and his men were shooting at us and Mario was shooting back. When I saw Mario get hit in the arm, I panicked. I knew it was time for me to run for my life. I jumped right back into the passenger side of the car and crawled over to the driver side. Thank God Mario left the key in the ignition with the car running because I didn't have a lot of time to get out of there.

Right before I put the car in gear I looked back at Mario as he ran for cover in the cornfield. I had to protect myself as well, especially after the windshield was shot out. Without giving it a second thought, I pressed down on the accelerator and bailed out of there. My heart was racing as I tried to dodge the load of ammunition that came my way. I couldn't look back to see what Mario was doing because my head was buried directly below the steering wheel. I couldn't even see in front of me, but somehow I managed to force my way by them. Bullet holes mangled the passenger side doors and all the windows were shattered to pieces. Maceo wanted me dead and he tried everything within his power to do it.

"Get her! She's getting away," I heard him yell, while shots were still fired.

Driving uncontrollably down the dirt road, the noise from the shots became less intense, so I knew I had passed them. And when I thought I was in the clear, I raised my head and then the back window came crashing down. "Ooooowwwww!" I screamed, and then I ducked my head back down. At that very moment I lost control of the wheel, and before I knew it, I ran into a nearby tree. BOOM!!!!!

Thank God I wasn't knocked unconscious, but I was banged up a bit from the airbag erupting in my face. I shook my head and immediately pushed the white plastic airbag away from my face and forced the driver side door open. I crawled out onto the ground but I couldn't stand on my feet because the impact from the car hitting the tree head-on damaged my ankle. The only choice I had at this point was to hop on my other foot or crawl. I decided the best thing to do would be crawl, since I was only a few feet from a cornfield. I heard Maceo's voice trailing down behind me, so I needed to make a getaway.

"You can run all you want to, bitch! But I got your ass now!" I heard him yell. He was running in my direction fast, so I knew it wouldn't be long before he and I would be face to face. I said another silent prayer, but this time I poured my heart into it. I had to let God know that if he got me out of this, I would return back to Miami to turn myself in, so I could deal with that situation. And in addition to that, I promised that I would turn my life around and start serving him. I was tired of being on the run and I was tired of running to protect my life. So many of my loved ones had been murdered because of me, and my heart couldn't take it anymore. More importantly, my heart was missing my mother. It took all this shit to happen to me for me to realize that I needed her in spite of all the bullshit I went through with her from my childhood. I also knew that she needed me as well, so I had to make a change.

I continued to crawl until my hands and knees couldn't take the hard sticks and the gravel that punctured me every time I pressed over top of it. I stopped for a second so I could hear how far away Maceo was from me. But I couldn't hear anything. He must've stopped moving, too, so he could hear or see my movement. At one point, I held my breath so he wouldn't hear me breathing. "Oh, my God! What am I going to do?" I said to myself. I was in the middle of nowhere. And it was pitch dark outside. The only light I saw was what came from the headlights of the car Maceo had driven. "Come out of there, bitch! You ain't got nowhere to run," he said, chuckling.

I didn't respond and remained still.

"I know you hear me! You better bring your ass out from there before I really lose my mind," he threatened.

I still remained quiet and I didn't make a move. After about five straight minutes of him trying to coerce me into turning my life over to his hands, he grew frustrated and started toward me. He had no idea where I was, but he made up his mind that he didn't have any more time to waste so he had to go after me. My heart started jumping around when I heard his footsteps coming in my direction. I wanted so desperately to move but I knew if I did, the corn stalks would move for sure and he would be able to locate me with no problem.

"You better say your prayers, bitch, because you are about to meet your maker!" he threatened me once more.

The closer he came to me, the louder his voice became, and I got more and more nervous. I wanted to move just a couple of feet to my right but, again, I didn't want him to see the corn stalks moving because that way he would definitely find out where I was.

Angry and frustrated by my disappearing act, Maceo continued to storm in my direction and then he fired a gunshot in the air. I jumped back and accidently pressed my hand against a sharp object. I couldn't tell what it was until I picked it up in my hand. I had no lights to see with, so I zoomed in on it and strained my eyes to see what it was. It didn't take long to figure out that I was holding a bear trap in my hands. The device had sharp iron jaws and was so heavy, I had to put it back down. The surface of it was rusty too. I could tell just by rubbing my hands across it that it had been out in the field for a very long time, but I could also tell that it still worked.

My mind started running sixty-five miles a second. I knew that Maceo would eventually find me because he wasn't too far from me now. But it was impossible for him to see what was before him, so I knew that when he did find me, it would only be because he walked into me. I immediately placed the trap on my lap so I could figure out how to set it. The bear trap could be my safeguard device to slow that maniac down in his tracks.

"Come on, please work," I whispered softly as I adjusted a few of the locks and switches. Finally, after about three consecutive minutes of messing around with the thing, I managed to set it. I laid it down next to me and waited patiently for that bastard to bring his ass my way. I was tired and wanted all this shit to go away. Maceo had to be stopped.

226 / Kiki Swinson

He'd caused enough pain in people's lives and tonight he and his mental health issues had to be put to rest. Seeing Carmen's limp body lying there on the ground gave me enough courage to stop this maniac from terrorizing anyone else. Aunt Sandra and Carmen were both gone and it was all because of me, so it was time for me to seek some revenge.

"I know you're out here. I smell your sweet perfume, you bitch!" I heard him utter.

The crackling noises from him stepping on sticks and dried-up leaves told me that he was only a few feet away. So, I turned on my stomach and lay completely flat on the ground. The anticipation of when he would finally run into me was about to drive me crazy. I really wanted this shit to be over right then.

"Come out from there, you fucking whore! I can make this a little less painful for you," he bargained.

When I lay down on my stomach, I was on top of a stick that was piercing the hell out my side. The pain was tearing through me like a sharp needle, so I moved just a little bit to my right so I could avoid touching the bear trap. That was a bad move. Because when I moved, my hand accidently hit the trap and the thing snapped back and almost took my hand off. I screamed to the top of my voice and fell back on my side.

Maceo heard me bellow out the scream and ran right in my direction. "I got you now, bitch!" he yelled.

My heart flipped over and took off running. I didn't know if I was coming or going. But I did know that I had just fucked-up and Maceo knew exactly where I was, so my life span was about to run out if I didn't do anything to prevent it. At that moment, I knew I had less than ten seconds to do something and since the bear trap was my only source of weaponry, I scrambled back up and grabbed a hold of the trap. I tugged at the switches a few times and then I locked it. "Yes," I stated when I realized it was set. I set it down and as soon as I did, Maceo appeared before me. My heart stopped the moment I saw his face. He had his gun drawn and pointed directly at me, so I sat completely up without saying a word. He took another step toward me and said, "I gotcha now, bitch! And you ain't got nowhere to run."

I looked down really quick to see how far away he was from stepping into the trap and when I realized he was only an inch away, I knew I had to get him to move one more time. So I said, "Why are you doing this to me? I wasn't even going to go to the police to turn you in."

"I ain't trying to hear that bullshit. Just shut the fuck up and die with some dignity."

"Please let me go. I promise I won't say anything," I whined, as I scooted backward.

"Where the fuck you think you're going?" he asked. And then he took one step. He didn't see the bear trap. So when he stepped into it, the jaws of it snapped around his right ankle and snatched him down to the ground. I guess he had no idea what he'd stepped in, but he did know that it caused excruciating pain. He screamed like a bitch and fell down on top of me and dropped his gun one foot to the right of me. I started kicking him in his face like I was losing my mind. He couldn't fight me back because he was so busy trying to extract the jaws of the bear trap from around his ankle. It was evident that his ankle was broken because this guy was screaming bloody murder. "Oggggggghhhh!" he screamed, lying in the fetal position. "Help me get this shit off my ankle!"

I ignored him and scrambled to get the gun. It took me about three seconds to grab it off the ground and when I did, I pulled back on the slide and pointed it directly at Maceo. True indeed, he was in a vulnerable position and had no way of getting out of it, but it was a prime opportunity for me to take that bastard out of his misery. While I watched him squirm like a fucking bitch, all I could think about was how many people he had killed throughout his entire life. My Aunt Sandra, Carmen, and Lil D were the only faces I could get a visual of. And just the thought of their lives being taken because of this fucking psycho made me furious. So without further hesitation, I aimed the barrel of the gun at the back of his head, closed my eyes, and fired. BOOM!!!! The explosion from the bullet made the gun sound like a cannon. And as soon as the bullet penetrated the back of his head, it exploded. When I opened my eyes, blood and parts of Maceo's brains were splattered on my face, my shirt, and all the dried-up crops that were within three feet of us. I looked down at Maceo and he was out cold. Part of his head was blown off and I could honestly say that I was happy with my efforts. And when I got up to scoot around his lifeless body, I kicked him right in his face. "That's for my family!" I said.

Knowing that he was dead and that there was no way he was coming back, I didn't fear him anymore. I turned over on my hands and knees and crawled out of there without looking back. I stopped a few times because I heard a couple of crackling noises coming from behind me. I hoped it was Mario looking for me. But when I realized that it was probably field rats, I kept it moving. The ground was unbearable from the cold and damp dirt. I knew it was going to take some time for me to recuperate after this ordeal but at this point, it didn't matter to me how much time it would take. I was just glad that it was over and he was one less person looking for me. All I had to do now was find Mario and get out of this godforsaken town. It was time for me to head back to Miami, where I could face Sheldon and the DEA. It might take me forever but I would die trying to clear my name once and for all.

Where to Go from Here

It took me forever to crawl back through that dried-up cornfield. The ground was rocky and cold and muddy, but I made it out. I came back out the side where I entered, so all I had to do was find a way to get back to the dirt road. I was tired as hell, but I knew I couldn't let that hold me back. I was alive and that's what I held on to.

Before I began to crawl to the main road, I turned my attention to the battleground. The headlights of Maceo's car were still beaming. The car was still running as well. My first thought was to crawl over there and get inside so I could drive away in it, but I was afraid that I was going to run into something my heart wouldn't be able to handle. I knew Carmen's body was over there and I wasn't sure how I would find Mario. I remember him taking one shot in his right arm, but anything after that, my mind drew a blank. "Lord, please give me the strength to endure what it is I am about to come upon," I said aloud, and then I took the first step in that direction.

I needed that car because I realized there was no way I could crawl back to the main road in the condition I was in. While I made my way back, I noticed two bodies lying on the ground. I knew they were two large men but I couldn't see the attire. My heart stopped because I was afraid that I would find out one was Mario. His body was the size of these two men, so to know that one could possibly be him made me want to cry out. I mustered up enough energy and willpower to get to them. They were lying perfectly still, so I knew they were dead. They couldn't do me any harm. After taking hundreds of steps I finally came upon the two bodies and realized that Mario wasn't one of them. And right when I was about to turn around to scan the area of where he fell, I saw something move through my peripheral vision. My heart jumped. I turned completely around to see what it was. And when my eyes landed on the object before me, I screamed, "Carmen!"

She was wiggling on the ground trying to sit her body up, while simultaneously trying to take the pillowcase off her head. I don't know how I did it, but I stood on my good foot and hopped right over to where she was. My heart was so overjoyed when I realized that she was alive. Seeing her kicking and moving made my fight with Maceo well worth it. When I finally got within arm's reach of her, I fell back down to the ground and struggled to untie the string around her neck. "Hold tight, cousin, I am going to get you out of this," I assured her.

It took me about three minutes of yanking and tugging to get the thing loose. When I pulled it from her head, she threw her arms around me and held me so tight. "You came back for me." She began to cry.

"You knew I couldn't leave you like that." I embraced her back.

"Do you know I thought I was going to die tonight?"

"Me too. But you will never have to worry about his ass again."

"Where is he?"

"He's lying dead over there in the middle of that fucking cornfield where he belongs."

"Who killed him? How did he die? Where is Mario?"

"It's a long story. I saw Mario run into the field, but now I don't know where he is. Let's get out of here." I tried to stand back on my good foot. I was struggling my ass off, so Carmen got up first and then helped me. We were only a few feet away from Maceo's vehicle, so it didn't take us long to get inside. Carmen got in the driver side and I got into the passenger seat. She didn't attempt to put the car in drive so we could leave. She just sat there and turned her attention toward me. "What are we going to do now?" she asked.

"We're gonna have to call the police."

"Do you think that would be a good idea?"

"We have no other choice."

"But look at all of these dead bodies out here. They ain't gonna believe our story."

"Yes, they will. And besides, there are some other things I've got to tell them, too."

Carmen looked at me strange. "What other things?"

I took a deep breath and then I exhaled. "Carmen, I've been living a lie since I've been here in Virginia and now it has caught up with me."

"What are you talking about?"

"Remember when I told you and Grandma Hattie that I left Florida to get a breather. You know, take a break from practicing law?"

"Yeah."

"Well, the truth is, I am on the run."

"What do you mean, you're on the run?"

"Carmen, somebody murdered my best friend and they pinned it on me. Now federal agents and the DEA are searching high and low for me so I can answer to those charges."

"Oh, my God! What's going to happen to you?"

"I'm gonna turn myself in and try my best to fight the charges."

"Oh, Yoshi," she said, and threw her arms around me once again. "Are you sure you want to do this? They may never let you out."

"I know that. But I'm tired of running. I just want to get this over with."

"Do you know if you turn yourself in here, they're gonna have to extradite you back to Florida? You might as well take a chance and drive back down there yourself, because Virginia might keep you for at least thirty days before they send you on your way."

I sighed. "Carmen, I don't care about any of that. I just want all this mess to be over. Come on. Let's get out of here."

"All right," she said as she put the car in drive. "You know you're gonna have to tell Grandma what's going on. She ain't gonna take it well if I tell her."

"Let's head over there first and then I've got to make that call."

"Okay," Carmen said, and then she pressed down the accelerator.

As we began to ride down the dirt road, I thought about Mario. Maybe he didn't make it. I wanted to see his face before I left, but if he was dead, I didn't want to remember him like that. He was a very good man and everything would have worked out as he had planned. I would have made him my man and perhaps after I got past my ordeal, made him my husband. He was the first guy in a long time that loved me for real. All those other idiots I used to mess with had motives, so our relationships didn't last a hot minute. With Mario, he wanted me for who I was and not what I had. That alone made all the difference with me. I'm just so sorry to know that he had to lose his life behind me. I swear I would have made him a very happy man.

After riding over miles of dirt road, we finally got to the

end. But when we got there, at least five police cars were waiting at the main road. Their lights were beaming very bright and their sirens were blaring like crazy. When I took a second look I noticed that every policeman was standing outside a squad car with a gun drawn and pointed directly at us. Both Carmen and I looked at each other without saying a word.

"Put the car in park. Turn off the ignition and get out of the car right now!" I heard one officer demand through his bullhorn.

"Oh, my God! What should we do?" Carmen whined.

"Do like they said," I commanded, so Carmen did just that.

After turning off the car, Carmen got out first and told them that I couldn't stand up on one of my legs, but they weren't trying to hear her. They still wanted me to remove myself from the car. I struggled for a bit, but I managed to get out. As soon as I stood up, I fell to the ground. One of the officers rushed to my side with his gun still drawn. I guess he had to use proper protocol just in case I wanted to try some funny business.

"Show me your hands," he demanded. I raised them into the air.

"You, too, put up your hands." He looked over at Carmen.

After she raised her hands in the air, another officer rushed toward her. "Do you have any weapons of any sort on you?" I heard him ask.

"No, I don't," she replied.

He turned her around and handcuffed her that instant. "Am I under arrest?" she asked him.

"No, you're not."

"Then why are you putting handcuffs on me?"

"So we can figure out what's going on."

Frustrated by the way he was handling the situation, she said, "You ain't got to figure it out, I can tell you myself."

"She hasn't done anything, officer. She was a victim of kidnap and the man who tried to kill us both is back there in the cornfield," I interjected.

"Is he dead?" the officer standing by my side asked.

"Yes, he is," I replied, as he pulled me onto my feet. Then he sat me against the hood of the car.

"Who killed him?"

"I did, because he was trying to kill me."

His questions continued. "Who are you? What is your name?"

"My name is Yoshi Lomax."

He looked at me strange. Then he looked back at his partner. "Are you the high-profile attorney from Miami, Florida, that the Feds are looking for?"

I nodded my head.

He smiled. "Oh shit, Bobby! We struck a gold mine tonight," he commented. And from that point, he didn't hesitate to handcuff me and escort me to his squad car.

"How many people are back there?" I heard the officer ask Carmen.

"Four."

"All of them are dead?"

"Yes."

"It can't be," I heard another officer yell. "The dispatcher said the person who made the call was a man."

My heart lurched and I forced the officer to stop in his tracks. "Did you just say a man made the call?" I yelled.

"Yes, I did," he replied, and then he turned his attention toward his fellow colleagues. "Where are the paramedics? They should've been here a long time ago." He tugged on the small radio attached to his shoulder. "Dispatch, this is badge number five-two-four-nine-one."

"Copy, sir, what do you have?"

"We have a one-four-seven and we need a paramedic out here. We also have victims of gunshot wounds." He gave the dispatcher the address.

"All right, I copy that," the dispatcher replied, and then she cleared the airways.

"Come on, let's go," the officer escorting me said as he tugged on my arm.

After he placed me in the backseat of the police car, I laid my head back against the headrest. I wondered to myself who could have made the phone call. While I sat there I noticed Carmen talking to the officer who had her detained, while the other officers got into their cars and headed back to the old house. I could see their flashing lights from where I was sitting. I took my attention off the police cars and looked back at Carmen. She seemed to be getting frustrating with the officer. By this time he had taken her cuffs off, so I assumed she was demonstrating the event that had just taken place, because her hands were moving right along with her mouth. This episode went on for at least ten minutes. He had his pen and pad out to write down everything she said.

The paramedics finally came and rode by. They didn't even stop to see if I needed any medical attention. They whisked right by us and went down the road toward the house. There was so much commotion going on, I couldn't think clearly. The radio in the police car was driving me crazy. The dispatcher would come on air, run down a few codes, and then a different police officer would respond. The shit was driving me bananas until I heard . . . something. . . . No. Could it be real?

I sat up in the seat and leaned over toward the fiberglass shield that separated the front seat from the back so I could decipher the police codes. "This is roger four-nine-oh-three-two. I'm located on the south side of the house. I found the gunshot victim that made the nine-one-one call. He needs medical attention immediately."

My mouth fell wide open. I turned my body toward the car door and yelled to Carmen. "They found Mario! He's alive!"

The officer who placed me in his car ran back toward me to see what my problem was. He opened the door in a flash. "What's your problem, miss? You can't be screaming like that," he snapped.

I totally ignored his ass and turned my attention directly to Carmen. "Mario is alive, Carmen!" I yelled once again. "I just heard an officer radio another officer that he found Mario behind the house back there."

The officer who stood before me slammed the car door in my face before Carmen could respond. She did, however, smile and wink her eye at me. I knew then that she'd heard me. I was fine now. My baby was alive and all I needed to do was see him for myself. Goose bumps spread over my entire body. Everything was gonna fall in its proper place and I was going to be all right.

I laid my head back against the headrest and before long, the officer who arrested me was in the driver seat of his car, escorting me down to police headquarters. Now I knew this sounded strange, but I was finally at peace with myself because the two people I just learned to love were alive and well. I couldn't ask for anything more. My job here was done.

The Life I Chose

I've been in Chesapeake's county jail now for about two weeks, waiting on my extradition papers to be processed. Everyone around the jail has been talking about me. The correctional officers look at me like I am some celebrity, and the female inmates have been worshipping me like I'm some goddess. I even had a guard bring me a fucking note from a male inmate who was being housed on another floor. The note stated that he would like to correspond with me if it was at all possible. I refused to reply to that nonsense, so I sent word back to him by mouth and told him to leave me alone. He must have gotten my message because I haven't heard anything else from him.

On to family matters. Carmen, Grandma Hattie, and Rachael have been up here to see me twice since this ordeal happened. They have been unbelievably supportive and I am constantly telling them thank you. I was told by Carmen that they had a wake service for Aunt Sandra, since the battery acid ate away at her body. There were no remains in the bathtub. The only thing the forensics team could go on were the blood samples they found mixed with the acid.

Mario came up here to visit me for the first time this morning. He was pretty banged up, but he assured me he was fine.

He suffered two gunshot wounds to his shoulder and chest, but after an intense surgery effort, he came out all right. He still has to wear bandages for his wounds to heal but other than that he's fine. Thank God he had a gun permit and that the pistol he had was registered to him, because otherwise he would have been locked up behind bars with me. We didn't discuss his brother Maceo at all.

We did, however, talk about my plans to go back to Miami. I told him I was ready to face the music so I could get this whole thing behind me. He told me that he'd contacted both attorneys he mentioned a while back, but only one of them was licensed to practice down south and that he wanted one hundred and fifty thousand dollars to retain him and his partner. Travel and hotel was not included. I told him I had a little over one hundred grand stashed away but that's all I had to my name. I did have money frozen in my accounts down in Florida. Mario told me that that wouldn't be necessary because he already took care of it.

My mouth flew open. I was shocked by his concern and his generosity. For him to hand the attorney and the attorney's partner that much money just like that told me one thing. And that was, this guy was really serious about me, so I knew I had to do everything within my power to help those attorneys win my case. My mind was set to come home so I could repay him for everything he had done for me.

What I loved about Mario was that he was very genuine. He never had an ulterior motive to be with me from the start. He presented himself as exactly who he was even though I played another role. Nevertheless, everything worked out and I wouldn't go back in time and change a thing.

Right before my visit ended, he kissed the tip of his fingers and pressed them against the glass partition. I blew a kiss back to him and smiled. And when it was time for him to leave, I told him I loved him and it wouldn't be long before he could hold me in his arms again.

"I can't wait until that day finally comes," he said, and then he left.

Dear Readers,

Thanks again for riding with me on yet another journey. I truly hope you enjoyed this story like you have all the rest. I do appreciate all the continuous support I've gotten over the years and the numerous blogs and e-mails I've received as well. To answer your questions, there will be a *Wifey, Part 5*. Also, you will see the *Wifey* series on television. Don't want to say too much, but it will be on a major cable network as a miniseries. So look out for it.

In addition to that, I am working on Part 2 to *A Sticky Situation*. I have had a lot of requests for that book, so you will get it sooner rather than later. Also, I just wanted to mention that I received a letter from a fourteen-year-old girl in Florida who says she spends her last dime so she can get my books. She sent the letter to Kensington Publishing and someone there forwarded the letter to me. I had to admit that really put a smile on my face. How sweet was that? And because of it, I had to show her some love and send her a couple of signed copies of my latest books. (I do that from time to time.)

Anyhoo, I don't want to talk your heads off. But I've got to end this by saying I LOVE ALL OF MY READERS! Especially those who look forward to my next book coming out! And because of that, people are calling out my name all over the place. That's real love right here.

Until next time,

Kiki Swinson

NOTORIOUS

Kiki Swinson

ABOUT THIS GUIDE

The following questions are intended to
enhance your group's reading of
NOTORIOUS.

Discussion Questions

1. How different was Yoshi's demeanor in this story compared to *Playing Dirty*?

2. If you were Yoshi, would you have hidden out among your long-lost relatives while they were living their lives in all that chaos?

3. Do you think Yoshi was too mild-mannered in this story?

4. Did you like the fact that Yoshi finally found someone to love? If so, do you think that it was a conflict of interest, considering her man's brother was the one trying to kill her?

5. Grandma Hattie had taken far too much from her family. Do you think Yoshi could have done more to make her grandmother's life run a little smoother?

6. Aunt Sandra spilled the beans on Yoshi to Maceo. Do you think she got what she deserved?

7. Was Rachael wrong for jumping on her mother for soliciting sex from her boyfriend, Rodney?

8. Do you think Carmen was jealous of her sister, Rachael? Or do you think Carmen only offered advice to her about the choices she was making concerning her boyfriend because she didn't want her sister to walk down the same path she'd walked?

9. Yoshi was a very selfish and self-centered person. Do you think she turned her views around because she was forced to or do you think she did it because she finally realized she had a heart?

10. Did you like the way the story ended? If not, how would you have allowed it to play out?

Want more Kiki Swinson?
Catch up with Yoshi Lomax in
PLAYING DIRTY

Available now wherever books are sold

From *Playing Dirty*

From the Beginning

"Okay, Yoshi, it's your time," I whispered to myself. I ran my hands over my Chanel pencil skirt to smooth out the wrinkles. Then I turned toward the large bathroom mirror and checked my ass—along with my silver tongue and beautiful face, it was one of my best assets. I stood in the old-fashioned marble courthouse bathroom, making sure I looked as stunning as always before I made my way to the courtroom. My assistant had just texted my BlackBerry to tell me the jury was back with a verdict. The jury had only deliberated for one day. For a defense attorney, that could spell disaster. But that rule stood for regular defense attorneys—and I'd like to think that I was in a class by myself.

The trial had had its moments, but through it all I shined like a star. On the second to last day, I had all but captured the jury in the palm of my hand. I used my half-Korean background and my native Korean tongue to appeal to the two second-generation Asian jurors. My mother would've been so proud. As a proud Korean, she always wanted me to forget that I was half Black. She spoke Korean all the time. It had everything to do with the volatile relationship she had with my father before he packed up and left New York to go back to his hometown in Virginia when I was only eight years old. Him leaving the family devastated my mother, but I was okay with it. I got tired of listening to them fuss and fight all the time. And it seemed like it always got worse on the weekends when he came home drunk.

That wasn't the life my mother's parents had in mind for her after they emigrated all the way from Korea to Brooklyn, New York. I'm sure they felt that if she was going to struggle, then she needed to struggle with her own kind. Not with some African-American scumbag, alcoholic, warehouse worker from Norfolk, Virginia, who only moved to New York City to pursue his dreams of making it big in the music industry. My mother, unfortunately, picked him to father me. When I got old enough to understand, my mother told me that as soon as my grandparents got wind of their relationship, they disowned her. But as soon as my dad packed his shit and left, they immediately came to her rescue and wrote her back into their will. They were so happy that nigga left, they got on their knees and started sending praises to Buddha.

I couldn't care one way or the other. I mean, it wasn't like we were close anyway. From as far back as I could remember, I pretty much did my own thing. After school I would always go to the library and find a book to read, which was why I excelled in grade school. After graduating from high school, I thought about nothing else but furthering my education in law. I had always aspired to be a TV court judge, so I figured the only way I could ever have my own show was to become an attorney first. So here I was defending my client, the alleged leader of the Fuc-Chang Korean Mafia, who was on trial for murder, bribery, and racketeering. Now I knew he was guilty as hell, but I pulled every trick out of the bag to make the jury believe that he wasn't.

"Ms. Lomax, the jury returned its verdict after just one

day of deliberation. Are you worried?" a reporter called out
as I made my way down the hallway toward Judge Allen's
courtroom. A swarm of reporters surrounded me, shoving
microphones in my face. I never turned down an opportunity to show up on television.

"A fast verdict is just what I expected. My client is innocent." I smiled, flashing my perfect white teeth and shaking
my long, jet black hair. And right after I entered the courtroom, I switched my ass as hard as I could down the middle
aisle toward the defense table. All eyes turned toward me. I
could feel the stares burning my entire body. My red Chanel
suit was an eye-catcher. It showed off my curves and it made
me look like a million bucks. When potential clients approach
me for representation, they are not surprised to learn that I
charge a minimum of $2,500 an hour. They don't even blink
when the figure rolls off my tongue. The way they see it,
you never put a price on freedom, and with my victory rate,
how can they lose?

Right before I took my seat at the defense table, I looked
at my client, Mr. Choo, who was shackled like an animal and
guarded by courtroom officers. He appeared cool, calm,
and collected, unlike the men in black across from him. The
prosecutors sat at their table and fiddled with pens, bit nails,
and adjusted ties. They looked nervous and frazzled, to say
the least. I was just the opposite. In fact, I was laughing my ass
off on the inside because I knew I had this case in the bag.

The senior court officer moved to the front of the jam-
packed courtroom, ordered everyone to stand, and announced Judge Allen. I looked up at Judge Mark Allen, with
his salt-and-pepper balding head and little beady eyes. Mark
is what I call him when he's not in his black robe. As a matter of fact, it gets really personal when he and I get together
for one of our so-called romantic interludes. Last week was
the last time he and I got together, and it was in his cham-

bers. It was so funny because I let him fuck me in his robe with his puny five-inch wrinkled dick. He thought he was the man, too. And when it was all said and done, I made sure I wiped my cum all over the crotch of his slacks. Shit, Monica Lewinsky ain't got nothing on me. I wanted him to know that I had no respect for his authority or his courtroom. After I let him get at me, and I bribed a few of the jurors, all of the calls in the courtroom went my way. The prosecutors never had a chance. . . . It was amusing to watch.

The judge cleared his throat and began to speak. The courtroom was "pin drop" quiet.

"Jury, what say you in the case of the *State of Florida* versus *Haan Choo?*" Judge Allen boomed.

The jury foreperson, a fair-skinned Black woman in her mid-fifties, stood up swiftly, her hands trembling. " 'We, the jury, in the matter of the *State of Florida* versus *Haan Choo*, finds as follows: to the charge of first-degree murder . . . not guilty.' "

A gasp resounded through the courtroom. Then the scream of some victim's family members.

"Order!" Judge Allen screamed.

The foreperson continued without looking up from her paper. " 'To the charge of racketeering . . . not guilty. To the charge of bribery . . . not guilty. And to the charge of conspiracy . . . not guilty.' "

Mr. Choo jumped up and grabbed me in a bear hug. "Yoshi, you greatest," he whispered in broken English.

"Order!" the judge screamed again. "Bailiff, take Mr. Choo back to booking so he can be released." He had to go through his motions to set Mr. Choo free. I looked over at the prosecutors' table and threw them a smile. I knew they all wished they could just jump across the table and kill me. Too bad they hadn't taken what I had offered them after the preliminary hearing. Both assistant district attorneys were new to the game and overeager to take on their first high-profile case. Out of the gate they wanted to prove to their boss that they both could take me on, but somebody should've warned them that I was no one to fuck with. With a smile still on my face, I strutted by them and said, "Idiots!" just loud enough for only them to hear. Then I threw my hair back and continued to strut my shit out the courtroom.

After I slid the city clerk's head administrator ten crisp one-hundred-dollar bills, it only took about an hour to process Mr. Choo's release papers. Money talks and bullshit runs the marathon! And before anyone knew it, Mr. Choo and I were walking outside to greet the press. He and I both were all smiles, because he was a free man and I knew that in an hour or so, I was going to be $2 million richer; that alone made me want to celebrate. But first, we needed to address the media. Cameras flashed and microphones passed in front of us as we stepped into the sunlight. Mr. Choo rushed to the huddle of microphones that all but blocked his slim face from view. "Justice was served today. I am innocent and my lawyer proved that. I no crime boss, I am family man. I run my business and I love America," he rambled, his horrible English getting on my nerves. I waited patiently while he made his grand stand and then I took over the media show.

"All along I told everyone my client was innocent. Mr. Choo came to the United States from Korea to make an honest—" *Bang, bang, bang, bang, bang, bang!* The sound of shouts and then screams rang in my ears. Then I heard someone in the crowd yell in Korean, "You fucking snitch!" The shots stopped me dead in my tracks; my words tumbled back down my throat like hard marbles, choking me. I grabbed my arm as heat radiated up to my neck.

"Oh shit, I'm hit!" I screamed. I dropped to the ground, scrambling to hide . . . and saw Mr. Choo, his head dangling and his body slumped against the courthouse steps. His mouth hung open and blood dripped from his lips and chin. Before I could figure out what to do next, someone snatched me up from the ground. I didn't know where we were headed—my thoughts were on my throbbing arm and my racing heart. Then suddenly my vision became blurry and the world went black.

My career changed after Mr. Choo's trial. Shit, after having almost lost my damn life, I would not accept anything less than the best.

After the shooting, the law firm of Shapiro and Witherspoon was thrown into the media spotlight like never before. I became known as the "ride-or-die bitch attorney" that would take a bullet to get a client off. I became the most sought-after criminal defense attorney in Florida. Sometimes I didn't know if that was good or bad. But one thing was sure, my life changed and my appetite for money and power grew more and more intense. I started living each day as if it were my last.

Years ago, I never thought I would have turned out to be the way I was today. When you look at it, I had become a heartless bitch! I could not care less about anyone, including my own damn mother. Even when having a nightcap with my flavor of the night, I never let my feelings get involved. Once I put the condom on him, I reminded myself that it was only business and that my client's freedom was on the line, so everything worked out fine. That's how I kept men in line. After the shooting, I vowed that my heart would remain in my pocket forever.

Enjoy the following excerpts from
Kiki Swinson's previous novels

Wifey
I'm Still Wifey
Life After Wifey

Available now wherever books are sold!

From *Wifey*

Tired of the Drama

It's 4:30 am in the morning and I've been pacing back and forth from my bed to my bedroom window, which overlooked the driveway of my six-hundred-thousand-dollar house, waiting for my husband Ricky to bring dat ass home. Who cared about all the plucks he had to make every other night? I kept telling him, all money ain't good money! But he didn't listen. Not to mention, I had to deal with all his hoes on a daily basis. We've been married for seven years now, and since then I've had to spend a whole lot of nights alone in this gorgeous five-bedroom home he got for us two years ago. That's how his three children came into play. All of them were by different chickenheads who lived in the projects. But one of them had a Section Eight crib somewhere in D.C. and she was ghetto as hell. Just like the other two, who lived not too far from here.

Now, Ricky didn't have enough sense to go out and donate his sperm to women with some class. Every last one of them were high school dropouts, holding eighth-grade educations and an ass full of drama. They figured since Ricky had a baby by them, that he was gonna leave me to be with their nasty tails. Oh, but trust me! It won't happen! Not in *this* lifetime. Because all they could offer him was pussy.

And the last time I checked, pussy wasn't in high demand these days like them hoes thought. That's why I could say with much confidence—that *Ricky needed me*. I kept his hot-headed ass straight. And not only that, I've got assets. I'm light-skinned and very pretty with a banging ass body! Niggas in the street said I reminded them of the rapper Trina because both of us favored each other and we had small waists and big asses. And to complement all that, I knew how to play most of the games on the street, as well as the ins and outs of running the hair salon I opened a few years back. Not to mention, Ricky gave me the dough to make it happen. Now you see, he was good for something other than screwing other chicks behind my back. This was why I was always trying to find reasons not to leave his ass.

So, after pacing back and forth a few more times, Mr. Good Dick finally pulled his sedan into the driveway. I made my way on downstairs to greet his butt at the front door. "What you doing up?" he asked as soon as he saw me standing in the foyer.

"Ricky, don't ask me no stupid-ass questions!" I told him with much attitude. Then I moved backwards two steps, giving him enough room to shut the front door.

"What you upset for?" he responded with uncertainty.

I'm standing dead smack in front of my husband, who is, by the way, very, very handsome with a set of six packs out of this world. I'm wearing one of my newest Victoria's Secret lingerie pieces, looking extra sexy; and all he could do was stand there looking stupid and ask me what I'm upset for? I wanted so badly to smack the hell outta him; but I decided to remain a lady and continue to get him where it hurts, which is his pockets. This dummy had no clue whatsoever that I was robbing his ass blind.

Every time he put some of his dough away in his stash I was right behind him, trimming the fat around the edges.

"Kira, baby don't give me that look," Ricky continued.

"You know I'm out on the grind every night for me and you."

"Ricky, I don't wanna hear your lies," I tell him and walk to the kitchen.

And like I knew he would, he followed in my footsteps.

"Baby!" he started pleading. "Look what I gotcha!"

I knew it. He's always pulling something out of his hat when I'm about to put his ass on the hot seat. He knows I'm a sucker for gifts. "Whatever you got for me, you can take your ass right back out in the streets, find all your babies' mamas, play Spin the Bottle and whoever the fuck wins, just give it to them." I fronted like I wasn't interested.

"Shit, them hoes wouldn't ever be able to get me to cop a bracelet like this for them!" Ricky tells me.

"They weren't hoes when you were screwing 'em."

"Look Kira, I didn't come home to argue wit' you. All I wanna do right now is see how this joint looks on your wrist."

Curious as to how iced out this bracelet was, I turned around with a grit on my face from hell. "You look so sexy when you're mad," he told me.

Hearing him tell me how sexy I looked made me want to smile real bad, but I couldn't put my guard down. I had to show this clown I wasn't playing with his ass and was truly tired of his bullshit. All his baby mama drama, the other hoes he was seeing and the many trips he took out of town, acting like he was taking care of business. Shit, I wasn't stupid! I knew all them trips he took weren't solely for business. But it's all lovely. While he thinks he's playing me, I'm straight playing his ass, too.

"Where you get this from?" I asked, continuing to front like I wasn't at all excited about this H series diamond watch by Chopard.

"Don't worry 'bout that," Ricky told me as he fastened the hook on it. "You like it?"

Trying to be modest, I told him, "Yeah." And then I looked him straight in his eyes with the saddest expression I could muster. I immediately thought about how I lost my mother to a plane crash just hours before I graduated from high school. I tried talking her into taking an earlier flight from her vacation in Venezuela, but she refused to leave her third husband out there alone and wanted to guard him from walking off with one of those young and beautiful women roaming around the beaches. So once again, she allowed her obsession for wealth to dictate her way of life. I hated to admit it but over the years, I had become the spitting image of her. I wanted nothing to do with a man who couldn't give me all the fine things in life. And since my mother had not been married to her third husband long enough, I got stiffed when his will was read. The only two choices I had was to either move in with my uncle and his family or my grandmother Clara, who were my only living relatives. So, guess what? I chose neither. I did this because I just felt like I didn't belong with any of them. I mean, come on. Who wanted to live in a house that always smelled like mothballs? Who wanted to live with an uncle who forced you to be in church every Sunday? Plus, you had to abide by his rules. And he didn't care how old you were, either. So, it had to be fate when Ricky came into my life.

He got me my own apartment not even a week after we met. The fact that he loved to spend his dough on me made it even sweeter. He tried really hard to make sure I got everything I needed, and I let him. Hell yeah! That's why most of the time when I'm upset, I can make him feel really guilty about how he's been treating me lately.

"Why do you keep taking me through all these changes?" I asked as I forced myself to cry.

"What you talkin' 'bout, Kira? What changes?"

"The constant lies and drama!"

"Tell me what you talkin' 'bout, Ma!"

"I'm talking about you coming in this house two, three, and four o'clock in the morning, every damn night, like you got it like that! I'm just plain sick of it!"

"Come off that, baby," Ricky said as he pulled me into his arms. "You know those hours are the best time for me to work. I make mo' money and get less police."

"Who cares about all of that? I just want it to stop!"

"It will."

"But when? I mean, come on, Ricky. You got plenty of dough put away. And I've got some good, consistent money coming in my salon every week. So, we ain't gon' need for nothing."

"Look, I'll tell you what? Let me finish the rest of my pack and make one last run down to Florida, then I'll take a long vacation."

"What you mean, vacation?!" I raised my voice because I needed some clarity.

"It means I'mma chill out for a while."

"What's a while?"

"Shit, Kira! I don't know! Maybe six months. A year."

"You promise?" I asked, giving him my famous pout.

"Yeah. I promise," he told me in a low whisper as he began to kiss my neck and tug on my ear lobe.

That instant, my panties got wet. Ricky pulled me closer to him. He cupped both of my ass cheeks in his hands, gripping 'em hard while he ground his dick up against my kitty cat. I couldn't resist the feelings that were coming over me. So when he picked me up I wrapped my legs around his waist, only leaving him enough room to slide his huge black dick inside my world of passion. I'm so glad I had on my crotchless panties because if I had had to wait another second for him to pull my thong off, I probably would have exploded.

"Hmmm, baby fuck me harder!" I begged him as I used the kitchen sink to help support my weight. His thrusts got harder and more intense.

"You like it when we fuss and make up, huh?" Ricky whispered each word between kisses. But of course, I declined to answer him. Swelling his head up about how I like making love after we have an argument, was not what I deemed to be a solution to our problems. After we got our rocks off, he and I both decided to lay back in our kingsized bed until we both dozed off.

Around 12:30 in the afternoon is about the time Ricky and I woke up. I hopped into the shower and about two minutes later, he hopped in right behind me. I knew what he wanted when he walked in the bathroom. It's not often that he and I take showers together, unless he wants to bend me over so he can hit it from the back. He knows I love giving it to him from the back, especially in the shower. The slapping noise our bodies make together in the water, as he's working himself in and out of me, turns me on.

After Ricky got his rocks off, he left the shower and returned to our bedroom to get dressed. "What you gon' do today?" I asked him as I entered into our bedroom, wrapped in a towel.

'Well, I'mma run by the spot out Norfolk and see why Eric and them can't get my dough straight."

"Please, don't go out there and scream on them like you got something to prove."

"I'm not. I'mma be cool 'til one of them niggas step out of pocket."

"See, that's one of the reasons I want your ass to stop hustling!" I pointed my finger at him.

"Won't you stop stressing yourself? Believe me, most niggas out there got nothing but respect for me."

"What about the one who don't?" I continued with my questions as I started to lotion my body down.

"I've got plenty of soldiers out there that'll outweigh that problem."

"Yeah, yeah, yeah!" was my response, hoping he'd catch the hint and shut up.

Unfortunately this wasn't the case. Ricky kept yapping on and on about how good his product was, and how the fiends were loving it. Once I had gotten enough of hearing about his street life, I grabbed a sweatsuit and a pair of Air Force Ones that matched my outfit and threw them both on. I scooped up my car keys and my Chanel handbag, and headed out the front door.

When I pulled up in front of my salon, it was packed. I knew I had at least four, if not five, of my clients waiting on me already. I know they were mad as hell, too, considering I was supposed to have been here three hours ago. My first appointment was at ten o'clock. Hell! I couldn't get up. After waiting up all night for my trifling-assed husband to come home and then after all the fussing I did, I still let him con me outta my drawz. As I made my way through the salon doors, I greeted everyone and told my ten o'clock client to go and sit at the washbowl. "Tasha, girl, please don't be mad wit' me," I began to explain as I threw the cape around her neck.

"Oh, it's alright. I ain't been waiting that long," Tasha replied.

"What you getting?"

"Just a hard wrap. I got two packs of sixteen-inch hair I wantcha to hookup."

"Did you bring a stocking cap?"

"Yep."

"A'ight. Well, lay back so I can get started."

Within the next two hours, I had all four of my clients situated. They were either under the dryer or on their way out the door. Seven more of my clients showed up, but three cancelled. I thanked God for that because I wouldn't be getting out of this shop until around ten or eleven o'clock tonight. That couldn't happen. I had to get home and wash those two loads of clothes I had packed up top of my hamper before I heard Ricky's mouth about it.

He loved for his house to be cleaned at any cost; if his ass wasn't so unfaithful, we could have had a housemaid, because nothing must be out of place. This fetish for absolute cleanliness got on my nerves sometimes. I mean, shit, ain't nothing wrong with leaving a damn dirty glass or a plate and a fork in the sink every now and then. As for certain garments in his wardrobe, I was forbidden to throw them in the washing machine. I was always reminded to read the label instructions for every piece of clothing he had. If it said "Dry Clean Only," then that's where it was going. I got a headache just thinking about it, so, I made a rule to put a big *"H"* on my chest and handle it.

A few more hours flew by and my other stylist's clients started falling out the door, one by one. This meant our time to go home was coming.

"Rhonda," I called out to one of my hair stylists, who happened to be one of the hottest beauticians in the Tidewater area.

"Yeah," she replied.

"You feel like giving me a roller set after I put my last client under the dryer?"

"Girl, you know I don't mind," Rhonda replied as she bopped her head to Lloyd Bank's single, "On Fire."

Rhonda's good people. I knew she was going to tell me yeah, before I attempted to even ask her. That's just her personality. She'd been working with me ever since I opened the doors to this shop four years ago. From day one, she's showed me nothing but love, even through all the drama her kid's father had been giving her. Her kid's father, Tony, is also a ladies' man; just like Ricky. I keep telling Rhonda to get him like I get my husband. Stick him where it hurts: either steal his money or his pack. It can't get any simpler than that. But nah, she ain't hearing me. That's why them hoes Tony's messing with was laughing at her, 'cause she was letting that nigga play her.

Now my other stylist, Sunshine, was working her game *entirely* different. She was your average-looking chick with ghetto-assed booty. Niggas loved her. Every time I turned around she had somebody else's man walking through my salon doors, bringing her shit.

Sunshine was strictly hustler bound. No other kind of man would attract her. You had to be driving a whip, estimating thirty Gs or better. And his dough had to be long. I'm talking like, from V.A. to the state of Rhode Island, to mess with that chick.

Oh, and Sunshine's wardrobe was tight, too. She wasn't gonna wear none of that fake-assed, knock-off Prada and Chanel that these hoes were getting from the Chinese people at the hair stores. No way. Sunshine was a known customer at Saks Fifth Avenue and Macy's.

I've seen the receipts. Sometimes I thought she was trying to be in competition with me, considering I was like a regular at those stores and all. But there can be no contest because when it's all said and done, I am and will always be the baddest bitch.

Since the day had almost come to an end, I sat back in Rhonda's station as she did her magic on my hair. We were in a deep conversation about her man Tony, when Ricky walked through the door. "Good evening," he said.

"What's up, Ricky!" Rhonda greeted him.

"Nothing much," he responded.

"Where you just coming from?" I wanted to know.

"From the crib."

"Our house?"

"Yeah."

"So, what's up?"

"I need to switch cars witcha," he said as he took a seat in one of the booth chairs across from me.

Something must be getting ready to go down. And he wasn't gonna spill the beans while Rhonda was sitting up in here with me. I let her finish my hair and in the meantime, Ricky and I made idle conversation until she left. After she finished my hair, it only took her about ten minutes to clean up her station. Then Rhonda said her goodbyes and left.

"So, what you need my car for this time?" I wasted no time asking Ricky the second Rhonda left out the door.

As I waited for him to respond, I knew he could do one of three things. He could either tell me the truth, which could probably hurt him in some way later down the line. Or he could tell me a lie, which would really piss me off. And then he could throw Rule #7 at me from the *Hustler's Manual,* which insisted that he tell me nothing. A hustler's reason for that was: "The less your girl knows, the better off ya'll be."

"I need it to make a run," he finally said.

"What kind of run?"

"You don't need to know all that!" Ricky snapped.

"Look, don't get no attitude with me because I wanna know where you're taking my car."

"And who bought you the LS 400?"

"I don't care who bought it! The fact remains, it's in my name. Just like the Benz and that cartoon character, Hulk–painted, 1100 Ninja motorcycle you got parked in the garage."

"And your point?"

"Look, Ricky just be careful. And please don't do nothing stupid."

"I'm not," he assured me with a kiss on my forehead.

"Don't have no bitch in my car," I yelled as he made his way out the door.

While he ignored me like I knew he would, I stood there and watched Ricky unlock my car door and drive off. At the same time, I wondered where he was goin'.

It Ain't Over

Can you believe it? After all the planning I did to leave my husband Ricky to run off with Russ, it backfired on me. It has been two-and-a-half months since the whole thing went down. Now I'm sitting here all alone, in my hair shop, thinking about what I am going to do about this baby I'm carrying.

Rhonda and Nikki both didn't believe me when I told them that I was pregnant by Russ. But after I pulled out a calendar and counted back the days from the last time we were together, it finally registered through their thick skulls.

"So, what cha' gon' do about it?" Rhonda asked me the day I got the results from a pregnancy test about a month ago. The first thing that came out of her mouth was for me to get an abortion since I ain't gon' have a baby daddy. God knows where he is. But I told her that was the furthest thing from my mind because whether I had Russ in my life or not, I was gon' have this baby. And then she said, "Well, what would you do if he found out you're pregnant and wants to come back with a whole bunch of apologies and shit?"

I told her that shit ain't gon' happen because first of all, Russ ain't gon' find out I'm pregnant 'cause ain't nobody gon' know I'm pregnant by him. And second, after that stunt he pulled on me to rob me for my dough, I know he ain't gon' never show his face around this way ever again. He would be a fool to. I mean, he don't know if I told Ricky that he robbed me or not. So to play it cool, he's gon' do like any other greasy-ass nigga would do after they pull a stick-up move, and that is to disappear. And even though he thinks he got away with it, he hasn't. 'Cause whether Russ knows it or not, karma is coming for his ass. And what will give me much pleasure is to be able to see it hit 'em.

Hopefully my day will come very soon.

Back at my place, which is a step down from my ol' two-story house, I decided to pop myself a bag of popcorn and watch my favorite show, *America's Next Top Model*. Afterward, I began to straighten things up around my two bedroom, two-bath condo until my telephone started ringing.

"Hello," I said without looking at the CallerID.

"Whatcha doing?" Rhonda wanted to know.

"I was just dusting the mantel over my fireplace."

"Girl, sit your butt down. 'Cause if my memory serves me, I do remember you being on your feet all day today."

"I'm fine. But what I wanna know is, why you didn't come back to work today?"

Rhonda sighed heavily and said, "Kira, if I could kill Tony and get away with it, I would do it."

"What happened now?"

"Girl, I caught this nigga talking to some hoe named Letisha on his cell phone."

"Where was he at?"

"He was in the bathroom, sitting on the fucking toilet, taking a shit."

I laughed at Rhonda's comment and asked her what happened next.

"Well, before I busted in on him and smacked him upside his damn head with my shoe, I stood very quiet in the hallway right outside our bedroom and heard this bastard telling that hoe how much he missed her and that he was going to get his hair cut at the barbershop. And right after I heard him say that, that's when I went off."

"So, what did he do?"

"He couldn't do shit with his pants wrapped around his ankles. So, he just sat there and took all them blows I threw at his ass. And then when he dropped his cell phone, I hurried up and snatched it right off the floor and cussed that bitch out royally."

"And what did she say?"

"I ain't let her say, shit. 'Cause after I told her who I was and that if I ever caught her in Tony's face, she was gonna get fucked up, I hung up."

"So, what was Tony doing while you was going off on that hoe?"

"Trying to hurry up and wipe his ass, so he can get up from the toilet and I guess take his phone back. But as soon as the bastard stood up to flush the stool, I threw his phone right up against the wall as hard as I could and broke that bad boy in about ten little pieces."

I laughed again and said, "Damn girl! That's some shit I used to do."

"Well, jackass didn't see it coming. So, it made it all the better."

"Where's he at now?"

"In the kitchen helping Ryan with his homework."

"So, did he ever go out and get his hair cut?"

"Hell nah. Shit, he knew better."

"Well, what kind of lies did he tell you about everything that happened?"

"Girl, that nigga ain't gon' volunteer no information. All he had to say was that I was crazy as hell. And then he went on about his damn business."

"Rhonda," I said before I sighed, "I know you're sick and tired of going through all that bullshit! Because I sure was when Ricky was on the streets."

"Hey wait," Rhonda interjected, "I forgot to tell you that he called the shop today while you was at lunch."

"Did you accept the call?"

"Yeah. But we only talked for a few minutes."

"What did he say?"

"He just wanted to know where you was and when was you coming in. So, I told him that you wasn't. And that's when he asked me to call you on three-way. But I told him the three-way call thing wasn't working."

"I bet he got real mad, didn't he?"

"Hell yeah!"

"So, what did he say after that?"

"Nothing but to tell you he called. And for me to tell you to come down to the county jail and see him before the U.S. Marshal picks him up and takes him off to the Federal Holding Facility in Oklahoma, because he has something very important to talk with you about."

"Well, he should already know that it ain't gon' happen. But, I am wondering what he's got so important to talk to me about."

"Girl, he's just probably saying that so he can get you to come down and see him."

"Yeah. You probably right," I agreed.

"Well, are you going to ever tell him that you're pregnant by Russ?" Rhonda blurted out of the blue.

"Nope. It ain't none of his damn business. All he needs to focus on is signing those divorce papers my lawyer is getting ready to send his ass."

"So, you're serious about that, huh?"

"You damn right!" I commented and then I said, "I'm

gonna get that nigga outta my life once and for all, so I can move on."

"Look, I understand all that. But I wouldn't let his ass get off that easy. Because the next time he calls the shop, I would make it my business to wreck his muthafucking ego and tell him, *'Yeah nigga, while you was running around behind my back with Sunshine's stinking ass, I was fucking your boy Russ right in your bed. And I just found out that I'm pregnant by him.'* "

"Oh my God! That'll kill him!"

"That's the idea," Rhonda told me.

I said, "Girl, that nigga gon' try and come through the phone after I tell him some shit like that."

"Well, no need to worry 'bout that. 'Cause it ain't gon' happen." Before I could comment, she told me to hold on because somebody was beeping in on her other line. When she clicked over, it got real quiet. But just like that, she was right back on the line and said, "Hey girl, one of Tony's home-boys is on the other end trying to holler at him. So, let me call you back."

"A'ight," I told her. Then we both hung up.

From *Life After Wifey*

Choosing Sides

Nikki Speaks

From the time I jumped into my car and left Syncere's house until the time I pulled in front of Kira's apartment building, I wrecked the hell out of my brain trying to rationalize and make sense of the text message I had just read on Syncere's T-Mobile.

The message was clear but I could not bring myself to believe that my man had something to do with Mark's murder, not to mention the fact that Kira had gotten caught up in the crossfire and lost her baby. I didn't want to sound stupid or naïve, but there had to be an explanation behind this whole thing. I needed to find out what it was and how involved Syncere was before Kira blew the whistle on him because whether she realized it or not, I needed my man. So, I was not letting him go that easy.

Immediately after I got out of my car I stood there on the sidewalk and took a deep breath. After I exhaled, I put one foot forward and proceeded toward Kira's apartment to confront the inevitable. Knowing she was going to bite my head off the moment I jumped to Syncere's defense was something I had prepared myself for. As I made my way down the entryway to her building, this fine-ass, older-looking Hispanic guy wearing a dark blue painter's cap and overalls came rushing toward me, so I didn't hesitate to move out of his way.

But, what was really odd about him was when I tried to make eye contact and say 'hello' he totally brushed me off and looked the other way. Being the chick I am, I threw my hand up at him and said, "Well, fuck you too! You ol' rude muthafucka!" I kept it moving.

Patting my right thigh, with my hand, to a rhythmic beat as I walked up the last step to Kira's floor, I let out a long sigh and proceeded toward Kira's front door. Upon my arrival, I noticed that her door was slightly ajar so I reached over and pushed it open. "Girl, did you know that your door was open?" I yelled as I walked into the apartment. I didn't get an answer, so I closed the front door behind me and proceeded down the hallway toward her bedroom. When I entered into her room and saw that she was nowhere in sight, I immediately called her name again and I turned to walk toward the master bathroom. "Kira, where you at?" I turned the doorknob and pushed the door open.

"Oh, my God," I screamed at the top of my lungs the second my mind registered the gruesome sight of Kira's body slumped over the edge of the bathtub, while her head lay in a pool of her own blood. I couldn't see her face because of the way her body was positioned. I rushed over to her side, got down on my knees and crawled over next to her. My heart was racing at the speed of light and my emotions were spiraling out of control as I grabbed her body and pulled her toward me.

"Kira, please wake up!" I begged her and began to cry hysterically. She didn't move, so I started shaking her frantically. "Kira, please wake up!" I screamed once again. "Don't die on me like this," I pleaded. Out of nowhere, her eyes fluttered and slowly opened. Overwhelmed by her sudden reaction, my heart skipped a beat and I pulled her body even closer. "Oh my God, thank you," I said in a joyful manner and cradled her head in my lap. "I almost thought I lost you,"

I told her and wiped the tears away from my eyes. Meanwhile, Kira struggled a bit to swallow the blood in her throat and then she tried to speak. I immediately leaned forward and positioned my ear about two inches away from her mouth so I could hear what it was she had to say.

When she finally moved her lips, the few words she uttered were just above a whisper and barely audible. I was about to ask her to repeat herself and she started choking. I panicked. "Ahh shit! Don't do this to me. Take a deep breath," I instructed her as I began to massage her chest. Then it suddenly hit me that I needed to call an ambulance. I retrieved my cellular phone from the holster on my right side and dialed 911.

"911, what's your emergency?"

"My cousin's been shot," I answered with urgency.

"What's your cousin's name?"

"Her name is Kira Walters."

"And what is your name?"

"My name is Nicole Simpson."

"Okay Nicole, I need for you to stay calm. Can you tell me if Kira is conscious?"

"Yes, she's conscious. I've got her lying in my arms."

"Okay, tell me exactly where Kira's been shot."

"In the left side of her head, right above her temple."

"Is that the only place she's been shot?"

"Yes ma'am."

"Nicole, I'm gonna need you to give me the address to where you are located. In the meantime, I'm gonna need you to remain calm and grab something like a sheet or a towel and press it against Kira's head to stop some of the bleeding. Has she lost a lot of blood?"

"Yes, she has," I assured the woman. Shortly thereafter I gave her the address.

The operator stayed on the phone with me until the police

and the paramedics arrived. Covered from the waist down in Kira's blood, I was ushered out of the bathroom and into the kitchen by this short, white, female police officer who had a ton of questions for me. I only answered the questions I knew the answers to. Once our little session was over, another detective—this time a white male—came in and asked me almost the exact same questions as the female officer did. I found myself repeating everything over again.

My back was turned when the paramedics took Kira out on the stretcher. By the time I realized that she had been taken away, she was already in the ambulance, headed to the nearest emergency room. The white, male detective informed me where they were taking her so I immediately called my family, told them Kira had gotten shot and that they needed to meet me at Bayside Memorial. After they assured me they were on their way, I hung up with them. On my way out, I noticed at least a dozen detectives and forensics investigators combing every inch of the apartment to collect evidence so there was no doubt in my mind that they were going to find her killer.

I got to the hospital in no time at all and to my surprise my mother, my father and my grandmother arrived shortly afterward. We all sat and waited patiently for one of the doctors performing the emergency surgery to come out and give us an update on Kira's condition. In the meantime, my grandmother had a few questions for me to answer.

"Nikki, are you sure Kira was conscious when she left with the paramedics?" she asked as if she was making a desperate attempt to find the answer in my eyes.

"Yes, she was," I replied in a reassuring manner. "She even tried to say something, but I didn't understand her. When I asked her to say it again she started choking and that's when I called the paramedics."

"Well, how was she breathing when they took her out of the house?"

"I don't know, Grandma. I was in the kitchen when they carried her out," I told her and then I put my head down in despair. Knowing that my cousin was in surgery fighting for her life and I couldn't do anything to help her put a huge strain on my heart. Not to mention the fact that if I would've gotten to her apartment a little sooner this probably would not have happened to her. In a sense I felt like her getting shot was partially my fault. Which was why I was feeling so terrible right now.

"What in the world do y'all got going on?" my father interjected as if the sight of me made him cringe.

"What are you talking about?" I looked at him with an expression of uncertainty.

"What kind of people are y'all mixed up with?"

"Come on now, honey, I know you're upset but this is not the time or the place," my mother spoke up.

"Yes, your wife is right," my grandmother agreed trying to keep the peace.

But my father wasn't trying to hear them. Their comments went in one ear and right out the other. "Whatcha trying to do, end up like your cousin in there?"

"What kind of question is that?" I snapped.

"Just answer the question," he commanded.

"No, I'm not," I replied, irritated with his questions.

"It's hard to tell," my father snapped back. "Because every time I turn around, somebody's either getting shot or killed. And if you keep walking around here like you ain't got the sense you were born with, then you're gonna end up just like your cousin back there."

"Alright now, that's enough! I don't want to hear another word," my grandmother whispered harshly with tears in her eyes. Her tone sent a clear message to my father that she was sincerely pissed and he'd better not utter another word.

But, knowing how much my father loathed when people told him what to do, the chances of that happening were slim to none. The moment she closed her mouth and rolled her eyes at him, he parted his lips and said, "You know what, Mama . . ."

But fortunately for us, he couldn't finish the thought because we were interrupted by an Asian doctor dressed in green hospital-issued scrubs, walking toward us. "Are you the family for Kira Walters?"

"Yes, we are," I eagerly replied.

"I'm Dr. Ming and I was called in to perform emergency surgery on Miss Walters."

"How is she?" my grandmother asked.

"Yeah, how is she? Can we go in and see her?" my mother asked.

"I'm sorry to inform you but Miss Walters didn't make it."

"What do you mean, she 'didn't make it'?" I screamed in disbelief.

"Ma'am," the doctor began in the most apologetic manner, "believe me, we did everything in our power but she was nonresponsive."

Hearing this man tell me that my cousin just died hit me like a ton of bricks. I couldn't believe it. I mean, there had to be some kind of mistake. Kira couldn't be dead.

I just had her wrapped up in my arms back at her apartment a couple of hours ago. Whatever this man was talking was pure nonsense and I couldn't accept that.

Meanwhile, as the thoughts of living my life without her started consuming me, my grandmother walked off in another direction, crying her poor little heart out. My parents got a little more in-depth with the complications Kira had and why they could not save her. I, on the other hand, just sat there in a daze.

My family and I left the hospital shortly after the doctor broke the news to us. Unfortunately, no one was able to see Kira's body except my grandmother. A nurse escorted her down to the morgue to ID her and get her belongings. My parents and I were cornered in a small room by the same two detectives from Kira's apartment. They didn't have much to say this time, so our little chat went by quickly.

When we arrived back at my grandmother's house I went off into a room by myself while my parents sat around in the living room with my grandmother. I heard bits and pieces of their conversations. But when they started talking about making Kira's funeral arrangements, I immediately turned a deaf ear to them because I wasn't ready to accept the fact that my home girl was dead. As it turned out, they ended up handling everything and I was truly fine with it because it took the burden off me.